USA TODAY BEST SELLING AUTHOR

KRISTEN PAINTER

BOOK ONE

THE TROUBLE WITH WITCHES

THE TROUBLE WITH WITCHES
Shadowvale, Book One

Copyright © 2019 Kristen Painter

This book is a work of fiction. The characters, events, and places portrayed in this book are products of the author's imagination and are either fictitious or are used fictitiously. Any similarity to real person, living or dead, is purely coincidental and not intended by the author.

Published in the United States of America.

Shadowvale isn't typical small town America. The sun never shines, the gates decide who enters, magic abounds, and every resident bears some kind of curse.

No one knows this as well as raven shifter Deacon Evermore, who, like everyone in his family, has a curse. While his position as Shadowvale's peacekeeper lets him use that curse for good, he'd rather live anywhere else. He stays for his family, but doubts he can last much longer.

Fledgling witch Emeranth Greer is determined to escape her past and make a fresh start in Shadowvale with the aunt she's never met. Her aunt and the town prove to be far better than she imagined. There's no way Em is leaving this magical place. Especially when staying means more time with the handsome Deacon.

But when Em's troubled past catches up with her and nearly destroys the romance budding between her and Deacon, her instinct is to run again. Except there's magic in the mix now and the town won't let her leave. Only Deacon can save her, but can a cursed man clear her name...or will her history destroy them both?

CHAPTER ONE

Countess Amelia Marie Antoinette Marchand left the warm embrace of her Egyptian cotton sheets to pull her velvet robe around her. She slid her feet into matching tasseled slippers, then sat on the edge of the bed for a moment. Age was a terrible thing.

With a wave of her hand, she brought the fireplace to life.

That was better. A little light and a little heat. Shadowvale's spring mornings still held a chill that seeped into her bones. She walked to her bedroom windows and drew back the heavy silk drapes to look out at the front of the property.

Another gray, sunless morning greeted her, fog rising off the ground like a host of specters come to haunt her. But that fog was nothing new. Neither was the gray, sunless morning. In fact, she took comfort in how firmly Shadowvale's magic held, just as it had for the past seventy-five years.

She stared out at the world she'd created. The town she was responsible for. She studied the enormous live oaks fringed in Spanish moss that

1

guarded the drive up to her home, Indigo House, and beyond the trees, the elaborate wrought-iron fence that bordered her estate's property lines. Then the street that ran past. The fog hid most of it, but then, it always did at this hour.

And over it all, the perpetual gloom. The permanent dusk that only really disappeared when night fell in its entirety. Then, and only then, did the clouds clear and the sky become discernable. Always. Every night. To Amelia, it seemed like the visibility of the stars was one of Shadowvale's ways of making up for the constant haze overhead.

Oh, the sky lightened considerably during the day. More than enough to show the passage of the sun that was hidden but indeed still present. But that solar beacon was forever filtered through the eternal, enchanted curtain that shrouded Shadowvale.

But perhaps *gloom* wasn't the right word. After all, this place had been painstakingly created as a gift of love. A safe haven for the man she'd treasured beyond all else. The man she'd traded her life to protect.

The man with whom she'd expected to spend her eternity.

It wasn't the town's fault that Pasqual had chosen to break her heart and reject her gift, leaving her a captive here. She'd known what she was getting into. Understood the deal she was making.

She just hadn't imagined he would grow tired of life here so quickly. Or at all, really. And then turn his back on her the way he had.

She put her hand on the windowpane, a little melancholy at the memory, but that soon turned to anger. Then resignation.

This was her town now. And it was a good place to live. The glass warmed under her touch. Yes, *her* town. Her home. Her life.

"Good morning, madam…"

She turned. Beckett stood at her bedroom door, eyes straight ahead. Of all his questionable qualities, he was at least a gentleman. Her warden, in a sense, but generally a polite one all the same. She waved her hand, using her magic to bring the chandelier above the bed to life. "Good morning, Beckett."

"Breakfast is ready."

She wasn't hungry. She rarely was. She would eat nonetheless. That was just the way of things. "Thank you. I'll be down shortly. Where's Thoreau?"

"In the garden pool."

She nodded. The pool was kept heated for him whenever the temperature dropped. "Did you feed him?"

"A side of beef. And his vitamins."

"Good. Thank you. I'll take my breakfast on the garden patio, then."

Beckett nodded and left. She imagined he waited in the kitchen with her tray until she was seated at the small café table where she ate whenever the mood struck her, which was usually when Thoreau was in the garden pool. He was quite something to see.

She dressed as she usually did. A long-sleeved top and leggings beneath a custom-made caftan from

3

Rajani Bhatt's shop in town. She paired that with silk slippers and a jeweled turban that was so much easier than coiffing her hair. The look was a bit eccentric, perhaps, but it suited her.

Pasqual would have hated it. Too theatrical for his taste, but she was a witch of considerable age, although she didn't look it, and great power lived within her. She would dress however it pleased her.

And for the past several decades, it had pleased her to dress the way her grandmother, Pavani, had. Even after years of living in the southeast of France, the only change Grandmama Pavani had made was to give up her saris for caftans. Amelia had loved both for their bright colors and sparkling adornments.

That thought put a smile on Amelia's face. It lasted all the way down to the garden patio, where the sight of her only real love these days greeted her.

Thoreau whuffed out a low, throaty noise from where he was reclining in the shallow end of the garden pool. Mist rose off the water, making him appear like something out of a maharaja's dream.

"Hello, my darling boy." Even in the watery light of a Shadowvale morning, his orange and black stripes were a gloriously brilliant spectacle. Proof that even Shadowvale's perpetually overcast sky could not diminish the natural beauty of things. She walked toward him, her slippers silent on the grass, but the crushed blades brought the reaffirming scent of green earth to her nose.

Already, the morning's chill was wearing off. It would be a pleasant day in Shadowvale. The kind where she could keep the windows and doors open to let in fresh air. That made her happy.

Once at Thoreau's side, she crouched and gave him a good scratch behind his ear. The velvet of his fur under her fingers was a privilege that gave her pause every time she experienced it.

He leaned his enormous head into her hand as he stretched his dinner-plate-sized paws out in front of him, rippling the water. Then he slow-blinked at her.

She returned the gesture. "I love you, too, my angel." The affection of a beast so great and mighty was all it took to fill her heart these days. Thoreau was enough. He had to be.

As for Pasqual...she couldn't help but wonder what had become of him. Had he met the sun in some cruel twist? Gone to ash with the morning's rays? She'd probably never know. It wasn't that she wanted him back. Not in the slightest. But she didn't exactly wish him ill either.

After all, she had this place because of him. Even if it had cost her everything.

"I have to eat my breakfast now, my darling." She patted Thoreau's big head, stood, and went back to the patio.

Beckett was coming out of the house with her morning repast. She took a seat at the small table and draped a napkin over her lap, her gaze on the pool again. Thoreau was fixated on a dragonfly. For all his size and majesty, he was at times just an overgrown house cat.

Beckett put a covered dish in front of her. "Will there be anything else?"

She glanced at the table, then frowned. "The paper?"

"Coming right up."

She sipped her tea, leaving the plate covered. It was steel-cut oatmeal with raw wild honey and Ceylon cinnamon. The same thing she ate every morning. Chef could make anything, but Amelia had become such a creature of habit that she seldom took advantage of the highly trained cook she employed.

Beckett left to get the paper. She amused herself by watching Thoreau until her warden returned.

With great pomp, Beckett held the paper over his forearm like some grand prize. "The *Vale Messenger*, madam."

She gave him a look as she took it from him, just to let him know she wasn't impressed with his theatrics.

He seemed amused nonetheless, and that amusement led to him dropping all pretense of formality. "What do you have planned for the day, Amelia? Perhaps a drive into the country yonder? A picnic in the sun, maybe?"

"If I want sun, I'll go to Nightingale Park." Because she wouldn't be venturing beyond the gates of Shadowvale any time soon. She narrowed her eyes at his nonsense. This game never got old for

6

him. Apparently. She flicked the paper open, ignoring his ludicrous suggestions.

He chuckled as he went back into the house.

She could possibly take a trip out to the mines to see how things were going, but if there was a problem, the manager would contact her. Those mines, deep in the mountains that surrounded Shadowvale, had never failed to produce a steady stream of gems. And those gems were what supported this town, so they were important.

But her presence there was never required.

She went back to the paper. Just a few thin pages, which was typical. There was only so much news a town like Shadowvale could produce on a daily basis. Most of it was meeting notices. The chess club, the quilters circle, the coven, the wolf pack, the gardening club, the curse support group. But it was news just the same, and she read every word of it every morning. Keeping tabs on things was important.

Gracie Evermore was listed in the birthday column. Her twenty-fifth. Amelia stared at the number. She'd been that age when she'd met Pasqual.

But Gracie had three older brothers to keep her from a similar fate.

Amelia made a note to send a gift. There would be a party, no doubt, but parties weren't really Amelia's style anymore. And attending could...dampen the festivities. She knew the effect her presence had on such events. Some perceived her power to be greater than it really was. Some feared her because of her power. Some would do anything to get her to use her power to help them.

Regardless, she was treated differently than other citizens. It wasn't enjoyable. All that fawning and flattery in hopes of swaying her to help. All those favors promised.

Favors she didn't want or need. Help she couldn't usually give. But no one believed her when she tried to explain.

She finished the paper and set it aside before turning to her breakfast. Thoreau was out of the pool now and sleeping in the grass at the edge of the patio.

She lifted the cover off her oatmeal and gave the porridge a stir. Was this really her life? The same breakfast, day after day. The same routine. The same everything.

Maybe she should go to Gracie's party. It would be a change, that was for sure.

She ate her oatmeal and sipped her tea, lost in her thoughts, as she was most mornings. By the end of the meal, she had convinced herself the party was something she might actually attend. She glanced down into her cup.

Fragments of tea leaves settled as she watched, forming a pattern that was undeniable.

She blinked, then swirled the cup again.

The same pattern formed.

She set the cup down and looked at Thoreau. Her breath felt tight in her chest. Maybe the party wouldn't be necessary after all if a change in her routine was what she was after.

Thoreau lifted his head as if sensing his mistress's unrest.

She met his gaze. "She's coming. How can that be?"

♪

There had been more than enough flashing blue lights in Emeranth Greer's life lately, but she could handle the ones in her rearview mirror. She hoped.

Em handed over her license and registration to the cop who'd pulled her over. *Please don't let me get a ticket.* She hadn't thought she was speeding, but the twists in these little country roads had a way of hiding speed-limit signs. Especially at night. She hadn't been sure if it was fifty or forty-five through here.

As it turned out, it was forty, and she'd been going eight miles over. Not any kind of real crime in her book, and she knew real crime well enough to compare it, but she was also smart enough not to make a fuss.

He stared at her documents. "Where are you headed, Ms. Greer?"

"To see my aunt." Great-aunt, really. Em had never met her, so she was taking a big chance that the woman would let her stay, but Em needed a fresh start so badly she could taste it. Her aunt had to let her stay. *Had to.*

"And where's she live?"

Em peered at the cop through the open window that was letting the car's heat escape. He was the color of midnight with arms like cannons. Seemed very no-nonsense. Not that she was about to offer him any. His badge said Baker. *Please don't give me a ticket, Officer Baker.* "In Shadowvale? I've never been there, but it's supposed to be right off this road and—"

"Ma'am, I see by your out-of-state license that you're not from around here, so I wouldn't expect you to know this, but no one lives in Shadowvale."

Except her aunt did. Em had the woman's address. She'd found it in her mother's ancient address book, the one with the leather flaking off the cover and the pages yellowed with age. "I...I'm not sure what you mean."

"I mean no one lives there. Shadowvale was a private community a long, long time ago. But now..." He shrugged and handed her documents back. "It's just an abandoned place. All shut up and forgotten. Owners ran out of money is the story. Not sure it ever even took off. Or who owns it now. No one I've met even remembers it being a going concern. What I do know is that the gates have been locked for more years than I've been alive."

She rubbed her arms to warm them up. That was the most disappointing news Em had heard in ages. Maybe since the last disappointing news she'd had, about her mother's string of cons finally landing her in jail. Em sighed and took her license and registration back. *Please don't give me a ticket. Please.* "Thanks for the information."

He gave her a strange look, shining his flashlight on her for a moment. "Since you're from out of town, I'll just give you a warning. Keep it to the speed limit."

"Yes, sir, Officer Baker. Thank you." No ticket. That was great. She couldn't afford it anyway.

"Drive safe and have a good night." He nodded and walked away.

She rolled up her window and cranked the heat up. It made a whining sound, then the air started coming out cold. Perfect. She sat there until Officer Baker pulled back onto the road and disappeared.

The GPS app on her phone was still showing Shadowvale 2.2 miles ahead. And despite what the cop had told her, she was too stubborn not to want to see for herself. Maybe she'd just drive through and have a look at where her aunt used to live.

Then she'd have to find a safe place to park for the night, because her car was going to be her bed this evening. Even without heat. A hotel room was too big of a luxury at this moment in her life. Especially if the aunt she'd been counting on to take her in was no longer around.

She checked her mirror, then headed down the road, driving a few miles under the speed limit and watching carefully for a sign that would point her toward the remains of Shadowvale.

The distance ticked away on her GPS, but no sign ever appeared. Maybe it had fallen down. The cop had made it seem like Shadowvale had ceased to be in operation long enough for that to have happened.

But the last few feet came and went, and no sign ever appeared.

She slowed down, crawling along the road as she tried to see any indication of where the town might be. Not easy on a country road with only the moonlight and her headlamps to go by.

She turned around and backtracked, following the GPS to the exact spot it claimed Shadowvale was located.

"You have arrived at your destination," the computer voice said.

"Thanks," Em answered. "But there's nothing here but trees and weeds and…"

She peered closer. Then shook her head. How had she missed that road before? It was a little overgrown, but it was plainly visible now that her headlights were shining right on it.

Too bad it wasn't lit. A couple of streetlights would make it a lot less creepy. But she'd come this far. She wasn't stopping now.

She turned down the narrow road. The trees were thick on both sides and dripping in moss. Creepy was right. But it was also kind of pretty. Like a film set. For a movie where everybody died.

She came to a gated entrance.

The metal gates were set in wide stone columns. They were twice as tall as she was and wide enough to let two cars pass, but they were also thick with vines and caked with rust. And closed. And locked.

The cop had been right. No one had been through them in many, many years.

She stared at the gates, leaning on the steering wheel to see the name Shadowvale spelled out in the wrought iron at the top. She sighed. Well, she was in the right place.

Too bad she was *years* too late.

She stared a few moments longer, then decided she might as well get a picture to prove she'd been here. To whom, she wasn't sure, but she needed some kind of proof that she'd made the attempt. Maybe for herself, for the future. As a reminder that she'd at least tried for a fresh start and hadn't failed for lack of ambition.

She grabbed her phone and hopped out of the car, then positioned herself in front of the gates, held her phone out, and snapped a couple shots.

The air was dry and cool, but scented with some kind of night-blooming flower. What kind of flower bloomed this early in spring? The South was a mystery to her. Spring here happened in a very different way than she was used to. Even the insect life was thriving. But the soft buzz of their wings almost sounded like a lullaby, reminding her she still had to find a place to park and sleep.

She scrolled through the pics she'd just taken to see how they'd come out. Decent. Although she looked a little tired, and her smile seemed forced. Which it was. She'd been driving for two days.

Only to discover it was all for nothing.

A faint creaking broke overtop the subtle hum of the evening. She looked up from her phone, unsure where the sound had come from. Nothing new that she could see. And thankfully, it wasn't her car rolling back toward the highway. Some bug, maybe? Or a frog? That was probably it.

She decided on one more selfie. One in which she looked a little more genuinely happy. One that might help her see the future in a brighter light.

She raised the phone again, smiled her best smile, and took the shot. She looked at it on her phone to see if it was better than the first ones.

She stared at the image, trying to understand what she was seeing. With two fingers, she zoomed in.

Was that right? How could it be? She turned around to look.

The gates were open.

CHAPTER TWO

Rumor had it that Shadowvale was the most cursed town in all of America. Deacon Evermore didn't know if that was true. He hadn't been to every town in America. And those he had been to, well, it had been a long time since he'd been outside Shadowvale's gates. He was busy enough in this town.

He did know that Shadowvale was definitely cursed. Though, maybe *cursed* wasn't exactly the right description. *Touched with questionable magic* was better. From the iron gates that opened when and if they wanted to, all the way up to the tops of the mountains that surrounded the valley the town sat in, then right back down to the magical meridian lines deep beneath Shadowvale's soil, everything was a little...off.

Some things were a lot off. Like how the sun never shone. Hadn't in as many years as anyone could remember. Because of a curse, naturally.

The vampires in town—and there were many—saw it as a major perk. It was their primary reason for moving to Shadowvale. A few of the witches (although not Amelia Marchand, grand dame of the town and the perpetrator of the sunless-existence spell) claimed they were working on a counterspell to undo the curse and bring the sun back to Shadowvale, but Deacon reckoned that was just a lot of talk.

Especially because the vampires were dead set against this. As a result, the feelings between the vampires and the witches ranged from mildly irritated to downright vexed.

Although there was the occasional pair who somehow looked past all that and got rather cozy with each other. But that wasn't his business, so he stayed out of such things. Preferred it that way, in truth.

Until he *had* to get involved.

The shifters and the other supernaturals in town didn't seem to care much about the sun one way or the other. After all, they had their own burdens to bear.

Everyone in town did, really.

Deacon was no exception, and proof that the curses came in varying degrees. Sometimes the curse was obvious because it was easy to see. Like with Mrs. Fitzwilliams in the black and gray cottage on Sorrows Lane whose hair set itself ablaze whenever she got upset. Or like with Fred Chimes, the butcher at the Green Grocer, who had a nervous condition that rendered him invisible during the peak of that condition.

Sometimes the curses weren't so obvious. Like Deacon's curse. Or all of his family's curses. They were very real, but nothing that could be seen. Thankfully. Small comfort, though.

But that's why people moved to Shadowvale. They had something to hide. Or they wanted to be left alone. Or they *didn't* want to be left alone, instead choosing to live amongst those similarly plagued by the misfortunes of life.

Curses, troubles, jinxes, plagues, miseries, traumas, plights, predicaments, whatever you called them, everybody here had one. Or they owned something cursed. Occasionally, someone just *thought* they were cursed, but even that was a sort of curse.

Whatever the reason they'd come to Shadowvale, something about that shared burden made the weight a little easier to bear.

Didn't mean getting a phone call from Amelia Marchand at half past ten in the evening was something he was thrilled about.

"Miss Amelia."

"Deacon."

"What can I do for you?" No doubt someone's curse had activated, requiring his services.

"I need a favor."

He took a breath. That was a better reason for her call than any he'd imagined. "I'll be happy to oblige if I can."

"My niece is arriving any moment now and—"

"The gates let her in?" The gates didn't just let people in. The gates were picky. And no one really

17

knew the how or why of their decision-making. (Or if the rumored gatekeeper really existed.)

"She's my niece. My blood is in her veins. I can't imagine they wouldn't. At this point anyway."

"Ah." He nodded for no real purpose, being that he was on the phone. "Makes sense."

"I need you to persuade her that Shadowvale is not for her."

That wasn't something he wanted to be on the hook for. "You don't think you can do that?"

"I love her. I don't want to hurt her. Or be the bad guy. And I will do my part, but I need someone more persuasive."

"I see. So I get to be the heavy."

Amelia sighed. "Is it so much to ask? You are the town's peacekeeper."

"True." But he wasn't a peacekeeper in the traditional sense of the word. Sometimes he was, taking care of things the same way any lawman would. Mostly, he fixed situations that had nothing to do with the law. And Shadowvale had a lot of those. This didn't seem like that kind of situation.

He made one last attempt to get out of it. "But I work for the citizens of Shadowvale. Technically, your niece doesn't quite qualify as—"

"I will make it worth your while."

"I'm listening." Not like he had a choice.

"You still want out of Shadowvale permanently? And to be free of your curse?"

He went silent for a moment. Moving out wasn't something he talked about. Mostly for Gracie's sake.

And because of the consequences that leaving would bring. "That's not possible."

"I can make it possible."

His breath caught in his throat. Was that true? It had to be if Amelia was saying so. But he'd heard her deny it before, too, so what did he believe? He shook his head. Amelia was the town's architect. If she said she could do it, she must really be able to. "Only if Gracie gets to go too. Same deal, free of her curse."

"That's a lot to ask for."

"It's not negotiable. We're a package deal."

Her sigh had an edge to it, like he'd asked too much. "I'll see what I can do."

He smiled. "When and where do I meet her?"

"Good." Satisfaction rang in her voice. "Tomorrow morning. Indigo House. Come for breakfast. Eight sharp."

"I normally eat here at the—"

"And listen, you're simply to show her around and persuade her this is not the place for her. No flirting, no amusing banter, no Southern hospitality. I don't want her to like you or this town."

His brows shot up, and he almost laughed, then thought better of it. For the reward Amelia was offering, she'd get what she wanted.

When he didn't answer, she sighed. "Do you agree or not?"

"I do. I'll be there." He hung up, wondering what he'd just gotten himself into. Amelia's niece. Had to be more like a great-great-great-niece. Amelia had been around for a long time. Unless this niece was on the upside of ancient, too.

Huh. He hadn't considered that. This might be trickier than he'd imagined. The blue-haired set was his best demographic. They loved him. Mostly because he loved them right back. Grandmas and aunties were his favorite kind of women, unless they were trying to fix him up with one of their much younger female relatives.

She was probably a witch like Amelia as well. That ran in families, from what he understood. Most supernatural abilities had a tendency to do that. It did in his family. Except where poor Gracie was concerned.

He rubbed the back of his neck. Squiring Amelia's elderly niece around town and keeping her from wanting to stay here might be the easiest thing he'd ever done, but he doubted that. Things were never easy where Amelia was concerned. That was the trouble with witches. They never seemed to give you all the details until you were too deep in to back out.

Gracie walked into the kitchen in her nightgown, her little white dog in her arms. "Trouble, Deac?"

"No, honey. Just setting up an appointment for the morning. Did I wake you and Tinkerbelle up?"

"No." She gave him a limp smile and scratched Tinkerbelle's head. "Couldn't sleep. Bad dream. Tink didn't have that problem, but I woke her when I got up."

"What was the dream about?"

She shrugged and put Tinkerbelle down. "You know."

He pulled his little sister into his arms and kissed the top of her head. "Let it go, Gracie."

She nodded against his chest. "I am. Just thought I'd make some tea and take it back to bed."

He released her. "Good idea."

She headed for the cabinets. Tinkerbelle stayed as close by as possible. "You going to bed soon?"

"In a bit."

She took a mug down, popped a K-Cup into the Keurig and pushed the brew button. Chamomile tea, by the smell of it. "Hey, what are you doing Saturday night?"

He almost answered her, then laughed. Saturday was her birthday, and he and his brothers had a party planned for that night. She'd been hinting around, trying for weeks to find out details. "Nothing much."

She frowned at him as she dumped sugar into her cup and stirred. "You boys are terrible."

"I know." He leaned against the counter, watching his baby sister. As much as he wanted to leave Shadowvale, that would mean leaving her. And his brothers.

Could he do that? He really didn't know.

Their father had left. And they all knew how that had ended.

With a funeral.

And as far as they knew, that had been their mother's fate, too, but she'd left right after Gracie had been born, and they hadn't heard from her since. The loss of her husband followed by the stillbirth of Gracie's twin had been too much for her, apparently.

He held a smile on his face even though he no longer felt it. He was trapped here. But if Amelia could find a way to change that…

Gracie lifted her mug. "Night, Deac."

"Night, Gracie."

With Tinkerbelle on her heels, she took her tea and padded back to her room, leaving him alone with his tortured thoughts and the feeling of guilt that had kept him rooted in this town for his entire adult life.

He stayed right where he was, hoping the feeling would pass, but it didn't. It never did. The Evermores had lived in Shadowvale for generations. They'd been its caretakers in one way or another for all that time, too.

How was he supposed to leave this place behind when it had its hooks in him so deeply? And how was he supposed to live anywhere else with the Evermore curse hanging over him? What other place would have him? And let him live in relative peace?

Resentment crawled up his spine, unsettling him more than he could put into words. There was only one way to combat a mood like this.

He pushed off the counter and strode out to the back deck. Stars filled the sky, and Shadowvale's constant fireflies dotted the woods beyond the house. A deep inhale of the night air helped, but what he really needed was that air beneath him.

With a few steps, he launched himself off the deck, shifted into his raven form, and soared into the darkness to fly and forget, at least for a little while.

♪

A dark shadow swooped past as Em inched her car down Shadowvale's main road. She checked the gates in her rearview mirror. They were already closing.

She really hoped she'd be able to get them open again. She didn't think Officer Baker would enjoy coming to rescue her.

But the gates had opened wide enough to grant her entrance, so she'd taken the opportunity. Hopefully, they'd let her out, too. How they'd come open, she didn't know, but she'd convinced herself they'd never actually been locked and that she'd leaned against them during her selfie, pushing them open in the process.

Nothing else made sense.

Except not overthinking it. Which was why she'd decided to focus on her current task.

Her plan was just to see her aunt's house. Maybe park in the driveway and sleep there, if it seemed safe. But the idea of spending the evening in an abandoned town wasn't all that appealing.

Still, staying somewhere for free was about all that fit her budget right now.

The road ahead went straight into the trees, then curved sharply. As she drove around the curve, she came upon the town. She frowned.

The town didn't really look all that abandoned. Shut down for the night, yes, but abandoned? Not by a long shot.

Actually, it didn't even look that shut down.

The street—Main, she guessed—was well-maintained, lined with shops that looked stocked. Some even had lights on. They weren't completely lit up, more like security lights. But enough to see that the stores weren't empty.

A sign confirmed that she was on Main Street. Softly glowing lamps sat at every street corner, giving off their dim, atmospheric light. Almost seemed like the lamps had been purposefully turned to half power. Or maybe the power grid was waning. More likely the lamps were just old.

Which made it odd that not a single one was burned out.

Odder still, what kind of abandoned town had an active retail presence and *any* electricity? None she'd ever heard of.

She kept driving and staring, but as she did, a new thought came to her. Maybe this place hadn't been meant as a town, but some kind of amusement. After all, she'd just passed a store called Bewitched Broomsticks. As if the place actually sold magical broomsticks.

She snorted.

Then saw another one. Varina's Potions and Spells.

And another. Professor Durrant's Impossible Tech. Whatever that meant. But judging by the android-looking creature in the window, it wasn't Radio Shack 2.0.

What kind of place was this?

She would have driven farther down Main, but her GPS spoke up, telling her to make the next left onto Hollows Lane. She did, quickly leaving the town behind to find a more residential area.

Lights filled quite a few of the homes, even at this late hour. And not dim lights either. She saw the blue flicker of a television through one window.

Clearly, that cop had been wrong. She squinted as she thought about how the gates had been rusted and overgrown with vines. And, she'd thought, locked.

But they had swung open, so maybe that was all a ruse. Maybe everyone who lived here had a clicker that opened them.

If that was true, they should clean those gates more often, because they looked like they'd been abandoned to time and the weather decades ago. Unless that was intentional.

Really, what was safer than living in a place no one thought was occupied? What better spot to be left alone. To be able to live your life by your own terms.

She smiled and nodded. Please let all of that be true. Please let Shadowvale be some secret community that had decided to hide itself away from the world. Because if it was, she was definitely in the right place.

Also, if they could be welcoming to newcomers, that would also be great. Because she might not ever leave.

Chapter Three

Em slowed down on pure autopilot. She'd gone a little distance without another house in sight, but now she'd found one and was too busy staring out the window to pay more attention to the car and her driving. This couldn't be right. Could it?

Specifically, the house in front of her was what she was questioning. Well, *house* maybe wasn't the right word. Mansion? Estate? Manor home? Whatever you called it, one word definitely applied. *Enormous.* Two sprawling stories of what she could think to describe only as a French chateau sat like a pale jewel at the end of a winding, tree-lined drive.

From the creamy stucco walls to the deep-blue, pitched roof, the entire house seemed to float above the pearly fog that draped the manicured lawn. Adding to that effect was the delicate illumination by landscape lighting so expertly hidden that it seemed as if everything just glowed because it was so beautiful.

If Cinderella herself had strolled out of the house in a giant ball gown and glittering glass shoes, Em would not have been surprised.

There was no way this was where her aunt lived. It didn't seem possible. Mostly because of what she knew about her aunt.

Em's mother hadn't liked to talk about Aunt Amelia, for some reason, but when she had, she'd always made it seem like Aunt Amelia was a poor relation. As if talking about her too much might make the woman suddenly show up, looking for a handout.

Which was pretty much what Em was doing here now. Okay, not a handout, exactly, but a place to stay, for sure.

She pressed down on the brake, finally bringing the vehicle to a complete stop. This was the right address. Seventeen Hollows Lane. She peered through the windshield. There was no name on the mailbox, just the house number.

She snorted. The mailbox alone probably cost more than her car. It was a beautiful wrought-iron thing that matched the fence around the property, all of which was decorated with a scowling-tiger motif. That had to be custom. She'd never seen anything like that at the DIY Depot in the eight days she'd been employed there before the news about her mother had hit and Em's position had mysteriously been downsized into nonexistence.

She tapped her fingers on the steering wheel. She had to make a decision. She couldn't sit in the middle of the road all night. And not just because this place probably had security that rivaled the prison where her mother was now serving six to ten.

With a long exhale, she shrugged and turned down the long drive. She rarely let adversity stop her. This situation was no different than any of the other things she'd faced.

But she drove slowly, trying to piece together what she'd say to whoever answered the door. *Hi, I'm Emeranth Greer. Is my aunt Amelia home?*

No, that wouldn't work. It was too assumptive. She'd just ask if Aunt Amelia lived here. That's what she'd do. Straight out with it.

And if Aunt Amelia didn't, well, then, Em would just—she braked suddenly as a realization hit her.

Of course Aunt Amelia didn't live here. Aunt Amelia *worked* here.

That had to be it. A house like this must have live-in staff, so maybe in a way, Aunt Amelia *did* live here. Maybe…there'd even be a job for Em. She could do anything if it meant paying her bills and keeping a roof over her head. Cook, clean, garden, run errands, scrub toilets, whatever they needed.

With new determination, she grabbed her purse and got out of the car.

She stood for a moment, looking at the house. This was going to be all right. It was going to work out. They wouldn't turn away the niece of one of their employees, would they? Em hoped not. She ran her hand through her hair, hoping she didn't look like a vagabond. She also hoped Aunt Amelia was a really, really good employee.

She bucked up her courage, put on her best smile, and headed for the front door. Which was really two doors. Beautiful blue arched doors flanked by carved statues of tigers done in some glittery blue-black stone that probably also cost a fortune.

The doors were mostly blue glass, but it was wavy and swirled and impossible to see more than shapes through. Despite the late hour, a chandelier in the foyer burned brightly, so someone was still awake, right?

She took a breath. She'd never been in a place this swanky. Heck, she'd never been *near* a place this swanky. She really hoped she didn't screw anything up.

She pushed the doorbell. Pretty chimes, muted by the house, reached her ears. Not long after the chimes faded, a figure appeared behind the glass. A man.

He opened the door. "Good evening. What can I do for you?"

He was trim, but barrel-chested and a little on the shorter side. Stocky. Like a bulldog. With neat, salt-and-pepper hair. Former military, maybe. Like, special ops military. Black ops. The kind where they killed bad people in secret places and denied all knowledge of—okay, she was working herself up now.

So much so, she almost turned and ran. "I, uh…I…"

He smiled. "There must be something I can help you with."

That smile somehow made everything all right. She nodded, her pulse slowing back to normal. "I'm looking for my aunt. Amelia Marchand. I think she might work here."

He let out a little snort, then schooled his face to eliminate the sudden smile, but the twinkle in his eyes remained. "I wouldn't say she works here, exactly."

"Oh. I guess my information was wrong." Em's heart sank, and she started to turn back toward the car.

"That's not what I meant. She is here. She just doesn't work here. The lady of the manor has staff to do the work."

Em stared at him. Her gaze narrowed. "The lady of the manor? You make it sound like...she owns this house? That can't be right."

"But it is." He nodded. "Amelia Marchand is the owner of Indigo House. Always has been. Would you like to come in, Miss...?"

"Oh, um, Em. Emeranth. But call me Em. Wow."

"Welcome, Miss Em. I'm Beckett. The majordomo. You can call me Beckett." The smile returned briefly. "I'll fetch your aunt."

Em stepped through the doors in a daze. Aunt Amelia owned this place. How was this possible? Also, what was a majordomo? "Thank you."

"If you'd like to follow me into the sitting room."

"Sure." It wasn't a question so much as a strong suggestion, but she was occupied with checking the house out and happy to comply. The foyer opened into a rotunda that had to be thirty feet high. Wrought-iron balconies looked down from the second floor.

She followed him, still feeling a little dumbstruck. The house was beyond words. Gorgeous thick crown moldings, beautiful furnishings, expensive art, inlaid marble floors in some rooms, gleaming wood in others, and all of it keeping the French chateau theme going.

He stopped and opened a set of double doors. "Please make yourself comfortable. I'll let her know you're here."

"Thank you." She walked into the sitting room. Wood beams, like something she imagined you'd see in an old French manor, braced the pitched ceiling. The beams looked well-aged, but maybe they'd just been finished like that on purpose, although she had a suspicion they were genuinely old. And expensive. As in imported from a French castle.

The wood floors looked a little like that, too, even though they were highly polished. The planks were laid in a herringbone pattern that gave the big room a more intimate feel. A broad carved stone fireplace sat at one end with a cozy seating area positioned around it. At the other end was more seating and a wall of shelves filled with books and objects.

Despite how high-end everything obviously was, the house had a comfortableness about it. Like it had been designed for the sole pleasure of those who lived in it, not to impress anyone. Em liked that. A lot. The idea that someone like her aunt could have so much money and so little care what others thought was completely charming. She couldn't wait to meet the woman.

Em sent a longing glance at the fireplace. How nice it would be to sit in one of those overstuffed chairs, curled up with a good book and a hot drink.

She'd never done anything like that, but people did it all the time in movies.

Life in this house must be amazing. Her aunt must be amazing. Em already adored the woman.

Em just hoped Aunt Amelia liked her in return. Enough to let her stay anyway. It wasn't like Aunt Amelia would even notice Em in a house this size.

*

Amelia stood in the doorway of the sitting room for a moment. She needed that moment. Needed to absorb the gift—and the burden—that had shown up at her front door.

She hadn't seen a single member of her family in nearly a century. Well, that wasn't exactly true. She hadn't seen a member of her family since Manda Greer had come calling for help, which Amelia had refused to provide, for a plethora of reasons. The primary one being Manda should have known better than to ask for something so...unsavory to begin with.

Now Emeranth Greer, Amelia's niece, was here. In her home. Amelia's heart strained with love. It didn't matter that she'd never met the child before. Although calling her a *child* wasn't fair. A woman stood before her. A beautiful creature with the dark hair and willowy frame and bronze skin that Grandmama Pavani had passed down.

Amelia saw herself in the young woman. Many, many years ago, but still, this was her blood. Her family. And one of very few left.

Amelia only hoped she hadn't come with her hand out like her mother had. At least not asking for things that were better left unspoken.

Either way, Amelia would have to send the woman away as quickly as possible. The dangers of being in this place with Marchand blood in her veins were too great.

Amelia took a breath. "Hello."

Emeranth whipped around, blinking like she'd been caught at something. "Aunt Amelia?"

Amelia nodded. "Yes. And you must be Emeranth."

"I am. But everybody just calls me Em. Your home is…" She shook her head and laughed softly. "It's so beautiful. I just love it."

"Thank you." Amelia gestured toward the sitting area in front of the fireplace. "Let's sit so we can talk. Old bones, you know."

Em moved toward the chairs, still smiling. "I was thinking when I first came in what a nice spot this would be to curl up with a book. Especially with a fire going."

Amelia smiled, overcome with feelings of generosity and affection. She waved her hand toward the fireplace, igniting a happy little blaze.

Em gasped and jumped back. "How did you do that?"

Amelia frowned. "With a touch of magic. How does a witch do anything?"

That did nothing to dissipate the fear in Em's eyes. "I'm sorry, what?"

Amelia realized all too quickly that her niece, no

matter what power might dwell within her, had never been initiated into the way of Marchand women. Manda had a lot to explain. And now Amelia did, too, because of her assumption that her niece had been raised as the witch she was. "It's okay. It's nothing."

Em shook her head. "Oh, it's definitely something. Are you saying you're a witch?"

Amelia sighed, folded her hands in her lap, and made a snap decision. "We are all witches, my dear."

"We?"

"The Marchand women."

Em snorted. "Um, maybe in, like, the metaphorical sense, but not—"

"Yes, we are. In the very literal sense. My grandmother was, my mother was, as am I and your mother. And you."

"No." Em reached for the arm of the chair nearest to her and held on. "That's not possible."

"Sit down, Emeranth. We clearly have much to discuss."

The woman didn't move.

"Oh, sit down. I'm not going to hurt you or turn you into a toad."

Em's brows rose. "Can you do that?"

"Yes. Now, sit. Please. I'm getting a kink in my neck from staring up at you."

Em sat, but the look of shock and confusion on her face remained. She stared at the fireplace. Maybe looking for answers in the flames. "I don't believe in witches."

Amelia laughed. "So you don't believe in yourself?"

"I'm not—listen, why do you think that about me? There's nothing witchy about me. Or my mother." She flicked a glance at Amelia. "And I don't know you well enough to make that judgment yet."

"It's nothing terrible, I assure you. And I didn't mean to startle you with the information. I just thought you knew. I thought your mother would have told you. Helped you understand your craft."

"My mother isn't exactly the nurturing type."

That didn't surprise Amelia. "I'm sorry to hear that. And I'm doubly sorry to know that she's never told you the truth about your nature. Maybe you should go home and have a talk with her. I'm sure she had a good reason for keeping things from you." Actually, Amelia wasn't sure of that at all, but she was trying to be kind.

Em grimaced. "That's not possible. Going home. Or talking to her."

Amelia felt a sudden panic. "Is your mother unwell?"

"You might say that." Em stared at the fire again, a frustrated bend to her mouth.

That didn't tell Amelia much, but she could see pain in her niece's eyes. "I'm sorry."

"Yeah. Thanks." Em was silent for a long moment. "If I'm a witch, wouldn't I know it? Shouldn't I be able to do magic and cast spells and turn straw into gold and all that?"

"Yes. Once you've been through the initiation. But I'm guessing your mother has never done that with you, so you've never experienced the true power that's inside you. You've probably seen small glimpses of things, depending on how much power you have, but without knowing what you were really seeing, you most likely found ways to explain them away."

"An initiation? And what kind of things?"

"The initiation for Marchand women is generally a bath of fire by moonlight."

Em's mouth twisted. "I'm afraid to ask what that means. Especially if it's exactly what it sounds like."

"It is. But don't look so skeptical. We are immune to the touch of fire."

Her brows bent doubtfully. "We are?"

Amelia got up, walked over to the fireplace, and thrust her hand into the flames. "See?"

Em's mouth fell open.

Amelia held her hand there a few seconds longer for good measure, then pulled it out and presented it to her niece. "Look at it. Not a burn. Not a mark. Not even a speck of soot."

Em took her aunt's hand in hers and inspected it, turning it over. "That's...amazing. Wait. Is that why my mother puts candles out by pinching the flame with her fingers? She always told me to try, but I was too chicken."

"Indeed. It's one of our many powers." Emeranth was the first person who'd touched Amelia in years. The warmth and softness of her niece's skin were almost breathtaking, but painful, too. It reminded Amelia how much she'd shut herself off.

Em looked up, still holding Amelia's hand. "Could I try it?"

"Not until you've been initiated." But she liked the woman's enthusiasm and willingness. And her lack of fear showed real strength of character. What had Emeranth been through in her life to be this bold?

Em shrugged and released Amelia's hand. "Then initiate me."

"It's really something your mother should—"

"She's kept this from me my entire life. You think that's suddenly going to change?"

"No. I suppose not." Amelia went back to her chair and sat. "What's brought you here? I'm not the easiest person to find."

"Neither is Shadowvale." Em smiled, her expression lightening considerably. "But I'm a little like a dog with a bone. When I want something, I go after it wholeheartedly."

That made Amelia smile, too. Em was so much like Amelia. "You'll make a good witch."

Em sat forward suddenly. "Are we really witches?"

"Yes."

She let out a fast exhale. "I've heard some crazy things in my life, but that takes the cake." She tipped her head. "You said I might have seen signs of my power already, but found a way to explain them away. What kinds of signs?"

Amelia was keenly aware that her question about how Em had found her had not been answered, but she understood the young woman's curiosity. "Perhaps you knew who was at the door before you answered it. Or what a letter was going to say before you read it. Maybe you wished for something and it came true. Or needed something that suddenly appeared. Or you saw something that no one else saw. Things like that."

"If you swap 'email' for 'letter,' then all of those things have happened. Are you saying those were actually manifestations of my power?"

Amelia nodded. "And chances are that it's considerable. It tends to ebb and flow from generation to generation. Your mother's power is decent, but nothing remarkable. Yours could be exceptional if things go as they normally do."

"Wow." She put her hand to her mouth for a moment. "Sometimes you just never know what the day's going to bring when you get up, do you?"

"Sometimes." Amelia paused for a breath. "Although I knew you were coming."

Em went back to her shocked expression for a brief second, then laughed. "Of course you did. Oh, Aunt Amelia, I'm so glad I found you. When can I be initiated?"

"First things first, dear." Amelia let her hands rest lightly on the arms of the chair. "Why did you come here to begin with? And what is it you hope to gain from this visit?"

CHAPTER FOUR

Em knew how to lie. Her mother had taught her. The lesson wasn't one Em had wanted or asked for, it was one she'd picked up through a life lived with a woman who painted in broad strokes and used those around her for everything she could by whatever means necessary. For Manda Greer, to breathe was to lie.

Em wasn't about to craft some tale that would make her aunt pity her. This was about a fresh start. One built on the truth.

But the woman before Em was incredibly wealthy, surprisingly beautiful, and had an air of power about her that Em hadn't expected. Was it any wonder Em was a little scared to tell her the truth?

There was no point in holding it back, though. Not if Aunt Amelia was really as powerful as she seemed to be.

And not if being here meant Em had the opportunity to see what that power was like for herself. A witch? Was that really possible? It seemed like it was. Especially if Aunt Amelia was supposed to be her great-aunt but looked young enough to be an older sister. If that wasn't witchcraft, some cosmetics company should figure out the secret and bottle it.

But then, Em had been conned before by flesh and blood.

She took a breath. "I'm here because I have nowhere else to go. That makes me sound like a charity case, I know, but it's where I'm at right now." How pathetic she must seem to a woman of means like Amelia. "I was hoping that maybe…"

Her words stuck in her gullet. It wasn't pride holding them there, but fear of rejection. She cleared her throat. "I was hoping I could get a fresh start here. That you might let me stay. Not forever. Just until I get my feet under me again. I won't be in the way. You won't even know I'm here. I swear it. And I realize that's a big ask from someone you've just met, but you're all I've got."

Amelia stared at her rather impassively. The jewels in her turban glittered, reflecting the firelight. Then something flickered in her gaze. Something that might have been consternation. Or disappointment. Or regret.

Whatever her aunt's emotions, Em understood perfectly that Aunt Amelia didn't want her here. Her heart sank as she dropped her head and let out a small sigh without meaning to. She could tell her aunt the truth, that Manda was in jail. But that felt manipulative, and honestly, Em was tired of people knowing about her mother's situation and judging Em as being cut from the same cloth.

That left only one more question. Where was she going to go?

"Three days."

At her aunt's words, Em looked up again, hope suddenly big and bright inside her. "You mean I can stay?"

Amelia nodded.

Em sucked in a breath. "Thank you. Thank you so much."

She wanted to beg for a week, but knew better. Besides, she would find a way to charm her aunt into more time. At least she'd try her very hardest. Maybe she could make herself indispensable in some way. "I won't be a problem. I'm quiet, and I don't eat much and—"

"My house. My rules. Do we have an understanding?" Her aunt's aloof demeanor remained for a few seconds more.

"We do. Totally."

At last Aunt Amelia's expression softened. "I'll have someone show you around town tomorrow. You'll see why this is no place for you. Why I'm doing you a favor by getting you out of here before—" She closed her mouth quickly, the unfinished sentence hanging there between them.

Em was dying to ask, *Before what?* But she didn't want to jeopardize the good news she'd just been given, so she tucked that question away for a safer time.

Amelia pushed to her feet. "It's very late. I need to go to bed. I'll have Beckett show you to a room."

"Thank you, Aunt Amelia. I appreciate it so much."

Movement caught Em's eye. Beckett was already at the door of the sitting room. How had he suddenly arrived without making a sound? He nodded at Aunt Amelia as she went by. "Good evening."

"Beckett," was all her aunt said as she left. How odd that Aunt Amelia would employ a man she seemed not to care for.

More questions. So. Many. Questions.

He glanced at Em now. "Are you ready to go up?"

Em stood, smiling a little nervously at the majordomo. "I have to go to my car and get my things."

"I'm happy to help you."

She was about to decline his offer, then realized she would be giving up valuable question-asking time. "Thank you. That would be great."

As in a great chance to find out more about this place and Aunt Amelia.

Amelia went up to her bedroom, closed the door, and leaned against it, exhaling the sob she'd been holding on to. Her hands went to her heart, her chest aching with emotions she hadn't felt in years.

Not since Pasqual had left anyway.

Family. Her flesh and blood. In her home. How cruel life was to give her such a precious gift she couldn't keep. It was almost more than Amelia could take. She'd barely restrained herself from grabbing the girl and pulling her into her arms just to feel the embrace of another human being.

When Emeranth had taken her hand to inspect it for burns, the rush of emotion she'd felt had been almost unbearable. Amelia had almost wept right then.

She tipped her head back. She hadn't felt this torn since Pasqual. She desperately wanted Em to stay. To live here, in this enormous, empty house. To fill this space with youth and laughter and beauty and life. Amelia craved the company, the conversation, the chance to mean something to someone once again.

But that would all vanish once Emeranth understood what staying here would mean. No, the burden that came with having Marchand blood in Shadowvale was too great.

Amelia had known her niece for only mere moments, but already she loved the child too much to lay that weight upon her.

For her own good, Emeranth would have to go. Three days should be safe enough. No more, though. Any longer and this place would get its hooks in her. Then there'd be no leaving. Ever.

She couldn't do that to Emeranth. But she also couldn't leave the girl uninitiated. That Manda had done that infuriated Amelia. No witch deserved to be left unattached from her powers.

Amelia would fix that. Then she would send Em on her way. At least with her power unleashed, she'd have a better chance at making her way in the world.

Amelia pushed away from the door and went to the bathroom to splash some cold water on her face. The icy water felt good, but it didn't dissipate her anger at Em's mother.

Was keeping Em from her powers some way of getting back at Amelia? It couldn't be. That was far too self-centered a thought on Amelia's part. More likely, it was just Manda's way of keeping Em attached to her.

Because there was no doubt in Amelia's mind that Em was the more powerful witch of the two. No doubt. And not just because the power had mostly skipped Manda. Amelia had seen the magic dancing and sparking around Emeranth like the fireflies that speckled the Shadowvale horizon at night.

Visible magic like that happened for only a few reasons—because a witch was very powerful, very upset, or the magic was suppressed.

In Emeranth's case, Amelia guessed it might be all three. Especially if the poor child really was homeless. That would distress anyone.

Amelia leaned on the bathroom's marble counter and stared at herself in the mirror. What kind of woman turned away one of her very few remaining relatives at a time of need?

She frowned. A woman who very much wanted to keep that relative from sharing her same fate.

Amelia left the bathroom and walked to the windows that overlooked the rear garden. Somewhere out there in the dark, Thoreau prowled. She'd have rather had him curled up on the bed beside her, but that hadn't been possible since he was very young. And much smaller.

Besides, if he wanted to be in the house, he'd be in the house.

She pulled off her turban and ran her hands through her hair. Enough wallowing. Time for bed.

Tomorrow would bring its own troubles. No point in bringing the ones from the past into it.

She climbed into bed, stared at the ceiling, and did something she hadn't done in a very long time—thought about a man who wasn't Pasqual.

The man on her mind was Deacon Evermore. He had to come through for her. Had to show Em what a terrible place Shadowvale was for her. How gray and depressing and soul-sucking it was.

Because if he didn't, Amelia might have to tell her niece the truth.

And if that happened, Deacon certainly wasn't getting a ticket out of here.

CHAPTER FIVE

Em and Beckett walked together through the house out to her car. She would have loved to ogle the place some more, but now that she'd secured a few days here, there'd be time for that later.

Instead, she glanced at the curious man beside her. He really didn't seem like the butler type, which was what she figured a majordomo must be. So what was he doing here?

He caught her looking at him. "Something on your mind, Miss Em?"

Beyond him? Fortunately, there was. "I was wondering if you want me to move my car after I get my stuff out of it. I'm kind of right there in the driveway. Probably blocking my aunt if she has to go anywhere."

"That would be highly unlikely—your aunt going anywhere—but we should still park it in the garage. I can handle that for you. If you trust me to drive your vehicle."

"Considering it wouldn't be most people's *last* choice for a joy ride, I don't think you're likely to do it any damage." She laughed. "I'll hand over the keys after I unlock it."

"Very good, Miss Em."

She went back to studying him as best she could without being blatant about it. The idea that there was something a little foreboding about him had been her first impression when he'd opened the door, and it was still her impression of him. In fact, he seemed almost dangerous. Or like he could be, if the need arose.

It was as if a darkness surrounded him, waiting to strike at his command. But, really, who commanded darkness?

That seemed like such a silly thing to even contemplate, but then, she'd just found out her aunt—and probably Em herself—was a witch. What else was possible if that was real?

Whatever or whoever Beckett was, he didn't seem like the kind of guy she'd want to get on the bad side of. Like, ever.

But maybe that was exactly why Aunt Amelia had hired him. For protection. And to make the kind of first impression that caused people to think twice. She did live in this big house by herself, after all. "Do you like working for my aunt?"

His smile was kind but a little thin. "Our relationship is a complicated one. But yes, for the most part, my life here is good. I enjoy your aunt's company. Although I'm not sure she'd say the same about me."

That wasn't exactly a rousing endorsement, but it wasn't a condemnation either. It pretty much confirmed what Em had picked up on earlier. Aunt Amelia wasn't that keen on Beckett. So odd. "How long have you worked here?"

"Close to fifty years."

"Wow." Em almost stumbled. For one thing, that was a long time to employ someone you didn't like. For another, he didn't look old enough to have worked here that long. He must have started very young. But then, Aunt Amelia didn't look her age either.

His smile broadened. "I'm older than I look. A common trait for many of us here in Shadowvale."

His answers were only giving her more questions. "Why is that?"

He went pensive for a moment as they went out the front doors. Maybe deciding what to tell her. Or how *much* to tell her. At last, he spoke. "This town was built over magical meridian lines. The lines are old and a little fragile, however, and they tend to leak magic into everything around us. A lot of people say that's why we age so slowly."

Then he laughed. "Of course, some of us have enough of our own magic to keep age from creeping up on us too quickly."

Meridian lines? She had no clue what he was talking about. "Are you one of those people? Do you have enough of your own magic?"

His eyes seemed to darken, but they were outside, and there wasn't much light beyond the landscaping, so it was hard to tell for sure. "I have enough, yes."

He turned abruptly as they reached the car. "How many bags do you have?"

Ready to change the subject, apparently. "A big suitcase and another smaller bag, plus my purse. I have a bunch of other stuff in a couple totes, but they don't need to come in tonight."

He glanced at the car's interior, then at her, brows lifted. "You plan on staying longer than three days, don't you?"

She weighed all possible answers, choosing the truth very quickly. "I really hope to, yes."

He laughed softly and nodded. "Good. If I can help, I will."

That wasn't the response she'd been expecting. "You will?"

"Of course. Your aunt has been alone too long. Your presence will be very good for her. I can see it already. And not just because of the company, but because you're family."

A wave of relief swept Em. With Beckett suddenly on her side, she felt herself warm to him considerably. Like they were allies. Even if there was something a little foreboding about him. "I would like that very much."

His amusement disappeared. "You need to know that this is not an easy place to live, however."

"Indigo House or Shadowvale?"

"Shadowvale."

"Aunt Amelia said the same thing, but she didn't explain it. What do you mean? What's so hard about life in Shadowvale?"

He glanced toward the house before answering her. "It's not my place to tell you. If you're meant to know, it'll be explained. But not by me. Your aunt has reason enough to dislike me. I'm not giving her another."

"Why did she hire you if she doesn't like you?"

"She didn't—" He shook his head. "You ask a lot of questions. Questions I shouldn't answer. How about we get your things inside and you let your aunt do some more talking in the morning?"

She frowned at him as she unlocked the car. "You're an odd man, Beckett."

"I've been called worse." He opened the back door and pulled her big suitcase out like it was filled with feathers and not packed with everything she owned.

She was impressed, but not enough to get distracted. "By who? My aunt?"

He snorted. "Yes. And that's the last question I'm answering this evening."

She smirked as she got her purse out of the front seat. "Beckett, I think we're going to be very good friends."

He straightened with a sudden look of surprise. "I would like that very much."

"Me, too." She took a few more things off the back seat, such as the book she'd been reading and a bag with some snacks from the last gas station she'd stopped at. Snacks that were going to be her dinner, actually. "Okay, got everything I need. How about I just leave the keys on the front seat?"

"Perfect. I'll come out and move it later." He had the handle of her big suitcase in one hand and a firm grip on her small carry-on bag with the other. "Let's get you to a room and settled, then."

She dropped the keys on the driver's seat and closed the door. "Great. I'm going to sleep like the dead tonight."

She just barely caught the odd expression that zipped across his face, but it morphed into an awkward smile too quickly for her to figure out what he'd reacted to.

He started walking, carrying her bags with little effort. "Would you like a drink or something to take up with you?"

She lifted the white plastic gas station bag. "Nope, I'm good. Still have some snacks left over, including a bottle of water."

"Snacks?"

"A candy bar, some chips, and a package of cookies."

He side-eyed the bag. "Those don't sound very…nutritious."

She laughed as they went into the house. "Yeah, well, it's hard to be nutritious on a budget."

"I'm sure it is. If you want something else, feel free to rummage about in the kitchen. I'm sure your aunt wouldn't want you going hungry. Chef usually makes breakfast around eight."

"Chef?"

"Yes. Your aunt has a chef. Vivian is a very nice woman and well trained. French cuisine is her specialty, but she can make just about anything."

They went down a long hall and came to an elevator. He put the carry-on bag down and pressed the button.

"That's something." She shook her head. "This house has *you*, a chef, and an elevator?"

"And a team of gardeners, two housekeepers, a handyman, and a pool service. But only myself, Chef, and one housekeeper live here. Oh, and the mechanic, who lives in the apartment over the garage."

The elevator doors opened, and they got on.

"This house isn't as empty as I thought it was."

"Oh, it's still plenty empty. Your aunt keeps to herself most of the time." He pressed the button for the second floor, but she noted there were also buttons labeled with an L and a three. "You'll see."

"What's on the third floor?"

"Nothing really. Finished storage."

The doors opened again, and they got out. A few yards down another hall, they went by one of the balconies that overlooked the rotunda.

After a couple more yards and a slight turn, Beckett opened a door. "The guest rooms haven't been used in a long time, but they're cleaned regularly, so everything should be in good order. If it's not, just let me know. You can reach me by dialing nine on the house phone."

Em walked into the room and gawked at the space. "This is a guest room?"

"Guest suite, really. The bedroom and bathroom are through this sitting room."

A little panic crept up Em's spine. "This is too much. I just need a place to sleep. I don't need all this. I don't want to be any trouble." Aunt Amelia wouldn't want her around if she was a bother.

He smiled. "It's no trouble. The housekeepers will be glad to have something to actually clean, I would imagine. And there's no smaller room to put you in, so this will have to do."

She did a slow turn, taking in the utterly charming decor of pale blue trimmed in gold with touches of ivory and rose. The crystal chandelier and gilded mirrors made her feel like she'd slipped off to some expensive little B&B in the South of France. If they had B&Bs in the South of France.

She put her hand on her cheek. "This is going to be really hard to leave."

Beckett carried her bags in. "Maybe you won't have to."

"Maybe I won't." That made her smile again. "I guess I'll see you at breakfast."

"I'll be there." He headed for the door. "And remember, if you need anything I'm just a phone call away."

"I'm sure I'll be fine. Anyway, you need to sleep just as much as I do."

He tipped his head, giving it a little shake. "Not really. But sweet dreams to you."

Then he was gone before she could ask what that was supposed to mean, closing the door behind him and leaving her to her thoughts.

Which were many, but she really needed to sleep.

But first, a more thorough inspection of the suite was called for. She'd stayed in a suite once before, although *stayed* was a rather questionable term since she and her mother had been forced to leave in great haste the moment the hotel manager had discovered the credit card her mother used belonged to someone else.

Borrowed, her mother liked to correct Em. But people didn't run in the middle of the night because something was *borrowed*.

She left her suitcases and the bad memories in the sitting room and walked into the bedroom. She flipped on the lights. It was equally as charming as the sitting room, and Em sighed at the sheer prettiness of it all.

There were two more doors. Had to be a closet and a bathroom. She opened the first one, and a light came on automatically.

"Wow. Now this is a closet." She walked in and stood in the middle of it, stretching out her arms. Her fingers didn't touch the sides. Didn't even come close. It was at least three times as deep, too.

She ran her hand along one of the empty racks. The thought of having enough clothes to fill a space like that was almost as daunting as it was thrilling. Em loved clothes and shoes and purses and all things girlie and beautiful. She'd never had much of any of them, but whenever she'd gotten a chance to visit a library, she'd pored over the fashion magazines to see what the latest was.

Maybe someday she'd fill a closet like this. Someday when she was settled and stable and her past was a long way behind her.

With a wistful smile, she went back out to see what was behind the second door.

A bathroom. Or a mini spa.

The claw-foot tub sat on gold feet that looked like a lion's paws. The tub was higher at the ends, and the faucet, a gold swan, was positioned right in the middle. A small table sat nearby with an array of bath oils and candles on it.

Em went closer. There was a silver lighter with the candles. She lit one, staring into the flame for a long moment as she gathered her courage. Then she pinched the flame out.

She hadn't felt a thing. She did it a second time just to be sure. A new lightness zipped through her. Amazing. And she was definitely taking a bath at least once while she was here.

The rest of the room—the shower, the double sinks set into the long counter, the floor—were all marble, too. Mostly, the colors were ivory and gold, but there were a few touches of blue that tied the space into the rest of the suite.

And the crystal chandelier that hung over the tub looked like a perfect half-size replica of the one in the sitting room.

If this was a guest room, what did her aunt's room look like? Em couldn't imagine.

But she was happy that her aunt had done so well for herself. She walked to a set of French doors and pushed the sheers back to look out. The grounds were beautiful and just as nicely lit as the front had been.

Em had a feeling why her mother had never talked much about Aunt Amelia.

Jealousy.

There was no way her mother hadn't known about Amelia's financial situation.

Manda Greer could smell money at the bottom of a wishing well two states away. There was also no chance that she hadn't come here and tried to get herself a piece of Amelia's pie.

The shiver of panic returned.

What if Aunt Amelia thought that was why Em had shown up, too?

CHAPTER SIX

Deacon wasn't in the mood to play tour guide to an old woman who would probably want to stop every fifteen minutes for tea and cake and would talk incessantly about her grandchildren and hip problems and which medication she was due to take next.

But he did want a ticket out of Shadowvale, so for that reward, he got up, showered, dressed, and prepared himself for a day of small talk and fake smiles.

Which he would do while somehow also convincing Amelia's elderly niece that Shadowvale was no place for her.

He stared out at the town that was just waking up, regretting his decision but knowing there wasn't much point in trying to say no to Amelia.

Why had he agreed to go to breakfast, too? He shouldn't have. He probably could have gotten out of that, at least.

Then he'd be sitting with his younger brother, Bishop, on the back deck with his feet kicked up, drinking a deep mug of black coffee.

Tinkerbelle would be running around the backyard, barking at squirrels and birds. Gracie would be in the kitchen, fixing more breakfast than three people could eat, just in case their other brother, Shepherd, stopped by. And she'd be fussing at them good-naturedly about getting chores done.

Bishop would make a crack about how he really needed to get married, or just move out like Shep had.

Then Gracie would remind them both that Shep still came back to eat more often than not and that if Deac and Bishop wanted dinner, they'd get the trash out and the yard mowed.

They'd groan, and she'd tell them dinner was meat loaf or pork chops or turkey with all the fixings or one of her other equally delicious dishes, and they'd promise to get things done right after breakfast.

He laughed to himself as he drove. Life, despite all the many ups and downs, despite all the issues their family had, was good.

But it would be better if he could leave this town. Find a place for himself beyond the boundaries of Shadowvale. Beyond the grip of the curse that held him here.

Because leaving Shadowvale would mean leaving his curse behind. Wouldn't it? That's what Amelia had implied.

It had to. He hoped. He just wanted a chance to live like a normal person. Sure, he'd come back and visit. He'd still have family here, after all.

But to live without the burden of his curse…even beyond that, to have a chance for a normal life. A wife. Kids even. So long as he could be sure he wouldn't pass some aspect of the Evermore curse on to them.

He couldn't be sure, though. At least not while living here. That's why he had to get out.

He pulled into Amelia's long drive, dreading the day that lay ahead of him, but knowing he would do it with a smile on his face for the reward it would bring. He'd get a good breakfast out of it, too. Amelia's chef could cook. Maybe not country cooking like Gracie did, but the woman had skills.

He turned the truck off, got out, and after a quick glance around for Thoreau, went up to the door.

Beckett answered before Deac had a chance to ring the bell. "Good morning, Mr. Evermore."

"Morning, Beckett." The man's sly smile told Deacon all he needed to know. This was going to be a long day.

"Breakfast is being served in the dining room."

With a sigh, Deacon nodded. "Great. I can see my way—"

"Oh, no. Amelia's asked that I bring you in."

Deacon doubted that. More like Beckett wanted to see Deacon's face when he met Amelia's niece and saw who he was going to be babysitting. "Lead the way."

Beckett closed the door and gestured toward the rotunda. Both men started walking.

"So," Deacon said, "what's for breakfast?"

"Croissants with jam and butter, poached eggs, sweet potato and turkey hash, bacon, sausage, grits, fresh fruit, a selection of cheeses, and of course coffee and juice."

Deacon's traitorous stomach rumbled before he could say a word. "That'll do."

Beckett laughed. "It'll start your day off right."

"Something had better."

Beckett shot him a look. "You're dreading this, aren't you?"

"Wouldn't you be? Or do you think spending the day convincing Amelia's niece this is not the place for her to retire sounds like fun?"

Beckett's brows pulled together. "Retire?"

"Isn't that why she's here? To spend her golden years near family?"

Beckett snorted. "Your head has taken you in a very different direction than reality." Then he chuckled to himself as he reached for the dining room doors. "This is going to be interesting."

He opened them with a great flourish. "Mr. Deacon Evermore has arrived. I'll let Chef know we're ready to eat."

"Thank you, Beckett." Amelia made eye contact with Deacon. "And thank you for coming. This is my niece, Emeranth Greer."

Her niece turned from the coffee station that was set up on the table against the far wall. "Good morning, Mr. Evermore."

Deacon looked at Emeranth and just managed to keep his jaw from unhinging and going south. "Call me, uh, Deacon."

She smiled and lifted her coffee to take a sip. "Call me Em."

She wasn't remotely elderly. In fact, she was closer to his age. And beautiful. Big eyes, dark hair, skin that seemed to glow. Or maybe that was her witchy aura.

He couldn't stop staring. Or keep his insides from tightening up in a way they hadn't since he'd been in high school and Carmela Westin had returned from summer break with a brand-new figure and no more braces.

Em's figure surpassed Carmela Westin's. And he wouldn't have cared if she'd had braces or not. Amelia's niece was a stunner.

Amelia cleared her throat. "Would you like to join us at the table?"

He nodded and finally got his eyes off Em long enough to realize there was also a maid in the room with them. Helen, he thought her name was. "Sure."

He was happy to sit, happy to focus on something other than the gorgeous woman he was going to be spending the next several hours with. Anything to get his pulse back to normal and his head on straight again. He had a job to do, and he was going to do it. Eye on the prize and all that.

This was still going to be a much longer day than he'd imagined, but for very different reasons.

Em wasn't entirely sure what her aunt was up to. If she was trying to dissuade Em from staying in

Shadowvale, Deacon Evermore wasn't helping her case.

The man was hot. And even better, he didn't seem to know it. Plus, he had that rugged, outdoorsy thing going on that seemed genuine. The flannel shirt and faded jeans he was wearing looked worn in from work, not because they had been designed that way.

He probably had a whole closet of those shirts. Hmm. No, he probably had enough to get him through the week. Same thing with the jeans. At least that's how he struck her. Practical. No-nonsense.

And a good kisser.

She almost choked on her coffee at that thought. Where the heck had that come from?

Amelia glanced at her. "Are you all right?"

Em nodded and took her seat next to Aunt Amelia and across from Deacon. "Just went down the wrong way."

She sipped her juice, but that did nothing to lower her temperature, which had shot up the moment Deacon had walked into the room. Helen, the live-in housekeeper who also helped with breakfast apparently, poured him a cup of coffee.

Beckett hovered nearby with a rather amused look on his face. He glanced down at his phone, then over at Helen. "Breakfast is up."

"I'll be right back." She returned the coffeepot to the burner and left for the kitchen.

Silence took over. Deep, prickly, uncomfortable silence.

Why Em felt the sudden need to fill that void, she had no idea, but she couldn't keep herself from speaking. "So, Deacon, where are we going today? Aunt Amelia said you'd be showing me around."

As if he didn't know that already. Thanks, Princess Obvious. And if her stomach could stop being all fluttery, that would be great. She was *not* interested in getting involved with anyone at this point. Not when she was dead broke. And at least not until she knew where she was going to be in three days' time. Her future had to come first.

His hand was on his coffee cup, but he didn't pick it up. "Downtown, I guess. Maybe the cemetery. Or the swamp."

The cemetery and the swamp? For real? She stared at him, wondering if Deacon was one of those superhot but also kind of dumb guys who basically got through life on their looks. *Please, don't let it be that.* She really didn't want to babysit him all day when she could explore just as easily on her own. "Well, downtown sounds nice. I drove through a little of that on my way in last night."

He nodded. "There's a lot more than what you saw."

"I can't wait."

The housekeeper returned, pushing a serving cart with three covered plates. She placed the smallest one in front of Aunt Amelia, then the two larger ones in front of Em and Deacon, taking the covers off as she did. "Enjoy your meal."

"Thank you," Em said. She was starving. Her cookies and chips hadn't gone very far last night. Her plate was full of all kinds of yummy goodness. She picked up her fork and was about to dig in when she saw her aunt wasn't eating the same thing. "Are you only having oatmeal?"

Aunt Amelia nodded. "I eat it every day."

"Doesn't that get boring?"

Aunt Amelia's spoon hung in the air, and she hesitated. "Yes, it does."

"Then why not eat something else?"

Deacon held a strip of bacon by the end. "Nothing wrong with routine."

"No, there's not," Em admitted. But his answer confirmed what she'd thought earlier. He was a practical guy. Probably not into frills and complications.

He wouldn't like her, then. Em was nothing but complications. Sure, she was trying to put all that behind her, but she couldn't magically erase her past or her connection to her criminal mother, no matter how much she wanted to.

Which made her realize that no matter how much she wanted to tell the truth as she started this new chapter in her life, her past was the one thing that was always going to trip her up. Always going to make people judge her.

Maybe a little lying wasn't such a bad thing…

CHAPTER SEVEN

Deacon had intended to take Em to Main Street first and show her the area everyone called downtown, then maybe Fiddler Street, the artsier part of town, but as he navigated Amelia's driveway, he realized it was a little too early for either of those places. Nothing would be open yet, except for a few offices. Even the shops that stayed open late had to close for a couple hours.

So when he hit the end of the driveway, he went left instead of right on Hollows Drive. "Change of plans."

"Oh?"

He glanced over and nodded. Outside of Gracie, he hadn't had a woman in his truck in a long while. Em made the old Ford look good. Or maybe it was just that she looked good. He'd seen Gracie in nearly the same outfit of black leggings, ankle boots, and big denim shirt, but he'd never realized how sexy it could be on someone who wasn't his sister.

The thought made him straighten up and refocus on the road. "We'll go by the cemetery first."

"Is that a big tourist attraction? I mean, is there someone famous buried there or something?"

"Shadowvale doesn't get tourists."

She laughed. "Well, I'm here."

He looked at her. "Is that what you are? A tourist?" Because *tourist* meant temporary. And if that's what she was thinking, he wasn't going to have to work as hard.

She held his gaze for a long moment. "No. At least I hope not to be. I want to live here. My aunt doesn't seem to think it's a good idea, but—"

"It's not. This town..." He shook his head, not quite able to find the right words in the moment.

Her brows furrowed. "Why isn't it? Everyone keeps telling me that about Shadowvale, but no one's told me why."

He gave it another second of thought, but if Amelia wanted him to persuade Em not to stay here, he had to be able to tell her the truth. The whole truth. "The town is cursed. So are the people in it."

She didn't say anything for a few long moments, so he glanced at her. She was staring at him like he was insane. "Cursed?" Her tone rang with disbelief.

"Mm-hmm. Jinxed, troubled, plagued. However you want to say it, there's a darkness that hangs over this place. In all sorts of ways."

"So you're cursed, then?"

"Yep." No point in pretending otherwise.

She crossed her arms and leaned sideways in the seat as she looked at him. "With what?"

He narrowed his gaze at her. "You don't ask people that. Also, in general, it's a good idea not to make physical contact with anyone you meet here. Don't fist-bump or shake hands or any of that. We don't do it. Too many things transfer that way."

Her eyes rounded, and a little alarm crept in.

He was sorry about that, but it was the truth. And what Amelia wanted him to do. Turn her niece off this place. Well, the truth seemed the best way to do that. And being honest meant there were no lies for him to get caught up in.

Seconds ticked by without another word from either of them. He turned onto Dusk Drive. They'd be at the cemetery in a few more minutes.

She made a small noise. "I'm cursed, too."

That caught him off guard. "You are?"

She shrugged, but she wasn't looking at him. Her gaze was fixed on the road ahead. "Sure. Who isn't?"

He frowned. "I'm not talking about occasional bad luck, or being unable to find love, or constantly losing things." Although those all existed in Shadowvale on grander scales. "This isn't just hitting a rough patch in life."

"No, I get it. You're talking about living under a cloud. The constant presence of something you can't change and can't get away from. I know what you mean."

He doubted it. Not many outside of Shadowvale could really understand it, not to the level that existed here. But he wasn't ready to debate the true meaning of *being cursed* with her. He wasn't sure it even mattered, because hopefully, he'd never have to. If all went well, a few hours of touring this place would be enough, and she'd hightail it back to wherever she'd come from.

Back to whatever guy was waiting on her. Because there had to be a guy. Or guys. He grunted. Yeah, that was more likely. Probably had a line of them waiting to take her out. A different one on the hook every night.

"What?"

He looked at her. "What what?"

"You grunted."

"I did?"

She nodded, lips pursed, amusement dancing in her eyes. "Or is that your curse? You make random noises without knowing it?"

"No."

"What, then?"

"I was just…must have been thinking about something." Like her abundant love life, which was inexplicably making him cranky. He really needed to change the subject. "Where's home?"

"Outside of Oklahoma City, last. Tiny place called Bethany."

Oklahoma. She probably preferred cowboy boots to work boots. Well, she was out of luck here. "Last?"

"We move around a lot. Moved. Hopefully, that's over."

We. So there was a man in her life. The muscles in his jaw tightened. "I see. Won't you miss it?" And him?

"All that flatness? And the tornadoes? Nope." She sighed. "Although the aquarium outside Tulsa was nice."

"We don't have an aquarium."

"I'll manage. I can always get a fish tank."

"We have a couple gators in the swamp."

She blinked. "For real?"

"Mm-hmm. Including one behemoth known as Brutus." He shrugged. "Never bothers anyone, though." Then he quickly added, "Yet."

The stone arch of the cemetery entrance rose up ahead. He drove through, slowing to a crawl as he headed for the center of the graveyard. "This is it. Last Rest."

She turned to see out the window better as they drove. "It's, uh, very interesting."

"You have no idea." He parked by the enormous mausoleum at the dead middle of Last Rest. "Come on, I'll show you a few things."

She looked less than ecstatic to be getting out, but did so anyway.

He walked around to meet her, and they took a few steps toward the mausoleum.

She read the words carved over the door. "In Memory. Who's buried here?"

"No one. It's just that. In memory of someone who disappeared."

"Who was it?"

More truth-telling, but what else was he supposed to do? Wasn't like she couldn't find out if she wanted anyway. "I guess the man who would have been your uncle."

Em looked at him. "Really? Why 'would have been'? Were he and Aunt Amelia not married?"

"No one knows for sure, and she doesn't like to talk about it." He was probably telling her too much, but he'd mentioned in front of Amelia that he was taking Em to the cemetery, and she hadn't told him not to. And Amelia had to know a visit here would lead to this conversation.

Em stepped up and put her hand on the door. "Uncle who?"

"Pasqual."

"Why did he disappear?"

"Not sure."

She glanced at him. "You don't know much, do you?"

He barked out a laugh. "Your aunt isn't the chattiest person. She keeps a lot to herself." He shrugged. "Which is fine. This is her town, after all."

Em's brows lifted slowly. "What do you mean 'her town'?"

"Shadowvale is here because of her. Her magic, her influence, her desire to create a place where Pasqual would be safe."

Em shook her head. "Okay, slow down. You're giving me a lot of information in a short amount of time. Explain. Why is this her town? And why would Pasqual need a place to be safe? Safe from what? Or who?"

He took a breath, again warring with how much to tell her. "This is your aunt's town because her magic created it and continues to protect it from

71

discovery. Her magic keeps all of us safe. As safe as we can be with the curses we carry."

She just stared at him, so he continued. "If we lived in the outside world, we'd be branded as freaks. Or forced to live our lives in isolation. For some of us, it would be worse."

"So Shadowvale is like a haven, then? For people who are outsiders for whatever reason?"

"That's a pretty good simple explanation, yes."

"And is that why Pasqual needed to be safe? Because of his curse?"

Deacon hesitated. "Not exactly…I mean, maybe. I'd say it was more because of who he was. Or what he was. Whether you'd consider that a curse is relative, I suppose."

"Okay, just explain it. Because I'm not following you at all. Who or what was Uncle Pasqual?"

This was going to be interesting. "He was a vampire."

*

Em stared at Deacon without saying anything while her brain tried to sort out what he'd just said, but the first thing her brain came up with was that she hadn't heard him right. "I could have sworn you said vampire."

"I did."

She went back to staring for a few seconds. "So you're saying vampires are real."

He nodded.

"Like, actual vampires? I realize that since I just found out there are witches, and that I might be one, this shouldn't be so hard to accept, but really? Vampires? Those seem so...so...I don't know...made up."

"They're not."

She sat down on the steps of the mausoleum. "Are they dangerous, or are they sparkly?"

"Well, they're not sparkly. But they're not necessarily dangerous either. They could be. Any of us could be."

"Whoa." Everything in her went on alert. "*Any* of us? Are you a vampire?"

"No."

"Good. I mean, it would be fine if you were. I guess." She wrapped her arms around her knees. "This might be a little bit much for me to take in."

He nodded and leaned against a nearby headstone. "Take your time."

She blew out a breath. *Time* wasn't going to answer her questions. Not with the kind of speed she wanted anyway. "Why was Shadowvale safe for Pasqual? Was he the only vampire allowed here?"

"It was safe for him because the sun never shines. And no."

She glanced up at the cloud cover. "Never? Or do you mean Shadowvale is like the Seattle of the South, overcast more often than not and always on the verge of a downpour?"

"It rains about the same as anywhere else, but the clouds are permanent until the sun sets. We almost

73

always have a clear night sky. It's one of the ways the town maintains a balance."

He made it sound like the town made that decision. She shook it off. "Are there other vampires in town, then?"

"Yes."

"And other witches?"

"Yep."

"What else?"

"That's a tough question. There are all kinds of supernaturals who live here, and not all of them fall into a distinct category. Then there are the humans who are just cursed and not really supernatural at all."

"Give me an example."

He hooked his thumbs in his belt loops. "Fred Chimes. He has a nervous condition that makes him invisible during times of extreme stress. Every time Lucy Smothers sneezes, lightning cracks the sky. Last time she had a cold, the park pavilion almost burned down and three blocks had no power for a day and a half due to a blown transformer."

She took all that in, trying to accept that these were real people with real problems, but it all sounded so crazy. "And there are lots of people like that in town?"

"To varying degrees, yes."

"What about the supernaturals who live here? You said they don't all fit into distinct categories. Like who?"

He glanced upward for a second, thinking who best fit that description. It wasn't a surprise who came to mind. "Nasha Black. She owns Black Horse Bakery here in town."

"What kind of supernatural is she?"

"I don't know what you'd call her exactly, but her father is one of the Four Horsemen of the Apocalypse."

Em frowned. "Come on."

"I'm being serious. Her father is the Harbinger of Famine. She opened the bakery as a way of getting back at him. Or counterbalancing his power. Something like that." He lifted one shoulder. "Whatever. Her stuff is good. She's making my sister's birthday cake."

Which was nice of Nasha, considering that she and Shepherd hadn't really worked out. Deacon didn't harbor any ill will. Shep was a tough nut to crack.

Em stood up and brushed off the seat of her leggings. "Great. Let's go there now. I want to meet this woman. See for myself. Maybe buy a cupcake."

CHAPTER EIGHT

Deacon checked his watch. It wasn't quite ten yet, but Nasha should be opening the bakery by the time they drove over there. He wasn't exactly done showing Em the cemetery yet, though. "Sure, we can go downtown next."

"Great."

He straightened up. "First, there's one more thing you should see here." Something that really ought to freak her out.

"Oh?" She looked around. "What?"

He made a little squeaking sound, then waited. It wasn't something he liked to do, but Em needed to see these wretched things for herself.

A few seconds later, a black-and-brown-striped meowl swooped in and landed on a headstone a few feet away. The beast was fifteen pounds, maybe bigger, and it looked straight at him, whiskers twitching like it could smell the raven side of him and thought it was delicious.

He glared right back at it. Creepy little thing.

Em's mouth came open. "Is that...a cat with wings?"

"Sort of. It's a meowl. They inhabit the cemetery mostly, although you occasionally see them in other parts of town and in the forest."

She didn't move. Obviously, she had the same feelings toward the meowl as he did. Good. That should help put her off Shadowvale.

The meowl blinked its big, round eyes at her, then lifted one taloned paw and gave it a lick, showing off an impressive set of pointy cat teeth.

Em glanced at him. "Are they friendly?"

"They're not house cats, if that's what you—"

"Hiya, kitty bird." Em stretched out her hand. "Who's a sweet little winged baby cat?"

What was she doing? "I wouldn't—"

The meowl flutter-jumped onto Em's arm and cooed at her.

Cooed.

Deacon growled a little. That hadn't gone as planned. Maybe it was a witch thing. Maybe meowls wouldn't bite witches. Or think they smelled like supper.

The meowl blinked at him and licked its chops.

That was enough of that. He pointed over his shoulder with his thumb. "Okay, we should probably go downtown now. See if the bakery is open. You know, cupcakes and all that."

The meowl was nuzzling Em's neck, and she was scratching its head. "What did you say this little cat-bird was called again?"

He frowned. "A meowl. And they can be *very* dangerous."

"Right. Like vampires are sometimes."

"Meowls bite."

She made a face that said she was clearly trying not to laugh. "Don't vampires do that, too?"

He made a face back at her, but she didn't see it because she was too busy petting and talking baby talk to the vile creature perched on her arm.

She scratched under its chin, making it purr. "Well, this meowl is a darling. Aren't you, precious?"

He refrained from making a gagging sound. "You can't take it home. They aren't domesticated." Plus, Thoreau would probably try to eat it. Or actually eat it. Either would be fine with Deacon.

"Okay." She kissed the meowl on the head. "You fly off now, kitty bird. I'll come back and visit you again. I'll bring you some treats, too."

"You're not putting live mice in my truck, so that's a return trip you can take on your own."

She tipped her head at him. "I'm not bringing it live mice. I was thinking more like regular cat treats from the store. You do have a grocery store in Shadowvale, don't you?"

"Yes."

"Good." She went back to smiling at the meowl. She lifted her arm. "Bye, sweetie."

Sweetie. Whatever.

The meowl stretched its wings and took off, soaring back into the trees.

She watched it go. "Are there any other interesting animals like that in this town?"

"We have droxes. I don't think those are too common elsewhere."

"I've never heard of a drox, so I'm gonna say yeah, those probably just exist here. What are they?"

"They're basically winged foxes. With dark green fur tipped in blue or purple usually."

"That sounds amazing. Why are they called droxes?"

"Because they've got dragon genes in them. Hence the wings. And their ability to breathe fire."

"Yeah, I was thinking it would be cool to see one until you added that part."

"They pretty much live in the enchanted forest." Along with some other creatures he wasn't going to tell her about since she was finding it all so fascinating and not the least bit scary.

"Are we going there?"

"At some point." If they really had to.

"Great." She rubbed her hands together, looking rather pleased with that answer. "All right, let's go get a cupcake from Famine's daughter."

"Maybe don't call her that, okay?"

"I won't. I was just teasing." She put her hands on her hips, grinning madly. "Boy, the cursed are a sensitive lot."

"Well, Nasha is. Sometimes." Deacon grunted and headed for the truck. This was not going as planned. The only thing she'd been put off by was the mention of vampires, and even then she hadn't seemed as freaked out as he'd expected.

His ticket out of here was looking more and more unlikely. He opened the passenger door for her, then walked around to the driver's side, racking his brain for where to take her that might turn her off of Shadowvale.

They hadn't been to the swamp yet. Maybe that should be their next stop after downtown. And cupcakes.

He rolled his eyes. There was nothing scary about cupcakes. Then he grinned a little. Nasha Black was pretty Goth and definitely had an unpredictable streak. Maybe she'd do something that would freak Em out.

He cranked the engine and left the cemetery behind.

She gazed out the window. "Always cloudy, huh?"

He nodded. That could be the thing that would get to her. Some people couldn't take days and days of no sun. And there wasn't much alternative in Shadowvale until you drove up the mountains past the twilight line to a place like Nightingale Park. Or went to one of the spots in town that offered artificial UV.

Gracie went to them sometimes.

Which was why he understood why some folks lived up above the twilight line. If you needed sun, you needed sun. But raven shifters were night creatures, and the lack of sun had never been a problem for the Evermores. Except for Gracie.

But then, Gracie was the exception to a lot of things.

He looked over at Em. She was still peering out the window as if she thought an errant ray of light might suddenly appear. Well, it wouldn't. Not ever. Not unless Amelia's magic suddenly stopped working. "You like your sun, huh?"

She shrugged. "I've never really given it much thought."

"The lack of it makes some people crazy."

She raised her brows. "How can you tell in a town like this?"

"Very funny. I just mean some people get that seasonal depression disorder. It's a real thing. Lack-of-sun sickness."

"I've heard of it. But I'm guessing those people wouldn't choose to live in Shadowvale."

She wasn't wrong. But she wasn't completely on target either. "You can't really just choose to live in Shadowvale. I mean, you can try, but it doesn't always work out that way."

"Why not?"

"Because the town doesn't let just anyone in."

"It let me in."

True. "You're a special case, being Amelia's blood relative and all. Most people come here because they're called here in some way. Because they need a place like this to be safe and free. Others have nowhere else to go. Some are chosen."

"Or maybe, like me, they need a place like this to figure out what comes next in their life. Where they can be with family and leave the past behind." She studied her fingernails. "I just want a fresh start, you know?"

He did know. He wanted that very same thing for himself, somewhere outside of Shadowvale. "I understand. I just think deciding to live in a place like Shadowvale is a big step. It's not like moving to any other town. Life here isn't normal."

She snorted. "Where exactly is life normal? Because I've yet to find it anywhere."

"I couldn't tell you. But I know it's not here."

Downtown was waking up, and the streets were getting a little busy. He realized they'd be seeing a lot of people. And while he'd warned her about not making physical contact with anyone, he hadn't said anything about not staring. That probably wasn't something she'd do anywhere else, but this was Shadowvale.

There was a lot more to stare at here.

"Listen, you might see some things today that shock you. Try not to react too much. Remember, people live here to escape the world's typical reaction to them."

"Got it." Her head whipped around like it was on a swivel. "Did I just see a guy with a tail?"

"Jason's in town?" Deacon glanced back, but didn't see the man. Then he frowned at Em. "What part of 'don't stare' was unclear?"

"Calm down. He couldn't see me in your truck."

"Let's hope not. Jason can be a little touchy." Deacon parallel parked two doors down from the Black Horse Bakery, put the truck in park, and turned it off.

"Why? What's his curse?"

"He's a minotaur. Which makes him a shapeshifter. And he has a bad temper. But since he's been keeping his horns shaved down, he's been a little more chill."

She twisted in her seat to face him. "A minotaur like from Greek mythology?"

"Yes. Shadowvale is an anything goes kind of place. You'll see."

"I guess I will." She canted her head to one side, giving him a curious look. "You know, you still haven't told me about your curse. I know you said it's not done—asking, that is—but we're friends now, right? And don't friends tell each other those kinds of things?"

Were they friends? He liked that. It was a lot better than being enemies. "Maybe I don't want to."

"Okay, that's fine. I respect that. Can you at least tell me if you're a cursed human or a supernatural? Or if you're hiding a tail? I'm guessing not. Those jeans are kind of tight, and I think I'd be able to see it."

She'd opened the door, so he walked through it. "You've been looking at my butt?"

She went red. "That's not what I meant."

He laughed and decided not to embarrass her further. "No tail. I'm a cursed supernatural."

"Oh." She didn't say anything more, but he could see the questions in her eyes, questions she had to be dying to ask, but her sudden mortification seemed to be keeping them at bay.

She was awfully cute when she was embarrassed. He pulled the key out of the ignition. "Let's go get your cupcake."

"Right." She reached for the door handle, letting her hair swing down to hide her face.

They got out of the truck, and he went around to the sidewalk, expecting her to make haste for the bakery, but she stood there for a moment, looking around.

A shop down the street had caught her eye. "So all these stores are really what their signs say they are? Like that place over there actually sells spell books?"

He glanced in the direction she was looking. "Spellbound? They sell more than spell books and grimoires. They sell magic accessories, too. Crystal balls, scrying bowls, wands, all that kind of stuff. A few ready-made potions and salves. But if you're looking for regular books, there's the Gilded Page. Other side of the street and down a few blocks."

"What's a grimoire?"

"A book of magic. Pretty much another kind of spell book." He cocked an eyebrow. "You're a witch. Shouldn't you know this stuff?"

"I'm not absolutely convinced I'm a witch, but even if I am, I just found out, so I don't know about any of this." She looked at the shop a little longer, squinting a bit. "And this is absolutely all for real?"

He nodded. Too real sometimes, in his opinion.

"Why isn't it better known, then? Why aren't witches and vampires and shapeshifters more mainstream instead of being the stuff of make-believe?"

"Personal protection, mostly. On several levels. If your friends knew you could create a love potion that would bring them their soul mate, don't you think they would ask?"

She pondered the question. "Can witches do that?"

"I'm not really sure. But let's say they can."

"Then my friends would probably ask. But that would be okay. I wouldn't mind doing it for them."

"I'm sure you wouldn't. What about strangers who wanted a spell to win the lottery, or heal their sick child, or remove an enemy from their life? Where would you draw the line? How do you know you wouldn't be hounded relentlessly for your abilities? Threatened because of them. And don't even get me started on vampires and werewolves and some of the scary supers."

"There are things scarier than vampires and werewolves?" Then she held up a hand. "Never mind, don't tell me. I don't think I'm ready for that yet. But I see what you mean about staying hidden. There'd be no peace."

"No. And most of the folks who live here now have already experienced that in some way. It's why a lot of them are here. They've been in fear for their personal safety. Or that of their families."

Compassion filled her eyes. "Wow. I guess Shadowvale is a lot more special than I imagined."

Inwardly, he groaned. He didn't need her thinking Shadowvale was special. He needed her to think it was awful and restrictive and dreary.

For the man in charge of solving problems, he was really screwing this up. "Come on, let's get a cupcake."

CHAPTER NINE

Em seesawed between overwhelming giddiness and absolute fright. Shadowvale seemed like the coolest, creepiest place she'd ever imagined. Actually, she'd never imagined a place like this. It was beyond anything her mind could have come up with.

But was it creepier than she could handle? So far, she didn't think it was. But then, she was still getting to know the place and had yet to see much of it.

What she did know was that being here in the midst of it felt different in a way she'd never experienced before. She knew the outside world existed beyond the gated entrance, but…did it? For the people who lived here, the outside world seemed to hold no importance.

Which meant if she lived here, she could leave the outside world behind, too.

That part made her almost breathlessly happy. Except when she thought about everything she'd be leaving. Like her mother, whom she loved even though the woman had ruined Em's life in so many ways.

After all, she only had one mother. And moving to Shadowvale would mean not just leaving Manda, but leaving her while she was in prison.

Just the thought of that filled Em with guilt, an emotion her mother shouldn't be able to stir up in her and yet did. In buckets.

Would she be able to visit on occasion? She couldn't imagine doing it more than once or twice a year. But still, not being able to visit at all would weigh on her, because despite all the chaos that Manda had created for Em, that parent-child connection remained.

Once again, more answers led to more questions.

Deacon held the door to the bakery open for her.

She smiled at him and put her questions away for the moment. "Thanks."

He grunted in reply.

She almost laughed. He was ridiculously good-looking, and his slightly grumpy demeanor was charming in a gruff kind of way. It was amusing, too, at least to Em, because some of it seemed like a big put-on. Like he was reminding himself that none of this was supposed to be fun.

Well, she thought it was fun. Especially because everything in this town was a revelation. From the meowls that she just wanted to pet and squeeze, to the store that catered to witches, to the citizens who got curiouser and curiouser. There was so much to learn and explore in this place. She could see spending days just looking through the shops.

Like this bakery, for instance.

The tantalizing smell of sugary baked goodness rushed her as she stepped inside. She took a moment to breathe it in while she looked around.

The interior was done in black and white with touches of deep purple and shocking green. She'd never seen a bakery that looked like this. Or had such morbidly interesting sweets on display.

Three long display cases made up the store's counter, and there were cupcakes, all right. Decorated with sugar spiders and fondant crows and wonky eyeballs. Some had cat faces (or maybe they were meowls) with whiskers that stuck out past the paper cups. The cakes next to them were the same way. One had tiny black ants marching across the frosting. It took Em a second to be sure those ants weren't real.

There were some standard things in the cases, too. Cookies, brownies, bars, and pies. Loaves of bread filled racks on the side wall, and they all looked pretty typical, too, although the dark rye was almost black.

Next to the bread racks, the wall was covered with chalkboard paint, and the menu was laid out. Pie of the Day was blackberry.

In front of that wall were some comfy leather chairs and small round tables. On the other side of the store was a big leather sofa with two more matching chairs and a coffee table in the middle.

For a place that seemed to specialize in darkness, it had a pretty cozy vibe. She could see hanging out here, for sure. She nodded at the chalkboard. "I bet that pie is good."

"It is," Deacon said. "But don't feel like you have to try it today. Blackberry is always the Pie of the Day."

"That could change at any time." A wisp of a woman walked out from the back. Strikingly pretty, she wore black pants, a black-and-purple-striped tee, and a white apron with the Black Horse Bakery logo on it. This close, Em realized the horse in the logo looked a little...possessed. "But it won't because blackberry is very popular. In fact, there's someone who comes in and buys six at a time."

"Who?" Deacon asked.

The woman's brows bent and she frowned. "I can't remember."

Her dark hair was pulled into a high ponytail about as thick as Em's wrist. She sported an extremely smoky eye and penciled brows that arched skyward. She put her hands on the counter, tapping her pointed, black nails on it, and looked at Deacon. "You didn't come in here to pick up the cake, did you? Because the work order says Saturday."

"Nope, just came in to show your bakery to a visitor," Deacon said. "Nasha, this is Emeranth. Amelia's niece."

Nasha's perfect black brows arched a little higher. "Didn't know Amelia had any family. Nice to meet you. Welcome to Shadowvale."

"Thanks," Em said. "Nice to meet you, too. This is quite a shop you have here. Smells like heaven."

Nasha's answering smile was sly, like maybe she thought Em had made a joke. "Thanks. Can I get something for you? Despite what Deacon may have told you, it's all good."

"Actually, he's been singing your praises." Em looked at the goodies on display again. "Say, is there anything in particular that my aunt likes? It would be nice to take something back that's one of her favorites."

Nasha glanced at the racks of bagged bread against the wall. "She likes the pumpernickel raisin. And Beckett likes the mocha cupcakes. Or any cupcake, really. Unlike your aunt, that man has a sweet tooth."

"Perfect. Then I'll take a loaf of the pumpernickel raisin and one of the mocha cupcakes."

"Oh, take half a dozen. He really likes them."

"Um, okay." That was going to cut into her budget, but cupcakes couldn't be too expensive, could they?

Nasha pulled on a pair of plastic gloves. "And for you?"

"I'm good," Em said.

Deacon turned to look at her. "You couldn't stop talking about cupcakes a second ago."

Nasha tipped her head. "If you don't see a flavor you like, I might have something in the back."

Em hesitated, biting her bottom lip. She definitely wanted to try something, too, but she wasn't exactly flush with cash. "How much is the bread and the cupcakes?"

"Nothing."

Em leaned forward. "How much did you say?"

"Nothing." Nasha waved her hand over the display case. "Everything in the shop is free."

Em almost wiggled her fingers in her ears to see if they were clogged. "It sounded like you said everything is free."

"It is." Nasha looked at Deacon. "Didn't you tell her how this whole shop is me getting back at my father?"

He closed his eyes and sighed out what sounded like a small profanity. "Yes, but I forgot the free part."

Em couldn't imagine why he looked so cross about that bit. "That's amazing. This place just gets better and better."

"Doesn't it?" he mumbled.

Nasha smiled at her. "So what'll it be?"

"Is it wrong that I want to say one of everything?"

Nasha laughed. "No, but's it going to take me a minute to box all that up."

"I can't do that, it wouldn't be fair. What's that chocolate cupcake with the sugar skull on it?"

"That's my Chocolate Reaper cupcake."

"Is that your version of death by chocolate?"

"It is. It's chocolate so dark it'll claim your soul."

Em snorted. "Sounds like my kind of cupcake. I'll have one of those."

"I'm on it." Nasha took a box from the shelf behind her and started filling it.

Em glanced at Deacon, who looked like someone had just kicked his dog. "What's got you all grumpy all of a sudden?"

"Nothing," he muttered.

But it didn't take an expert in people to see he was bothered by something. What that was, Em had no clue.

Nasha handed over a white shopping bag with the bakery's logo on it. "Here you go. I took the liberty of adding a few more things I think you might like."

"Thank you. That was so nice of you."

"No problem. Tell your aunt I said hi. And come back again before you leave. There are always new things on offer."

"I will, but I don't think I'm leaving." Em grinned. "This place is starting to feel like home."

Home?

That was not what Emeranth's reaction was supposed to be.

Deacon was failing. Hard.

It was definitely time to take a trip to the swamp.

Em put her bag into the truck's back seat, then climbed into the front of the cab. "Where to now?"

He got in and shut the door with more force than he'd meant to. Whatever. He wasn't here to make friends even if that's what Em thought they were. He cranked on the engine. "The swamp."

"Where the gators are?"

There was a teasing lilt to her voice that made him want to tease right back, but what was the point of that? To make her like him? That wasn't productive. So he kept his grump going. "Yes. And the vampires."

The amusement drained from her face instantly. "There are vampires in the swamp?"

"Not in the swamp. They live there." He turned down Main Street. The swamp was on the opposite side of Shadowvale from where Amelia lived.

Her forehead was bunched into lines. "Vampires live in the swamp? With the gators?"

"No. In houses." He sighed. "You'll see."

She frowned and looked out the windows, watching the shops go by. "But there's so much here I haven't seen yet. Look at all those stores."

"There are stores everywhere. There's nothing unusual about them."

"Oh, really? Because where I come from there aren't any shops that sell Bewitched Broomsticks. Is that really a thing? Can witches ride broomsticks?"

"Beats me. Ask your aunt. I'm not up on what witches can and can't do."

She went silent for a long moment, then finally asked another question. "Did I do something to upset you? Your mood has changed since we were at the bakery."

Maybe because he knew he was losing his fight to get out of here. But now he felt bad for making her think his attitude was her fault. Crud. He hadn't intended that. He hadn't really meant for his last comment to come out quite so sharply either. He softened his voice. "No. You didn't do anything."

"Then what upset you?"

He couldn't tell her. "I'm just a cranky guy."

"Is that your curse?"

He almost laughed, biting his cheek instead to keep the chuckle from rolling out of him. "Something like that."

She nodded with sudden understanding. "Well, I won't hold it against you."

"Thanks."

She was really something. Pretty and sweet. Accepting and forgiving. Easy to like. He made himself focus on the road. He was a cursed man from a cursed family. She was a talented witch from the most powerful family in Shadowvale. He was supposed to be turning her against this place, not making googly eyes at her.

"Do you think we could go back to Main Street after the swamp?"

He laughed, unable to hold it in any longer. "You must really like to shop."

She shrugged. "I do, but just window-shop. That's all my bank account allows for. I'm just fascinated by all the magical stuff. I mean, until last night, I didn't even know I was a witch."

CHAPTER TEN

Deacon pulled off the road and threw the truck into park, then turned to look at Em. "You keep saying you just found out about witches and that you are one. How did you not know that they existed if you're one yourself?"

She shrugged. "Aunt Amelia said I never knew about my own powers because my mother never did the initiation ritual with me. Or told me we were witches. So I had no idea. I wasn't even sure I really believed Aunt Amelia, but she did a few things that were undeniably witchy, so yeah, she's got some kind of magic skills for sure. Thankfully, Aunt Amelia's going to do the initiation for me. Then I'll be able to access my powers. Crazy, huh?"

Crazy wasn't the word. He got back on the road, gripping the steering wheel a little tighter. "You've spent your entire life not knowing?"

"Whole life, no clue. But Aunt Amelia told me a few things that were probably indicators of my magic, things I never really gave too much thought to before, but that make sense now. My magic has always been a part of me. Just a closed-off part. She's going to help me open that door."

"Indicators like what?" The moss hanging from the trees grew more frequent, a sure sign they were approaching the swamp.

"Like how I always knew when bill collectors were calling before I answered the phone. Or when the landlord was at the door asking for the rent. Stuff like that."

How odd. Those things confirmed the sense that she was struggling with money. And had been for some time. She'd also asked Nasha how much the stuff at the bakery was going to cost. And had made the comment about her bank account not letting her shop.

Combined with her wanting a fresh start in Shadowvale, he now understood that Amelia's niece was in financial trouble. Maybe that's why Em had really come here. To get help from Amelia.

He'd never known Amelia to be stingy. Not even remotely. She'd poured tons of money into this town, and continued to do so, donating much of the money made from the gem mines to make sure the town was well supplied with everything. Top-notch schools, a fire department that lacked for nothing, a hospital equipped with state-of-the-art facilities, perfectly maintained roads even here in the back country, a library that was as beautiful as it was functional…this town put most normal ones to shame.

Shadowvale might be cursed, but not when it came to its standard of living.

So why would Amelia withhold funds from her niece? There was only one answer Deacon could think of. Amelia didn't know that Em was struggling. But that excuse felt thin. Amelia knew a lot. She could sense things like that. Anticipate them, even.

What was holding her back from helping Em, then? He turned onto Orleans Road, and they entered the swamp proper.

Em put her hands on the dashboard and leaned forward like she was trying to get a better look at things. "Is this it? The swamp?"

"It is. Part of it anyway. This is Bayou Orleans."

"Shadowvale has mountains and an enchanted forest and a swamp and bayous? Just how big is Shadowvale?"

"How did you know the forest is enchanted?"

"I saw the sign when we left the cemetery. The arrow in the opposite direction said Enchanted Forest. Or is that like a kids' playground or something?"

"No, it's a real enchanted forest. And that sign's really more of a warning."

She laughed. "Of course it is. So really, how big is this place?"

"No one knows. The place has been surveyed three times. All three results have been different. Shadowvale is as big or small as it needs to be. But yes, we have all those things. There's a lake, too. And a river."

Her brows went up, and she returned to studying the scenery. "Okay, so Bayou Orleans. This is where the vampires live?"

"It's one of the main places they live. Bayou Orleans is primarily home to the Thibodeaux family."

"And they're vampires? Why here?"

He nodded. "Every last one of them. I suppose this area reminds them of their roots in Louisiana." He slowed down as they approached the first of the Thibodeaux homesteads. "That's one of their houses now."

She turned to look. "That is *not* what I thought a swamp house would look like."

"Around here, that's what's known as a low-country-style house."

"And it's built up on stilts like that to avoid flooding?"

"In theory. We don't really get flooding in Shadowvale. Mostly, I think the Thibodeauxes built it like that because it's the kind of house they grew up in, and it gives them an added level of security."

She glanced at him. "Are vampires in danger here?"

"No. But old habits die hard."

"Are they the only ones who live in the swamp? I mean, Bayou Orleans?"

"No. Anyone who wants to can live out here." He drove on, and more houses came into view.

She studied each house with genuine interest. "Do the people that live here have to contribute in some way? I mean, do they work? Or are most of these people independently wealthy?"

He snorted. "Most of us work. There are a few who choose to be left alone, and everyone respects that. And yes, a few are independently wealthy." Like Amelia.

"So are the vampires loaded?"

"They have money, but most of them still work. The Thibodeauxes' eldest son, Valentino, runs the jazz club in town. The second-oldest son, Constantin, operates the other bookstore I mentioned, the Gilded Page. The eldest daughter, Daniella, grows orchids and some other exotic plants that she sells through the town florist. The youngest, Juliette, is a painter."

"Those all seem like interesting professions."

"When you're hundreds of years old, I imagine you need something interesting to do to keep from getting bored."

"Good point." She kept looking at him, then narrowed her eyes a bit. "What do you do?"

He'd been wondering when she'd get around to that. "I'm Shadowvale's peacekeeper." He didn't like to call himself the law, even if he was. The town didn't have a regular police force. There was no need. Yet.

She nodded, taking that in. "So you stop fights and stuff like that?"

How much did he want to tell her about himself? That wasn't an easy question to answer, but he wanted to be truthful. No real reason not to be. "I can if called upon, but primarily what I do is—"

His phone rang with the siren ringtone. "Sorry, I have to take this."

But that ringtone meant only one thing. He was about to show her what he did.

Em went back to looking at houses while Deacon answered his phone. She tried not to listen to his call, but she couldn't help it. They were in the same vehicle. It was impossible not to.

And while the houses were beautiful (she could definitely see the appeal of living up on stilts like that), they weren't as interesting as finding out more about the very curious man beside her.

"This is Deacon," he said into the phone. He kept his right hand hooked overtop the steering wheel, right at the apex of it, his arm stretched out and slightly flexed. There was something very sexy about that casual position.

She swallowed and did her best to look like she wasn't listening.

"Again? Okay. Where? Right. Sure, I understand. Give me a few minutes. I'm in Bayou Orleans." He hung up and made a three-point turn in the road, sending them back toward town. "You want me to drop you off on Main Street? I need to take care of something."

No way was she letting him ditch her now. "No, I'm fine to ride along."

He gave her a look that showed her he clearly had not been expecting that answer.

Adorable. "Is there something confidential about peacekeeping work that I'm not aware of? Some kind of client-peacekeeper privilege?"

"No. But what I do isn't typical peacekeeping work."

"Then what is it?"

"What I do is more personal."

She crossed her arms. "Such as?"

"When a person's curse gets too much for them to handle, or becomes a danger to them or those around them, I step in. To keep the peace."

"You fix curses?"

"More like I help the person get rid of them. Temporarily."

"Wow, that's amazing."

He sighed. "If you're that person, I suppose it is."

"But not...for you?"

His jaw tightened, and he didn't answer right away. "My curse is the ability to take on another person's curse. I absorb it. It only removes their curse from them temporarily."

"And for you? Are you stuck with it?"

"Until the moon rises, yes."

That seemed a lot more troublesome. "Do you feel the effects of their curse?"

He nodded. "I feel the effects, but I always survive them."

"Ouch. What particular curse are you going to take care of now?"

"Frieda Ruhday's. She's broken out in spines again. It happens every couple of months. Usually, she just stays in until it passes, but—"

"Spines? Like a porcupine?"

"Close. But the spines are short, deep blue, and venomous."

Em jerked back. "What? That doesn't sound good at all. Why do you have to take this on? You said she normally stays in until it passes. Why not this time?"

"Because her daughter has a recital tonight."

"Yikes, she has a kid? What if the kid gets stuck by one of those poisonous spines?"

"Brianna's immune."

"Does this woman have any other children with the same curse?"

"No, Brianna's an only child."

Em cringed as a new thought occurred to her. "Please don't tell me the little girl has the same curse."

"We don't know yet. Nothing's manifested, but then, curses don't always show up right away. Sometimes they arrive later in life."

She was fascinated. "Was yours like that?"

"No. I was born with it."

This was the most he'd shared about himself so far. It felt big. Like he was trusting her. She loved that. Trust wasn't something she got a lot from people. Not those who knew who she was anyway. "Are you an only child?"

"Nope." He turned back onto Main. "Two brothers, one sister."

"Big family. Where are you in the bunch?"

"Second oldest. Shep, then me, then Bishop, then Grace. Well, we all call her Gracie. Most folks do."

103

"Shep, as in…?"

"Shepherd."

She pondered that. "Shepherd, Deacon, Bishop, and Grace?"

"Uh-huh."

"Is your father a pastor?"

He laughed. "No. Our mother was a very religious woman. Almost became a nun, actually." The lightness in his eyes faded. "But then she met my father, and he talked her out of it. Talked her into marrying him instead of the church."

He blamed his father for that. Or for something. She didn't know what, but she could tell by the way his gaze went distant and his jaw tightened back up. There was some bad blood there. Maybe his father was a hard man.

She'd never known her father, so she couldn't relate, but she knew what it felt like to have a difficult parent. That much she could understand. "Sorry."

He glanced at her. "For what?"

"For whatever it is about your father that makes you unhappy."

His eyes narrowed. "Don't do that."

"Do what?"

"Use your magic to figure me out. Stay out of my head." He made a sharp turn off Main, the momentum pushing her into her seat.

"I wasn't—"

He straightened the truck as they entered a residential area. "Just don't."

She kept quiet then, mostly because she wasn't sure saying anything more was going to help, but also because she couldn't be certain she hadn't used her magic to read him. She'd been so good at figuring people out all her life that she'd taken it for granted, until her aunt's explanation that something like that might actually be her magic at work.

So maybe she had done that to him. She hadn't intended to. "If I did, I didn't mean to. Honestly. I don't know how to use my magic that way yet. But I'm sorry anyway."

He frowned. "Sorry I snapped."

She nodded. "It's okay. We all have a tender spot."

He pulled into the driveway of a little yellow house with white shutters and a green door.

The front door opened as he shut the truck off.

A very worried-looking woman covered in short, thin, deep-blue spines stepped out onto the porch.

"Oh my," Em whispered. She knew she shouldn't stare, especially not with her mouth open, but it was impossible to do anything else. "I'd say less porcupine, more puffer fish."

Deacon shot her a glance. "Don't touch anything."

"You don't have to tell me twice."

CHAPTER ELEVEN

Deacon wasn't really worried about Em being there. She was smart enough to know how to handle herself and seemed like she'd err on the side of politeness when in doubt.

He just didn't want Frieda to think he'd invited someone along to rubberneck during her time of misfortune. "Frieda, this is Emeranth, Amelia's niece. I'm showing her around town today, so I had to bring her with me. I hope that's okay."

Em stuck her hand up in a tentative little wave.

"Amelia's niece?" Frieda glanced at Em. "Hi. I, uh, don't usually look like this."

"Deacon told me," Em said. "No worries."

"Yeah," Deacon said. "I explained." Em still looked a little lost in the reality of what was happening. Which was probably a good thing. Maybe this would be the straw that kept the camel from moving here permanently. Not that she remotely resembled a camel.

Frieda offered Em a tense smile, then looked back at Deacon. "Thank you for coming. I'm sorry to call, but with Brianna's recital tonight…"

"Stop apologizing," he said. "That's what I'm here for."

She sighed. "I really thought it would have cleared up by now."

"When did it start?"

"Two days ago." She wrung her hands together. "Seems like it lasts longer and longer each time it happens."

Em stayed by the truck. "What makes it happen? If you don't mind me asking."

Frieda shrugged. "It just comes on."

"Next time, call me sooner. You don't need to deal with this." Deacon knew from experience that only her palms and the soles of her feet were untouched by the curse.

Frieda shrugged as best she could. "But then you have to deal with it. And that's not fair either."

Fair wasn't something that had applied to the Evermores in a long time. "Still. I'm here to help. So call me. Now let's get it taken care of so you can get ready for that recital."

"Thanks again." Frieda started to move back toward the house. "Should we go inside?"

He shook his head. "We can do it right here."

"Okay." She came down the porch stairs to stand closer to him.

Em hadn't budged from the side of the truck. He was good with that.

"You know the drill." He lifted his arms, palms up. "Give me your hands."

Frieda held hers out as she moved toward him, finally making careful contact.

Deacon took a breath and flipped the little mental switch inside himself that opened up his curse vacuum.

Frieda's trouble hit him like a baby grand piano, nearly flattening him with the impact. He laced his fingers with hers to hold on so he could be sure he took all of it. Finally, the onslaught turned into a trickle. Instinct told him that was the last of it.

That and the woman across from him no longer resembled a pin cushion.

He let go of Frieda. A second later, his body went numb. Then a familiar tingling spread over him. He knew what was coming next. He rolled his shoulders and braced himself as every nerve ending erupted in fire and the spines burst through his skin.

Em's sudden gasp barely registered over his own grunt of pain.

In a few more seconds, the pain subsided, and the curse was fully realized.

In front of him stood Frieda, looking how she usually looked. Like a middle-aged mom. She smiled at him. "Thank you so much."

"You're welcome."

"I would hug you, but..."

"Yeah, I know. Enjoy the recital."

She headed back inside. "I will now."

He turned to Em. Her eyes were rounded and filled with concern and questions. "Yes, I'm okay. Yes, it hurt, but it doesn't now."

She kept staring. "I know those spines are deadly, but I still want to touch one. Like when you're a little kid and the stove is hot, but you have to see for yourself? It's kind of like that."

He put his hands up. "Don't."

"I'm not going to." She pulled out her phone. "But I have to get a picture of this."

He snorted. "Good luck."

"What's that supposed to mean?"

"You won't be able to."

"Sure I will." She wiggled her phone. "I've got my camera right here."

He put one hand on the hood of his truck and leaned. "Try it."

She lifted the phone and snapped a picture, then looked at the screen. "Hang on, I hit the wrong thing."

"No, you didn't."

"Yes, I did. Let me try it again."

He rolled his eyes, thoroughly amused. "Have at it."

She snapped a second picture and checked again. She frowned. "Okay, what's going on?"

"Told you. The town protects those who live here."

She stared at her phone a second longer before looking up at him. "Are you kidding me? The town is making my phone malfunction?"

"Yep. Well, those meridian lines are." He glanced down. And was suddenly glad she hadn't let him drop her off on Main Street. "Hmm. I don't really want to get into my truck like this. The leather seats will never be the same."

"You want me to drive?"

He nodded. "Would you?"

"Sure, but won't you just tear up the passenger's side?"

"No. I'm going to ride in the back."

She looked at the truck. "So…standing up and holding on to the roll bar?"

"Pretty much." He checked over his shoulder to get a better look at his backside. "Sitting doesn't seem like a smart move."

She was grinning, but trying not to.

"It's okay," he said. "You can laugh. I know you want to."

"It *is* kind of funny. I mean, it's also amazing that you did what you did for Frieda, but now it's just funny. Unless you accidentally stick someone. Then it would be tragic."

"Which is why today's tour is over. And I need to go home."

"Got it. How will I get back to my aunt's, then? I'm guessing Uber doesn't cover Shadowvale?"

"It doesn't. But I'm sure Beckett will come and get you."

She nodded. "Right. He will. I have no doubt." She held her hand out.

He backed up. "I told you, no touching."

She sighed and shook her head. "Keys?"

"Oh. Right." He made a face. "Thankfully, they're still in the ignition."

"Then hop on up and let's go. Of course, I don't know where I'm going."

"It's not hard to find. You can program the address into your GPS if you want."

She squinted at him. "So the town allows that, but not me taking a picture of you like this?"

"It's all about protecting the citizens. Using your GPS to get me home isn't harmful, so I'm sure it will work."

"Let's see." She pulled her phone out again. "Address?"

"Thirteen thirteen Pitch Lane."

She punched it in. "Yep, there it is." She looked at him, then the spines.

He stepped back. "You can't."

"I know, I know. But it's still tempting."

Before she changed her mind, he went around to the back and climbed into the truck.

She got into the cab, and off they went. She drove slowly, probably because she was following an unfamiliar route, but he still appreciated it, seeing as how he was upright and falling would be disastrous.

It was interesting seeing the town from this angle. He sort of felt like a one-man parade. Especially when people started waving. Out of obligation and politeness, he waved back, but he cringed inside every time. Not just because he disliked so much attention, but because this was Frieda's curse on display, and being so open about it felt like a disservice to her.

Truthfully, taking on her curse was the exact opposite of a disservice, but he couldn't help the discomfort it gave him to be so visible.

Relief swept through him when Em finally pulled his truck into the driveway of his family house. He jumped down, closed the tailgate, and walked around to the passenger's side to keep a safe distance from Em.

She got out and met him around the front. "Are you going to be here by yourself?"

"No, Gracie's probably here. Maybe Bishop. He lives here too."

"Good. I hate for you to be alone like this."

That was sweet of her to care. "I'll manage. But remember what I said about not touching anyone. That applies to my family, too."

Almost on cue, a curious light lit her gaze. "Got it."

He knew she wanted to ask why and what curses his sister and brothers had, but she didn't. For whatever reason.

The front door opened, and Tinkerbelle came running out to the edge of the porch. Gracie stood in the doorway, staring at Deacon. "Frieda?"

He nodded. "Brianna's recital is tonight."

"Poor woman." Her gaze shifted to Em. "Hi."

Deacon spoke up. "This is Emeranth, Amelia's niece. She was kind enough to drive me back so I wouldn't have to perforate my upholstery."

"You must be Gracie," Em said as she headed up the steps.

"I am. Nice to meet you. I didn't know Amelia had any family left. Or in town."

"I just got here yesterday."

"How nice. I bet she's so glad to have company."

Em shrugged. "Not entirely sure about that, but I'm here now, so she's stuck with me."

Deacon stayed at the bottom of the stairs, not wanting to risk accidentally brushing against either of them. "Em needs to use the phone to call Beckett so he can come pick her up. Or just give her the number. She has her cell phone."

Em turned toward him. "Either way, I need the number to my aunt's. I don't know it yet. I should have programed it into my phone."

Gracie smiled and scooped Tinkerbelle up. "I can help with all that. Come on in, and we'll give Deac a wide berth until he can get out of our way."

"Sounds good. Thank you." She followed Gracie in. "What's your dog's name? He's such a cutie."

"He's a she, and her name is Tinkerbelle."

Deacon waited until they were well into the house, then came in behind them, shaking his head. He hadn't intended for the day to go like this. Now Em and Gracie were going to be friends, and Em would have one less reason to want to leave.

He sighed. He was never getting out of here.

Suddenly, Em appeared in the hallway again. The stairs to the second floor—and his bedroom—were between them.

He stiffened. "What's wrong?"

"Nothing. I just forgot my stuff from the bakery in the truck."

"Oh. I'm gonna go upstairs and stay out of the way for a bit."

She nodded, looking him over. "Until the moon rises, huh?"

"Yep."

"What time is that?"

"Tonight?" He thought for a second. "Around two a.m."

"Long night."

He nodded and should have excused himself and gotten moving, but something kept him there. Facing her. Breathing in the scent of her. "Thanks for driving me and my truck back."

"You're welcome. Thanks for giving me a tour of Shadowvale."

"Half a tour, really."

Her lips pursed. "Then I guess I'll see you tomorrow for the rest of that tour."

"I...okay." Why he agreed, he didn't know. He shouldn't have. All he would do was make her like the town more. And Amelia was not going to be happy with that.

Neither would he, really. But he liked Em. And spending another day with her wouldn't be a hardship. Even if it meant his and Gracie's ticket out of this town would be a lot harder to earn.

"Good." She smiled.

He'd expected her to move then, but she stayed put. "Is there something else?"

"Nope."

He frowned.

"Just waiting for you to move so I can live long enough to eat one of those cupcakes."

"Oh, right. Yeah. Sorry." He tipped his head toward the stairs. "Heading up. See you tomorrow."

She pulled her bottom lip through her teeth. "Tomorrow."

He closed his eyes as he took the first few steps, suddenly mortified at what a bumbling moron she'd turned him into. That was not good. That meant something. Maybe that her magic was affecting him?

Or maybe…something else entirely.

CHAPTER TWELVE

Gracie was still on the phone when Em walked back into the kitchen, carrying the shopping bag from Black Horse. Tinkerbelle was sitting at Gracie's feet with her tongue hanging out and a cute doggy smile on her face.

Maybe when Em got herself straight, she'd get a pet. Weren't witches supposed to have cats anyway? Oh! Maybe she'd get a meowl!

Gracie hung up. "Okay, all set. Beckett said he'd be here in a few minutes." She spotted the bag. "Oooh, I love Black Horse. Their black-and-white cookies are just the best. What did you get?"

"Pumpernickel raisin bread for my aunt, mocha cupcakes for Beckett, and a Chocolate Reaper cupcake for myself. Plus, Nasha said she threw in a few other things she thought I might like, but I don't know what they are yet. And if I had known I was going to end up here, I would have gotten you something. You want to see what the extra goodies are? Maybe pick something?"

Gracie waved the comment away. "No, you should try them. And how could you have known?

Although for future reference, I'm partial to the strawberry bombs." She grinned. "Nasha's making my cake."

"Deacon mentioned that. I assume it's for your birthday?"

"It is," Gracie said. "Hey! You should come to my party. It's this Saturday. It's also a surprise, so you didn't hear about it from me." She winked.

Em laughed. Saturday was two days away. The end of her expiration date. "I would love to, if I'm still here. Thank you for the invite."

"Still here? You just got here yesterday. That's a quick visit."

"It is, but I'm hoping that won't be the case. I'd like to move here, actually. But I have to work all that out with my aunt."

"I see." Gracie rolled her eyes playfully. "I know all about family stuff."

Em wanted to ask what that meant, but plying Deacon's little sister for info felt wrong. And she didn't want to upset him. She wanted him to like her. Maybe enough that he'd put in a good word for her with Aunt Amelia about staying. "How old are you going to be?"

"I'm going to be twenty-five. A quarter of a century." Gracie laughed. "I know it's not that old, but right now it feels ancient."

"It's a great age." Em smiled. It really hadn't been for her.

When she was twenty-five, her mother had disappeared for two weeks only to return with the news that every cent they'd saved had been lost in a long con that had gone south so fast Manda hadn't even gotten out with her seed money.

But Em still smiled, because that was all behind her now.

"What kind of work do you do?" Gracie asked.

"I'd pretty much take anything I can get. I've done all sorts of things. Mostly retail and restaurant work." She'd never gotten the chance to go to college. And moving around so much had meant that building up experience was a hard go, except for the times she'd worked at coffee shops. "Do you know anyone who's hiring? For anything?"

"Not off the top of my head, but I'll ask around."

"That's very kind of you." Em liked Gracie. She'd never had much in the way of friends. Another thing that moving around so much made difficult. And at a certain point, she'd stopped letting people in. Maybe Gracie could be her first real friend.

Gracie got a coy look on her face as she leaned against the counter. "So." She paused to raise her eyebrows. "Deacon."

Em nodded, not quite sure where this was headed. "He's a nice guy."

Gracie's coy smile hitched up a little higher on one side. "Just a nice guy?"

Em wondered if this was how her own questions made people feel. Squirmy. And on the spot. "He's a little grumpy. But I don't mind it."

Gracie snorted. "He's terribly grumpy, but most of it's a big show. And seriously, don't you think he's handsome? I know he's my brother and all, but—"

Tinkerbelle barked suddenly, and a knock at the door followed, turning both their heads. Tinkerbelle took off for the front door.

"Must be Beckett," Gracie said.

"I can see myself out." Em lifted her bag of bakery goodies and headed for the door. "Thanks again. See you Saturday, maybe."

"I'd love that. I hope you can make it." A certain gleam lit her eyes. "I'm sure Deacon would like that, too."

With a small chuckle, Em paused and glanced over her shoulder. "Yes, I think he's handsome. But holy smokes, don't tell him I said that."

Gracie burst out laughing.

Em hurried to the door before Gracie could see her turn red. She slipped outside, making sure not to let Tinkerbelle out, and found Beckett waiting on the front porch. "Thank you for coming to get me."

"Happy to do it. I understand Mr. Evermore was pressed into service today?"

"Yep. Boy, was that interesting." They walked down the steps and to the car parked next to Deacon's truck. It was a sleek, deep-blue Rolls-Royce.

Beckett opened the rear passenger-side door for her.

She frowned. "Would it be okay if I ride up front with you?"

He seemed taken aback for a moment. Then he smiled. "By all means, if that's what you want."

"It is." Aunt Amelia might be used to people waiting on her and deferring to her, but Em had a long way to go before that would feel comfortable.

Still grinning, he closed the rear door and opened the front one. "There you are."

"Thanks." She got in, putting the bag on her lap.

He came around and slid behind the wheel.

She patted the bag. "I understand you like the mocha cupcakes."

"I do." He put the car in reverse. "You certainly know the way to a man's heart, Miss Em."

She laughed. She liked Beckett. He was still intimidating as all get-out, but she wasn't afraid of him anymore. "I wouldn't have known, but Nasha told me. Speaking of, Deacon told me her father is one of the Four Horsemen of the Apocalypse. That's wild."

He nodded slowly, eyes on the rearview mirror as he backed out of the driveway. "Shadowvale is home to all sorts. But I'm guessing you learned that today."

"I did. At least as much as Deacon could show me until he got called to help Frieda. He'd just been showing me where the vampires live."

"Bayou Orleans?" Now on Pitch Lane, Beckett shifted into drive and headed for Amelia's.

"Yep. Do you know any of them?"

"I do, a little. I go to Club 42 when I can. Isabelle Lagasse is a beautiful woman with a beautiful voice."

"Which one is she?" Em wondered if Beckett was sweet on her. His expression had gone a little dreamy all of a sudden.

"She's a cousin. Josephine Thibodeaux's cousin, actually. Josephine's the matriarch of the clan." He shook his head. "It's a big family. You'll meet them."

"I can wait on that." She grimaced. "I'm sure they're nice people, but vampires might be something I need to take slow."

"Understand." He glanced at her. "Now that you've seen Deacon's curse in action, what do you think about it?"

Em shrugged. "Doesn't seem like that bad of a curse to me. It makes it possible for him to help people, so that's a good thing, right? But I suppose it's not much fun for him to live with the curses he takes on until they go away." She thought about it some more. "Makes him a very sympathetic guy. He's a hero, really."

"He is. He's helped a lot of people in this town. Saved countless citizens from really bad situations."

"Does he have a girlfriend? Wait, never mind." Em's eyes went wide. "I do not know why I asked that."

Beckett laughed. "No, he doesn't."

She put her hand on her head. "I'm not interested. I'm really not. I have a lot to take care of before I even think about getting involved with someone."

He made a little face and kept his eyes on the road. "There are worse choices than Deacon Evermore."

"Shh."

"I'm just saying, he—"

"He lives at home with his sister and a brother. Not saying that's necessarily a bad thing, but it's not exactly a sign he's looking to move beyond that either. At least it isn't to me."

"The Evermore boys are very protective of their sister."

"Must be nice." Em frowned. "Did I just say that out loud? Apparently, I'm all about oversharing today."

"You did. And it's okay. Sometimes you just need to talk."

He wasn't wrong. And it had been so long since she'd had someone to talk to. She sighed and watched the scenery go by. "I never had any brothers or sisters. No father. And not much of a mother either. No one to look out for me, you know?"

He didn't answer right away, then softly said, "I'd be happy to look out for you, Miss Em. As long as I'm able."

Her heart knotted up at his sweet words, then she replayed what he'd just said. "What do you mean, as long as you're able? Are you...unwell?"

"No, nothing like that. But someday my job here will be done. And then I'll have to move on."

"You think my aunt is going to get rid of you?"

"That's...not what I mean."

She peered at him. The darkness she'd seen around him before had returned. The intimacy of their conversation made her bold, sudden courage loosening her tongue. "What are you, Beckett? I mean, besides the majordomo of Indigo House."

He kept his gaze straight ahead. "I'm not sure you want the answer to that."

"I do. I really do. I sense darkness around you. Almost see it, really. I want to know why that is. What you are."

He sighed as he pulled down Aunt Amelia's drive. He parked the car by the front doors, turned off the engine, and finally looked at her. "I like you, Miss Em. I don't want to frighten you off liking me."

"I like you, too. I won't be frightened by whatever kind of supernatural you are."

He smiled, but there was sadness in it.

"You are a supernatural, aren't you?" Her breath caught in her throat. Was he a vampire? Was that what all that darkness was?

"I am."

"Are you a vampire?"

"No."

She didn't say anything else. Just let the silence hang between them. It was a trick she'd learned from her mother. People would usually tell you what you wanted to know just to fill the silence.

At last, Beckett sighed. "I was assigned to your aunt about fifty years ago. But when I came here, I didn't understand the depth of the job I'd been given. Nor how powerful she is. Or how powerful this place is. Because of all that, I haven't been able to do the job I was sent to do. Instead, I've been forced to wait until she's ready. Or until she chooses to leave this bewitched ground. It's rather intent on protecting her."

Em tried to understand what he was telling her, but it didn't quite click. "I'm sorry, I'm not sure I get what you're saying. What kind of job were you given?"

His gloomy smile went flat, and a new sadness filled his eyes. "I was given the job of collecting your aunt's soul."

Em's mouth came open, but her brain was struggling to process what he'd just said. "Her soul? But she'd have to be...deceased for that to be possible. Right? Or am I missing something? I really don't understand."

He nodded. "I think you do, Miss Em. Yes, she would have to be deceased. I'm a reaper. Her reaper, to be exact."

She shivered without meaning to. Death. Beckett was Death. And she was in the car with him. Her throat closed up, making words impossible.

"You're afraid." He frowned. "I knew you would be. I won't hurt you. I can't hurt you. You're not my assignment."

She found her voice. "You want to kill my aunt?"

"No, not at all."

"Then what? Explain it to me."

"This isn't my story to tell."

"It is now that you started it."

"I suppose that's true." He took his hands off the steering wheel and rested them in his lap. "When her beloved left her—"

"Pasqual?"

"Yes. When Pasqual left, she was ruined. Heartbroken beyond repair. She decided that without him, she didn't want to live. She cast a spell to end her life. I was assigned to collect her soul, and so I came to Shadowvale. Of course, seeing me made her regret her actions, but what was done was done. Not all spells are reversible."

"But...she's not dead. Anyone can see that."

"You're right, she's not. Shadowvale won't let her die. She's too much a part of the magic that keeps this town going. She created Shadowvale. It's her magic that gave it life. And so despite her spell to end it all, the town had other ideas. And so she remains. As do I, unable to complete my task."

Em wiped a hand across her mouth. "She's alive because of the town?"

"Yes. But the moment she leaves the boundaries of this place, the instant she steps outside of those gates, the town's protection of her ends. And my job will be complete." He looked at the house. "In the beginning, I did everything I could to make that happen. Now I don't care if it ever does, although I do tease her about it a bit."

"That's why she doesn't like you. You remind her of the mistake she made. Not to mention her impending death, and how she's basically a captive here."

He nodded. "Yes. And I can't leave until my job is done. We're stuck together."

Em sat back. "Wow."

"Indeed."

"Does all of that have something to do with why she doesn't want me to live here?"

"I can't say it's not related, but there's more to it than that. But that story really is hers to tell."

"Thank you for sharing all that with me." She looked sideways at him. "A reaper, huh?"

"Yes."

"And you're really not dangerous to anyone else?"

"Don't misunderstand. I can wield great power when needed, but I have no need. I live very peaceably here. We all do, for the most part. But my sole purpose here is to collect Amelia's soul. That's all I've come to do. Bringing back a different soul would not go well for me."

"Can I ask you one more question?"

He laughed. "Would it matter if I said no?"

She grinned. "Probably not. How did you end up as her majordomo?"

"Indigo House is a beautiful place, but when I arrived it had already begun to show signs of neglect. With nothing but time on my hands, I took it upon myself to change that. Eventually, your aunt started paying me. Then giving me directions on what to work on next. I'm sure she thought if I was occupied, I'd forget why I'd really come."

"But you won't, will you?"

He shook his head. "I can't. That's not how a reaper is built."

"Well, I hope your job isn't done for a very long time."

He smiled without sadness. "Me, too, Miss Em. Me, too."

CHAPTER THIRTEEN

Deacon stared at himself in the mirror. Most curses didn't change his appearance so drastically. Or at all. But this one...this was a doozy.

He brushed his fingers over the spines on his cheek. Experience had taught him that he was immune to the side effects of the curses he took on. That was one upside of his own curse. But that didn't negate the fact that he was going to have to remain like this until Frieda's curse wore off.

He glanced at the bed. Lying down would mean poking holes in the sheets and mattress. Not something he wanted to do. Sitting in any of the upholstered chairs would have the same result.

There was one spot he could think of that would be okay for sitting. And now that Em had left, it would be safe.

He went back downstairs and outside to the deck. The breeze whistled through his spines. Not an experience he had often, to be sure.

He took a seat on the wicker glider, hoping his spines were mostly going through the small holes in the weave as opposed to making new ones. He stretched his arm along the seat, tipped his head back, and closed his eyes. Even with the cloud cover, there was some warmth coming through. It felt good.

Today had been an interesting day. All because of Emeranth, who was easily the most stimulating person he'd met in a long time. Which was saying something, considering where he lived.

She looked at Shadowvale with a completely different viewpoint than he did. That was because she was new to town. He understood that. But it was still curious to him how desperately she wanted in, while he so desperately wanted out.

Why? What was she running from? It wasn't his business. Everyone had baggage, and everyone had a right to their privacy, but he couldn't stop himself from wondering.

An ex, maybe? She was beautiful. It wouldn't surprise him to learn that there was a jealous man in her past, still burned by losing her.

That thought made him bristle in a way that had nothing to do with his current status. He felt oddly protective of her even though they'd just met. Maybe that was just something she inspired in those around her.

Gracie was like that, so he understood. His little sister had an effect on people that made them want to give her things and be extra kind to her and protect her. It was lovely, except when it wasn't. Like all the overzealous boyfriends he and his brothers had dealt with throughout the years.

Now Gracie mostly kept to herself. Not just because of how men responded to her, but more so because of her particular curse. Keeping some distance from others was an easier way for her to live.

Although he knew that was getting old for her. As much as she seemed excited about the prospect of a party on Saturday, she might not be when she saw how many people were there. He sighed, a little worried about how that was going to go, but everyone in town abided by the general rule of not touching others.

Except that it was Gracie's birthday. And such an occasion could make people act differently than they normally would.

He and his brothers would just have to be extra vigilant.

Or maybe one of the witches in town could put a little spell on Gracie to keep her curse from working temporarily. Was that possible? He didn't know, but it was worth talking to Amelia about.

He groaned. Amelia. He was going to have to call her and tell her today had been a bust.

A soft squeak was followed by, "Hey."

He opened his eyes. Gracie had the screen door open and was leaning out. "Hey."

"You hungry? I was about to make myself a sandwich. I could make you one, too."

He nodded. "I could eat. Thanks." He normally made his own lunch. He wondered if Gracie was up to something.

She smiled a little too big. "Turkey or roast beef?"

"Roast beef." Definitely up to something.

"Coming up." She went back in, then popped out again a second later. "Em's nice."

"She is." He wasn't sure where that had come from, but now his suspicions about Gracie's sandwich offer felt more on point. He decided to test the theory. "Do we have any of that grainy mustard left? If so, I'll take some of that on my sandwich."

She laughed. "You're changing the subject."

He'd been right. "Actually, you're the one who changed the subject. We were already talking about sandwiches."

She rolled her eyes at him. "Well, I like Em. She's nice and not that much older than me, and I think we could be friends."

"She's probably not staying." Reason enough for neither of them to get involved with her. Not that he was considering it. "Just so you know."

Gracie took a step outside to see him better. "That's not what she said. The way she talked, she's trying to move here."

"I know, but Amelia doesn't think Shadowvale is a good place for her. And Amelia usually gets what she wants."

Gracie folded her arms. "How about that. Someone trying to dictate what's good for another person."

He sat up, alerted by the sudden edge in her voice that the conversation had taken yet another turn. "What's that supposed to mean?"

She shrugged. "You know what it means. You guys are always trying to tell me what to do."

"Gracie, we're not trying to tell you what to do. We're trying to protect you."

"Yeah, I know. But that's not always what it feels like."

He frowned. "I'm sorry. I'll try to be better about that."

"Thanks. But tell Shep and Bishop, too, will you? Bishop already said he isn't going to leave my side at the party. I'm going to be twenty-five. Not even remotely a kid anymore. I love him, but a girl needs to breathe, you know? I'd like to be able to talk to people without one of you hanging over my shoulder."

"I can understand that." Although he wondered if by *people* she meant those of the male variety. Was she sweet on a guy? Who could it be? "I'll tell him to give you some room. We all will."

She smiled. "Thanks. Sandwiches coming up."

As she went back inside, he stared into the woods behind the house. He and his brothers were going to have to be less obvious about protecting her. They'd have to find a way to give her space.

And if a couple people forgot themselves and touched her...well, it had happened before, and they'd all lived through it. They'd deal with it again.

But the idea of letting Gracie just be was hard to wrap his head around. The four of them were all the family they had. Their bond was tight. And with good reason.

Truth was, Gracie was the tether that kept him in Shadowvale. He was sure his brothers felt the same, not that either of them had expressed a desire to leave.

Shepherd seemed content in charge of the fire department. Bishop had his tree-trimming service. Gracie ran the house and handled the books for Bishop, plus a few other small businesses in town. That let her work from home.

And helped keep her isolated.

Poor kid. No wonder she was itching for a change.

The door opened, and she came out with a plate for him in one hand and a bottle of soda in the other. "Here you go. Lunch is served."

"Thank you. I could come inside and eat with you." He took both from her, careful not to make contact.

"And put holes in my kitchen chairs? No, thank you." She winked at him. "Besides, I'm working at my desk. The dry cleaners just sent their quarterlies over."

"Okay. Thanks again."

"You're welcome. Maybe tomorrow when you're yourself again, the three of us can have lunch at the diner."

"The three of us?" He really hoped she meant the two of them and Bishop.

"You're giving Em the rest of the tour, aren't you?"

No such luck. "Yeah, I guess so."

"Great. It's a date!"

"It's not a—" But she'd already disappeared back inside. In fact, she'd gone so quickly he was certain she'd done it just so he couldn't argue.

It wasn't a date.

He frowned, staring down at his sandwich and chips. Clearly, sweetening him up with lunch had been all about the real lunch Gracie wanted.

He understood her wanting to get out of the house, but she also wanted to get him and Em together. He could feel it. Sense it, really.

She'd done this same thing with Shep and Nasha. You'd think the way that had gone would be lesson enough for her to stop trying to fix her brothers up, but apparently it wasn't.

Well, he wasn't about to get involved with Em. For one thing, she was a little out of his league. Sure, he knew he was a decent-looking guy, but she was a different level of pretty. Secondly, she was Amelia's niece, and Amelia probably had very different ideas about who Em should be with.

Lastly, Em wanted to be in Shadowvale, and he didn't. What was the point of attaching himself to someone here when he wanted out? It would only end badly.

And there was enough in Shadowvale that ended that way as it was.

He took a bite of his sandwich. Roast beef with grainy mustard, just the way he liked.

Well, Em might be getting the rest of her tour, and Gracie might be getting her lunch out tomorrow, but he was not about to be suckered into anything else where the two of them were concerned.

For all he knew, Em and Gracie were in this together.

Maybe he'd get lucky and someone else would need some curse relief.

He snorted. Wasn't often he had a thought like that.

Crazy what women did to a guy.

Maybe instead of calling, he should go over to Amelia's and talk to her in person. He lifted his sandwich for another bite and caught sight of the spines.

He groaned. He'd actually forgotten about them for a second.

He wasn't going anywhere.

Except out to lunch with Em and Gracie tomorrow.

CHAPTER FOURTEEN

Despite the overcast sky, the afternoon was still bright and warm in that way of early-spring days that teased summer's impending arrival. Really, it was lovely, and Em was surprised she wasn't missing the sun more.

She took her chocolate cupcake, which she'd decided would be lunch, and went into the garden. If she ate it while she walked, that practically made it calorie-free.

Of course, she would have rather spent time with her aunt, or even had lunch with Beckett the reaper, but he was doing a wine inventory, and Aunt Amelia wasn't readily available. Em was sure she was in the house somewhere, but wandering around in search of her seemed impolite.

If Aunt Amelia had things to do, Em didn't want to get in the way of that. Being a pest wasn't going to win her any points toward staying. Aunt Amelia would find Em when she was ready.

So the garden it was. Not a hardship. The place was abundant with beautiful plants, gorgeous flowers, and the loveliest, green floral scent.

Em wasn't sure how the garden grew so well without the sun, but her knowledge of plants was minimal. Maybe it was Amelia's doing. Some kind of spell that kept things green and growing, no matter the conditions.

That would be a good spell to learn. Really, any spell would be a good one to learn. A witch had to start somewhere.

She peeled back a little of the paper sleeve holding the cupcake and took a bite. The perfect bitterness of the dark chocolate mixed with the creamy sweetness of the frosting made a wonderful mouthful. She let out a little sigh of pleasure. So good. She could see daily trips to Black Horse Bakery becoming a thing if she moved here.

When, she corrected herself. *When*. Not *if*. Because she had to think positive. She had to cling to the hope that this was all going to work out.

That hope was all she had right now. She didn't even want to think about leaving. Where would she go? She had no ready answer to that question.

A stone bench sat by the garden pool. Em took a seat and stared at the water, trying to think about her next steps while she devoured the remains of the cupcake.

Maybe Nasha was hiring. Couldn't hurt to ask. Em hadn't seen any staff in the store with her, but she couldn't be producing all those goodies on her own, could she? The woman had to have some kind of help. Unless she was using magic, too. No way to know if there was a chance for a job except to ask.

Em sat up a little straighter. Maybe what she ought to do was finish this cupcake, then change into something more professional and head back downtown to do some serious job hunting. She would check every single shop if time allowed.

She nodded. She would, too. Every single one. Somebody had to be hiring. Even a part-time position would be better than nothing. And that could lead to more. Or maybe she could find two part-time jobs. That would be okay. Even three. She'd work as much as she could.

Building up her reserves so she could get a place of her own and start her life anew was what mattered. Not how hard she had to work or what kind of jobs she had to take. She wasn't a proud woman. Not where self-preservation was concerned.

This was a good plan. She felt encouraged. Buoyed, really. Aunt Amelia, and to some extent Deacon, might not want her to stay here, but they'd just have to get over it.

She was going to get a job, and she was going to put down roots and learn to be a witch and change her life.

She popped the last of the cupcake into her mouth, folded up the paper wrapper to throw away in the house, and got to her feet to go back inside. Nothing was going to stop her.

She turned toward the house and froze.

She was pinned by the gaze of the biggest tiger she'd ever seen. Her pulse jumped. Was it real? It certainly looked real. Just like the gates had appeared to be locked.

She couldn't tell and didn't want to find out if she was wrong, so for what seemed like an eternity, she and the tiger just stared at each other.

Its nostrils flared. Like it was sniffing her.

That looked very real.

"Please don't eat me," she whispered. "Please be a magical hallucination. Or something equally magical that also isn't dangerous. I really don't want to die today."

The tiger didn't move.

She gathered her courage and whispered as loudly as she dared, "Beckett."

The minutes ticked by, and he didn't show. Not that she'd expected him to hear that, especially while he was in the wine cellar.

"Nice kitty. Pretty, pretty kitty." A bead of sweat trickled down her back. Her voice was as trembly as the rest of her. "I am not delicious. I promise. Please don't eat me."

"Thoreau." Aunt Amelia's voice rang through the garden. "Emeranth is a friend."

The tiger turned to look at Amelia, then let out a whuff and lay down.

Em almost fainted with relief. Instead, she took a deep breath and tried to exhale the quivers from her body. "You know this tiger?"

Amelia walked toward them. "He's my companion."

Em swallowed. "You might have mentioned that sooner. You know, before I came out here and almost became his lunch."

Amelia stooped to scratch the tiger's head. "Thoreau wouldn't hurt you."

"I'm glad you think that. He was looking at me like he was hungry."

"Nonsense. He's fed on a regular basis. He was just trying to determine who you are. That's all." Aunt Amelia smiled. "But my apologies all the same. I should have told you. I'm sure running into a beast like Thoreau gives one pause."

"If you're talking about my heart, then yes, it definitely paused." She glanced at the enormous cat. "How did you end up with a tiger as a companion?"

"Beckett. He started feeding a stray cat that was hanging around the kitchen door. The cat ended up making a home here in my garden. He was a friendly little thing, and I took a liking to him. He was cautious at first, but after a while came closer."

She smiled down at Thoreau. "As soon as he let me pet him, I knew he was no ordinary cat, but that he'd been enchanted. I cast a spell to free him, only to discover my stray friend was this beast. Although he was a much younger tiger then and not nearly so large."

"How does that even happen?"

Amelia shrugged. "That's Shadowvale. It draws the cursed to it. Chances are someone turned him into a house cat to hide what he really was, but Thoreau took the opportunity his smaller size presented to escape his captor's clutches. And then he found his way here."

"So why not send him off to a big-cat rescue or sanctuary where he can hang out with his own kind?"

A little sadness filled Amelia's eyes. "I wish I could, but there's more magic stuck to him. Magic I haven't yet managed to remove. I'm not sure this is his final form. When I can completely free him, then I'll know what to do with him. But until then, he stays here. With me. Protected."

And yet, Em thought, her aunt wanted to send *her* away. The thought caused a wave of bitterness to wash through her. It was so strong and sudden, it spilled out in words. "So the tiger gets to stay, but I don't?"

"Emeranth, you don't understand—"

"You're right. I don't. But I'm happy to listen."

Amelia's mouth firmed into a hard, unhappy line. She opened her mouth to speak, but Beckett's voice interrupted her.

"Amelia, phone call."

Amelia sighed. "Coming." She shook her head. "We'll talk later, I promise."

Em didn't say anything. Just watched her aunt go.

And realized Thoreau still sat between her and the house.

"Oh boy." She smiled at the tiger, then stopped, thinking maybe you weren't supposed to show your teeth to a big cat. Would that be a sign of aggression? She did not want him to think she was challenging him. "Good kitty. Nice Thoreau. I'm just going inside, okay?"

Thoreau sighed, put his head down, and closed his eyes.

She stood there for a second. Was he really sleeping? Maybe. Maybe not. Either way, she held her breath as she snuck past him, tiptoeing like her life depended on it. Which maybe it did.

When she reached the patio, she slipped inside and shut the door, taking a much-needed deep breath. Beckett was going to hear about this. How had he not mentioned a tiger lived here? Wasn't that kind of an important detail?

But that talk could wait. She had work to do. And a job to find.

She jogged upstairs and got herself presentable. Her wardrobe was limited, but she had a decent pair of black pants and a simple silk blouse her mother had given her (probably stolen) as a Christmas gift a few years back. A little jewelry, some fresh makeup, and she was out the door, keys in hand.

Downtown wasn't hard to find, and neither was parking. There were no meters either, which was nice.

She parked as close to Black Horse Bakery as she could, making that her first stop.

Nasha was behind the counter when she went in. "Back for more?"

"Not exactly. That cupcake and the extra goodies were delicious, but I don't want to take advantage of the free stuff. That wouldn't be fair to everyone else."

Nasha shrugged. "Eh. It's first come, first served. You want another one, then have another one. That's how it works. Everybody knows that."

"I'll remember that. But that's still not why I came back. I was wondering…are you hiring, by any chance?"

Nasha shook her head. "I have enough employees at the moment."

Em had a hard time hiding her disappointment. "Oh. Do you know of anyone who might be looking for some extra help?"

Nasha squinted like she was thinking extra hard. "You might try Deja Brew, the coffee shop down the street." She pointed left. "But that's just a guess. I'm not sure. Sorry. There's not a lot of turnover in this town, so the job market can be a little stagnant."

Deja Brew would be perfect for Em if they were hiring. She nodded. "Yeah, Deacon said you don't get much in the way of tourists."

Nasha snorted. "No, we don't. There's a decent influx of new people, folks who find their way here one way or another, but Shadowvale isn't exactly a boomtown."

"Understood. Thanks."

"Hang on." Nasha fiddled with something behind the counter, then handed over a small bag. "Have that second cupcake. You might need it."

"Thanks." Em took the bag, feeling glum. She'd had such high hopes, not really thinking what the economy might be like here.

"Anytime."

An older man came in. Em gave Nasha a smile and slipped out. She put the cupcake in her car, then glanced both ways on Main Street. There were a good number of people walking around, so the shops weren't empty, but Em hadn't thought about how the lack of visitors might affect things.

Well, she needed to snap out of her mood and get cracking. She lifted her chin and headed in the direction of the coffee shop Nasha had suggested. All it would take was one place with one opening.

No job was too small.

She paused as she walked by Bewitched Broomsticks. She knew nothing about broomsticks. Especially if they were for riding.

But now was not the time to be picky. And hey, she knew how to sweep. Maybe that would count?

CHAPTER FIFTEEN

Deacon was in no mood to talk to Amelia, but it had to be done. He at least had to tell her how the day had gone. He extricated his cell phone from his back pocket, thankful the hard case had prevented damage from the spines, and dialed her number.

"Hello?"

"It's Deacon." The wicker glider creaked as he shifted forward to rest his elbows on his knees, then creaked again as he realized the spines weren't going to let that happen.

"Ah, yes. How did Emeranth respond? I saw her, but haven't had a chance to talk to her yet."

No point in delaying the inevitable. "Not great. The things I thought would bother her didn't seem to at all. Or at least not enough to turn her off this place."

A heavy sigh was her first response. "Is that why she was home so early?"

"No. Frieda needed some curse relief, and once I took that on, it was best I not be around anyone."

"Frieda. Poisonous spines, if I recall. I can see why you'd call it a day. How did Emeranth respond to all of that?"

"It was one of the few things that seemed to really make an impact. I'd go so far as to say it scared her a little." That was his best guess anyway, judging from how she'd kept her distance. But then, he'd told her to keep her distance. He shook his head. He wasn't going to explain all that to Amelia. Better to go with Em being scared.

"Then perhaps she needs to see more of that. More of why people come to this town."

"I can't make people's curses activate."

"No, but maybe you'll get lucky and get called in on another one."

"Yeah, that would be *lucky*."

"No, I don't suppose it would be. Well then take her to see some of the more egregious cases in town. Some of the more...famous. Either way, I'm sure I could persuade her to do another tour tomorrow."

"You won't have to. It's already arranged." He left out the part about having a lunch date with Gracie. That didn't seem remotely like the kind of thing that would cause Em to dislike Shadowvale. And Amelia wouldn't be happy about that.

"Good. You're the peacekeeper, Deacon. I expect you to find a remedy. I don't want my niece to suffer because of this town."

"I understand, Amelia." Except he didn't. Not exactly. If Em really wanted to live here, what was the big deal? Just because he wasn't happy here didn't mean most others weren't. Em might really like it here. And she was a grown woman. Shouldn't she be able to decide for herself? Granted, it was Amelia's right to say who lived in her house. But Em could live anywhere.

"Then we'll see you for breakfast again."

"I guess so." Amelia hung up, but his thought process kept going.

If Em decided to stay, and Amelia wasn't on board, the elder witch could make life here pretty hard for her niece. He wasn't sure Amelia would do that—Em was family, after all—but Amelia pulled a lot of weight here.

So did the Evermores, to some extent. But not like Amelia. Not like the woman who'd brought Shadowvale to life.

Deacon realized the phone was still in his hand. He laid it down next to him on the glider as Amelia's suggestion for the next tour swirled in his head.

Taking Em to see some of the most-cursed residents in town wasn't exactly an easy thing to do. Most of them had zero interest in being gawked at. They'd come here to be left alone.

And some could be downright dangerous.

He'd have to do some more thinking. Make a plan. Maybe a few phone calls. If Amelia really wanted Em to see the underbelly of Shadowvale, he supposed he could make that happen.

So long as he was there to protect her.

But some of those curses were hard-core. If he had to take them on to keep her safe, he would. He just hoped that wouldn't cause him to become a danger to her as well.

He shook his head. Was getting out of here really worth all this?

A long, difficult moment passed. The freedom to leave Shadowvale was worth it. Especially if he could take Gracie with him.

He was going to have to up his game if he really wanted to turn Em off this place.

◆

The broomstick store, which actually sold broomsticks for witches to ride, wasn't hiring. Neither was the curiosity shop, the café, the bistro, the gift shop, the crafter's corner, the apothecary, the dentist's office, the kitchen store, the deli, the health and beauty boutique, the chemist, or any of the other number of stores she'd gone into.

She walked through the door of Deja Brew with her hopes of employment fading, even though it was a business she was familiar with. She'd ask, of course, but maybe she'd get a coffee, sit down for a few minutes, and fortify herself to fill out yet another application.

The job hunt wasn't going the way she'd planned.

Not even remotely.

Fortunately, there were only a handful of people in the place to see what a sad case she was. She went to the counter, ordered an indulgent caramel latte she couldn't afford, then went to wait at the end of the counter for her order to be ready.

While she inhaled the comforting smell of java, she checked out the narrow glass display case and its sampling of treats. Biscotti, cookies, muffins. All probably delicious, but nothing on the level of what Nasha was offering. Probably why the selection here was so small.

If you really wanted something good, you got your coffee here, then went to Black Horse for the real indulgence to go with it.

She watched Joaquin, the barista who'd taken her order, make her drink. Em had worked at two coffee shops in her life. One for a brief six months in Bend, Oregon, then the last one for three years in Bethany, Oklahoma. She'd even made third key manager in Bethany.

She'd lost that job only because her mother had used that key to get a little more familiar with the store after hours. Em sighed. The manager had been kind but foolish not to press charges. Of course, Em had been the one who'd paid for that, with the loss of her job.

Then she'd gotten a part-time shift at the DIY Depot and promptly lost that eight days later when her mother had been arrested for another con gone wrong.

Em shook her head. She didn't want to think about all that now. She needed to focus on the future.

Making coffee was a job she could easily do. But what was the possibility that this place was hiring? She almost didn't want to ask.

But when the barista came with her latte, she did anyway. "Thanks. Any chance that you guys are hiring? I'm new in town and looking for work, and I have experience as a barista."

He slid her drink toward her. "Not right now, but you could fill out an application if you want. We keep them on file, so…" He shrugged.

She made herself keep smiling. "Okay, thanks. That would be great."

Actually, it sucked. But it was the best thing she had going right now.

He found an application and handed it over. She took it and her latte to a small table near the window and got to work filling it out. The latte was good and went down fast.

With a sigh, she filled in her aunt's address as her own. She had no reassurances she'd be in Shadowvale after Friday, but it was all she had at the moment.

The latte was half gone, but it would have been better with a Chocolate Reaper cupcake. Too bad hers was in the car.

Her pen stopped moving, and her head came up. She looked at the people coming in. And those already seated around her.

More than a few had bags from Black Horse.

"Holy smokes," she whispered as the thread of an idea began to unfurl in her mind.

She got to her feet, almost knocking her latte over, grabbed her drink and the application, and headed for the door.

Once on the sidewalk, she stuffed the application into her purse, then downed the last of her latte and tossed the cup into a trash can.

She didn't exactly jog toward her destination, but she passed all the slower walkers. As she traveled, she pleaded with the universe to let her have this one thing. *Please let this happen. Please please please.*

She pushed through the door of the bakery and took a breath of the delicious air filling the space while putting on her best smile. Nasha was bent down, adding more cookies to a tray. "Hi again."

Nasha stood up, but it wasn't Nasha. "Hi."

"You're not Nasha." Em's smile faltered.

"Nope. I'm Clara."

"Is she here?"

"Sure, she's in the back frosting a cake. I'll go get her."

Em wanted to stop Clara. Interrupting Nasha might put her in a bad mood. But this was an all-or-nothing kind of moment, and if she didn't do this now, she might lose her nerve.

Clara came back out with Nasha behind her.

The woman laughed when she saw Em. "Changed your mind about another cupcake, huh?"

Em swallowed. "Actually, I wanted to talk to you about something. I know you're busy, but do you have a minute?"

"For Amelia's niece? I do. Come on back."

Em followed her into the heart of the bakery. Long stainless-steel tables and shelving filled most of the space. Three giant mixers sat on the floor side by side by side.

In a lonely corner, covered with plastic, was a very familiar-looking machine. A veritable sign from the universe. She hoped.

Em stopped and pointed. "Is that what I think it is? Why isn't it out there being put to good use?"

Nasha glanced over and gave a little snort of disgust. "Because no one knows how to use that thing. It might be a transformer, for all I know. It was a gift from an ex when I opened this place. Pretty pricey, I think, but I haven't had the heart to sell it."

"Do you mind?"

"Be my guest."

Em went over and lifted the clear plastic sheeting to have a better look. "Wow."

Nasha came closer. "Wow, huh? I take it you know what it is?"

"I do." Em pulled the plastic back even farther, revealing the sleek chrome beauty underneath. "This is a La Pavoni three-lever espresso machine. Old-school Italian coffee company. This thing is built like a tank. Probably weighs about the same, too. You could make enough drinks on this to keep the whole town up for a week straight. It's beautiful."

"It is pretty snazzy, I'll give you that. But it looks so complicated."

Em touched one of the levers. "Not if you know what you're doing."

"And you do?"

Em nodded, her gaze still on the machine. "I've spent a lot of time working in coffee shops." She glanced at Nasha. "Why don't you serve coffee, by the way?"

"I always meant to. I just never got around to it. And like I said, none of us know how to use this thing. Setting up a regular old coffeepot seemed pointless with Deja Brew down the street, so I figured it was this or nothing."

"I don't disagree with that. Deja Brew's coffee is pretty good." Em grinned. "But you know most of what the people in there are eating with their coffee? Black Horse Bakery goods. I saw the bags myself."

"Oh yeah?" Nasha's gaze shifted from Em to the espresso machine, then back to Em. "You really know how to work this monster?"

"I know how to operate it, how to maintain it, and how to clean it."

Nasha folded her arms, but brought her hand up to tap her bottom lip with one finger. "Are you still looking for a job?"

Em laughed, almost giddy with nervousness. "As a matter of fact, I am."

"How'd you like to be the Black Horse Bakery's first barista?"

Em took a breath so she wouldn't squeal with joy. "I would love that. I will work so hard for you, I swear. Thank you. I can start immediately. Or as soon as we can get supplies."

"Good. I have cups and all that since I was planning on selling coffee someday. Just need to order beans. Right? Beans?"

"Right. Beans."

"Tell me what kind, and I'll get them in. We'll have to rearrange some things, but I think we can be selling coffee by the weekend."

"That would be amazing. Thank you."

"No, thank you. This thing's been sitting here for way too long. Knowing it's finally going to get put to work makes me happy." She tipped her head. "Hey, what did you want to talk to me about? I forgot you came in here for something."

Em laughed softly. "Believe it or not, I was going to see if you were interested in putting me to work selling coffee. I got the idea sitting in Deja Brew and watching all those Black Horse bags come in."

"How about that?" Nasha raised one shoulder. "That's Shadowvale for you. Sometimes this town just has a mind of its own."

CHAPTER SIXTEEN

Deacon's morning was off to a good start. He was spine-free as of 2:17 a.m., and now he was walking into Amelia's dining room, about to see Em again.

While he wasn't exactly looking forward to what today was going to bring, he was happy to see her. And happy to be spending the day with her, such as it was.

He liked her. There was no denying that. And spending time with her wasn't hard.

Too bad his future, and Gracie's, depended on getting her to leave.

Beckett announced him as he entered. "Mr. Evermore is here."

Amelia nodded. "Good morning, Deacon."

Em twisted in her chair to see him. "Hey."

"Hey. Morning."

"Are you hungry? Em asked. "There's all kinds of good stuff. Ham and cheese quiche, to be exact."

"I ate at home, but I'm always up for another cup of coffee."

A wide grin spread across her face. "I love coffee."

He did, too, but her expression seemed a little over the top. Maybe she'd had a few too many cups already. Didn't bother him. Who didn't get a little overcaffeinated sometimes? He took a seat next to her. Helen, the housekeeper, came over and filled his cup.

The sparkle in Em's eyes remained. "Where are we off to today?"

He glanced at Amelia. The look in her eyes was dark and certain. "Couple places," he said. "Mostly just around."

How did he tell her they were going to see some of the town's most infamous residents? The ones that existed only in myth and legend outside these walls? He couldn't really. It would be easier to show her.

And hope those particular people didn't take offense to being used as a deterrent, supposing they found out.

"So mysterious," Em said.

"I don't mean to be. It's just hard to explain where we're going when you've never been there before." He took a big gulp of coffee and checked his watch. "Actually, we should get going."

The first person they were going to see required proper timing.

Em frowned. "I'm not done with my breakfast."

"I'll get you a snack." He stood. "Come on."

"Fine, but I'm bringing it with me." She stood, picking up her remaining slice of quiche. "See you later, Aunt Amelia. Dinner tonight, right?"

"Yes." Amelia nodded. "Have a safe day."

Em's expression turned curious. "I'm sure we will."

Deacon tipped his head toward the hall. "My truck's out front."

She followed him out of the room. "Kind of strange, don't you think?"

"What?"

"'Have a safe day.' That's not what people usually say. Have a fun time, have a good day, that's what people say." She looked at Deacon. "Why would she say 'safe'?"

He grunted. "It's Shadowvale. 'Safe' is the right word."

That seemed to end the conversation until they were in the truck and headed toward their destination. By then, Em had finished her breakfast.

She tucked one leg under her and shifted in her seat. "So. Did you know my aunt has a pet tiger?"

"Thoreau? Yes. I think everyone knows."

She clicked her tongue against the roof of her mouth. "Well, I didn't until I came face-to-face with him in the garden."

Despite his best intentions, Deacon laughed. "I wish I could have seen that."

"It freaked me out!"

"I'm sure it did. It would have freaked me out, too." He glanced at her. "You don't seem to be any worse for the encounter."

She gave him a withering look. "All my scars are mental and emotional."

"Good to know your beauty remains unscathed." A second after the words were out of his mouth, he realized what he'd said.

Her silence melded with his until the space inside the cab pushed toward uncomfortable.

She suddenly held her hands up. "Okay, you think I'm cute, that's cool. Where are we going? Into the woods? If so, is this the enchanted forest or just a regular old—"

"Not cute. Beautiful. And yes, I do think that about you." Why pretend he'd said something different when he hadn't?

"Oh." She stared at her hands, which were now in her lap.

"Don't tell me you've never heard that before. I'm sure a lot of men have said the same thing. And probably a lot more than just 'you're beautiful.'"

She nodded. "Yeah. I've heard it. For whatever it's worth. I just didn't expect it from you. I didn't think you liked me enough to even notice anything about the way I look."

"I like you." And he had noticed. It was impossible not to. Especially when she was right next to him.

She lifted her head. "You do? I thought you were just, I don't know, tolerating me because my aunt is making you take me around."

"Maybe a little in the beginning. But you've grown on me."

Her brows canted inward, and her mouth quirked up on one side. "Like a fungus."

He snorted. "I did *not* say that."

She shook her head, still smiling. "Thanks. For the record, I think you're a very handsome guy."

He didn't drive off the road, which was nice. She thought he was handsome. So she'd actually looked at him, then. But handsome? That wasn't a word he'd ever use to describe himself.

She went on when he didn't say anything. "I mean, you're kind of grumpy, too, but I get that it's sort of your thing."

"My thing?" His brows lifted as he looked at her. "I'm not grumpy."

"Oh, you're totally grumpy. Even your sister agrees."

"You talked to Gracie about my grumpiness?"

"Among other things." A sly, knowing light danced in Em's eyes.

He shifted uncomfortably. "What other things?"

She casually lifted one shoulder like she couldn't quite recall. "Nothing much. But your sister is definitely trying to hook you up."

For the second time, he managed to keep the wheel steady. "What?"

Em nodded. "That was my take anyway."

"I do not want to be set up." Getting into a relationship with anyone was out of the question. It was pointless. He was trying to leave Shadowvale, not find a new reason to be anchored here.

"If she brings it up again, I'll tell her."

"Thanks." He was lost in his thoughts for a moment and almost missed the turn.

Em leaned forward. "Are we going back downtown? I didn't think anything would be open at this hour."

"We're going close to downtown, and you're right that nothing's open, but we're just going to observe."

"Observe what?"

"You'll see."

She scrunched up her face. "Still with all the mysterious stuff."

He pulled into the shadowy depths of a back alley and parked. He tipped his head forward. "Can you see the landing there on the second floor?"

She looked up. "With the stairs leading up to it? Yes."

"Good. Keep watching." He checked the time. Only a few more minutes, unless Henry was off his schedule for some reason.

But the good doctor was on time, as usual, and came lumbering up the stairs in his cursed form.

The hunched bulk of the man reached the door, a slab of reinforced steel, and began pawing at it, trying to pull it open with hands the size of baseball mitts. When he had no luck, he leaned his mountainous shoulder against it and pushed with a grunt that reverberated through the alley.

Em sat up. "Who is that?"

"That is Dr. Hendrick Jekyll. Henry to those who know him. But as you see him now, he's at the tail end of his cursed state. In that form, he prefers to be called Edgar Hyde."

As Hyde grew weary of the effort, he gave up and slumped down against the door. Beneath the thick ledge of his brow, his eyes closed. His time was nearly up, and his energy was going with it.

Em stared at Deacon. "You mean as in Dr. Jekyll and Mr. Hyde?"

"Yes. He's a descendant."

"But that's just a story."

"Is it? Keep watching."

Hyde began to change. His body lost all of the extra musculature, his bones shrank, and his features returned to their human state.

Em was at the edge of her seat. "He looks... normal now."

"Happens every morning at this time. He won't allow his cursed self into his apartment, so he spends the night in a basement cell beneath his laboratory and shop."

The now transformed doctor opened his eyes. He patted himself down, then ran his hands over his face. Satisfied he was himself again, he stood and placed his hand on the electronic panel next to the door.

The door unlocked, and he went in, shutting it behind him.

Em blinked and shook her head. "Did I really just see that?"

Deacon started the car. "Yes, you did."

"Has he ever not spent the night in the basement?"

"Yes. It takes several of us to contain him. Still happens on occasion." He backed out of the alley. He didn't want to drive past Hendrick's and alert him that they'd been there. The man had enough on his plate.

She looked pale. "Does he do anything...bad when he's out?"

"I guess 'bad' is relative in this town, but he tore down seven lampposts on Main. Chased Maggie Thorpe into the river. He's afraid of water, apparently, and that was enough to get him to leave her alone. Wiped out half of Skeet Lander's chickens."

"Wiped out?"

"Ate." He turned onto Main and headed for the forest.

She grimaced. "What other things that I've spent my whole life thinking were made up are actually real?"

"That's a tough question for me to answer. I don't know what you've thought was made up."

"*The Little Mermaid.*"

"Can't say about that story, but we do have mermaids. And mermen. They're beautiful, if you're into fish, but some of them are also very dangerous."

She stared, openmouthed. "And where do they live? In the river? Or the lake?"

"They live wherever they want. Like Frieda. She's half mermaid and can't really shift. That's where the spines come from. But quite a few live in Bayou La Mer." He watched while she took that in. "Does that make you think twice about living here?"

"I…" She shook her head. "No, it doesn't. Nothing is going to make me leave. Not when I have so many reasons to stay."

The way she said *reasons*, it was like there was something more to it than what he already knew. Whatever. He'd see what he could do about changing her mind. With a nod, he took the next turn into the enchanted forest. The neighborhood they were headed to wasn't a place anyone went unless they had a very good reason.

The Dark Acres. He went if he was called. But otherwise, no. He didn't even fly over in raven form.

"You never did answer my question earlier."

He glanced at her. "About what?"

"Are we headed for the enchanted forest or a different forest?"

"We're going to part of the enchanted forest. One that I don't recommend you ever come to on your own. Actually, you shouldn't come to any part of the forest by yourself."

She settled back in the seat, slouching down a bit. "So you're just bringing me here to put some fear into me."

He wasn't surprised that she'd picked up on that. It *was* what he was doing, after all. He was a little surprised she'd called him out on it. "You need to know who lives in this town. That's all."

And then, hopefully, be scared enough to not want to move here.

CHAPTER SEVENTEEN

She watched him for a bit, trying to read his expression, but he didn't have much of one. Unless *poker face* qualified as an expression. It should, because it was one he was really, really good at. In fact, he seemed to be deliberately holding on to that look *because* she was scrutinizing him.

Yep. She kept staring, and there was no change.

Fine.

She let out a little sigh and went back to watching the scenery. They had been driving through a residential area with some lovely parks, then had passed a high school—home of the Tigers, interestingly enough—but now what they were passing was just landscape. Lots of trees, the occasional bridge over a small stream, a field here and there. Pretty standard stuff.

A new question popped into her head. "Hellhounds?"

"What?" He turned. "Where?"

"I guess that answers that question. Those are real."

"Yes. But rare."

"Yikes. Even so, evening strolls are out of the question. How about the boogeyman?"

"Depends on your definition."

"Freddy Krueger?"

"No, he's not real or the boogeyman."

"Good. That would be super weird and terrifying." She thought a little more. "Spice worms?"

"What?"

"You know, from that series *Dune*. Never mind. Dragons? Bigfoot? Giant spiders?" A thick wall of trees had sprung up next to them. Their leaves, despite the lack of sun, were the most brilliant green.

"Yes, yes, and not giant, no."

"So just standard spiders?"

"There are some large ones in the Dark Acres."

She shuddered. "I don't love giant spiders. Or any spider, really."

He shook his head. "And yet you liked the meowls."

"Hello, they're kind of the opposite of spiders. They're adorable cats with wings. What's not to like?"

He just grunted like he couldn't understand why that was even a question. Then he slowed and turned down a road cut between the trees. What light there was went green.

She glanced up through the window. The leafy canopy grew over the road, making a tunnel. No sky was visible, just leaves and branches.

It was pretty. And definitely seemed magical. "Is this the enchanted forest?"

"Yes."

"What makes it enchanted?"

"The biggest meridian line runs beneath it. Look closer at the trees." He slowed a bit.

She turned, concentrating her efforts out the window. She squinted. Was she really seeing what she thought she was seeing? "Are those...faces? On the trees?"

"On some of them, yes. That's an indicator that a wood nymph lives there."

She had no clue what a wood nymph was. "Is that so the tree isn't accidentally cut down?"

"It helps, yes. Not that we harvest any of these trees."

Deeper in, where less light reached, a faint glow seemed to cling to the trees. "What are the spots of light I see on some of the trees?"

"Sprite moss. It's naturally phosphorescent. Only place I know that it grows is in this wood."

"Wow. That is really cool."

"It is. But don't get romanced. This is an easy place to get lost in."

"Got it." Every once in a while, a small unmarked road diverged from the main. There were a few footpaths, too. "I'm not doubting you about getting lost, but who uses those paths, then?"

"Desperate people."

She looked at him. "What does that mean?"

He shifted his hands, putting one on top of the steering wheel and the other on his leg. "There's a very special book somewhere in this forest. Legend says your best chance of finding it is during a full moon. Anyway, if you *can* find it and you write your name in it, your curse will be gone. The book absorbs it. Or so the story goes."

"But you don't believe it."

"I want to, but..." He shrugged, a little anger tugging at his mouth.

And suddenly she knew why. "You've tried to find it, haven't you?"

Silence answered her for a few seconds. "Everyone did in high school."

She wanted to ask him if that was the only time he'd looked, but she wasn't sure he'd want to tell her the truth. "What kind of book can do that?"

"A magical one. Just like everything else in this town." He turned down another road. It was wider than any of the others she'd seen and had a sign. Blackthorn Drive. "Ask your aunt about the book. She's supposed to be the one that found it."

"Really? I—" The woods around them changed, thickening as the trees grew more twisted. The light dimmed further. In fact, everything dimmed. Or darkened. She moved closer to the window. The brilliant green leaves looked almost black, and the bark now resembled charcoal, burnt and gray. "Was there a fire here?"

"No. This is just very cursed ground."

And yet, while she didn't see much glowing moss, she did see something else. "Are those fireflies? I've never seen red ones before."

"Not in the Dark Acres. Those are either will-o'-the-wisps or lightning bugs. Wait, red? Lightning bugs."

"Aren't fireflies and lightning bugs the same thing?"

"No. The lightning bugs carry a charge, like an electric eel. And they *will* zap you."

She took her hands off the truck door and placed them on her lap. For the first time, she was having second thoughts about Shadowvale. She didn't like that. Not when she'd been so certain this was her new start. "Why is there so much here that can do harm?"

He glanced at her, maybe a hint of sympathy in his gaze. "I told you, this town is a cursed place."

She looked straight ahead, trying to see where they were going. An iron arch crossed the road ahead. Dark Acres was spelled out in the top curve, but there were no gates to keep anyone out. Or in. "Where are you taking me?"

"As I said, the Dark Acres."

"I see that. But why? Who lives there?"

"Nasha's father, for starters."

"One of the Four Horsemen of the Apocalypse lives here? In Shadowvale?"

"All of them do, actually."

"Do they still…" She paused to choose her words better. "What do they do here? Do they work? Or don't they do anything?"

"Thanos—he's the Horseman of Death—runs the funeral parlor. He's a mortician by trade."

She stared at Deacon. "Are you playing with me?"

"No. That's really what he does."

They drove under the Dark Acres arch.

She wrapped her arms around herself. The woods here could be described in one word. *Creepy.* "Great. Good to know Death is active in the community. Does he know Beckett?"

"I take it you've discovered what Beckett is?"

"Yes."

Deacon nodded. "They know each other. Very different lines of work, though."

She sighed, shaking her head at it all.

"You asked."

So she had. "Who else lives here?"

"Medalina, Medusa's younger sister."

"The chick with snakes for hair? The one that turns people to stone with a look?"

"Same. For the record, they're Gorgons. Not just chicks with snakes for hair."

"Right. Thanks."

Signs of a house loomed in the distance. Then another. Then another. All Em could see was a chimney here, a weather vane there, the peak of a roof. But it was enough to know that beings lived in this place.

Beings that she hoped never to meet. But how could she hope that and still want to live here?

She swallowed down her burgeoning fear. "If these people are really so dangerous that they have to live in this part of town, separate from everyone else, how are people not dropping left and right because of them?"

"People do what they have to do to get by. Medalina never goes out without dark glasses and her hair covered. The banshees only speak in whispers when they're in town. The Horsemen just go about their business."

"Then there's nothing for me to be afraid of." Except he hadn't mentioned banshees before. Still, she managed to keep herself from reacting.

"Not really—" He stopped suddenly, pulling the truck over with a soft groan. "Yeah, actually there's a lot for you to be afraid of."

"At least you seem to think so."

He twisted to face her. "Why can't you just do what your aunt wants and go live somewhere else?"

The words struck her. She'd thought he liked her, but he clearly just wanted her gone. "For a lot of reasons. One, I'm my own person and I can do what I want. Two, I could really use a break in my life right now. And three..." She hadn't been planning on telling anyone about three just yet.

"What? Go on." Frustration sparked in his eyes. "What's your all-fired-up third reason?"

She glared right back at him. "I got a job."

"You got a—where?"

She lifted her chin a tiny bit, unable to hide her pride. "At the Black Horse Bakery. I'm going to be a barista. That's a professional coffee preparer."

"I know what a barista is."

She crossed her arms. "Well, you had a look on your face like you were confused."

"I was. Because Black Horse doesn't serve coffee."

"They do now. Or they will. I'm just waiting for Nasha to call me that the supplies have come in."

He sighed and slumped back in his seat. "You really aren't going to leave, are you?"

"Look, I've already told you, I don't have a lot of other options."

"And what if your aunt won't let you live with her?"

Em hadn't wanted to think about that, but it was a very real possibility and one she had to consider. "I'll figure something out. I'll...sleep in my car if I have to. Or find a cheap room to rent. I'm not picky. I can survive on cold showers and ramen if I have to. Or cupcakes. Especially since those are free."

He slanted his eyes at her, nodding a little. "You're tough, I'll give you that. And I mean it as a compliment. Gracie would screech to high heaven if she had to take a cold shower."

"Which you've made sure has never had to happen, am I right?"

"Yes."

Em knew her tone had some bitterness in it, but she couldn't help it. "I wouldn't know what that's like."

"What?"

She stared out the windshield. "Having someone watch over me. Look out for me. My life has always been my responsibility. If I'm really being honest, at times it's seemed like things have been stacked against me, you know? But I don't like even putting that into words, because that feels like a defeatist attitude. Like I'm accepting that I've been handed the short stick. And I refuse to feel sorry for myself."

"What about your parents?"

She barked out a soft, sad laugh. "Never knew my father. And my mother..." She sighed and shook her head. She wasn't interested in opening the Manda chapter for a public reading. Not now. Not to Deacon.

She cared what he thought about her, so telling him about her criminal mother was never going to happen. Not if she could help it. And really, if it didn't come from her, how would he find out?

CHAPTER EIGHTEEN

A sharp pang of protectiveness and anger zipped through Deacon's gut, as if a lightning bug had landed on him.

All because of Em's confession that she'd never had anyone to look out for her. How could that be? How could the world be such an unfair place?

He wanted to fill that role for her. To show her how different life could be with someone in her corner.

And yet, here he was, actively trying to get rid of her.

Sure, he had a good reason. But that didn't take the sting out of it.

Watching her, seeing the sadness in the set of her mouth and the utter determination in her eyes, just made him ache to fix things. That was what he did, after all. But this wasn't a curse he could take away.

This was her past. And nothing could erase that. Maybe this fresh start could fade the memory of it, though.

So did he continue to stand in her way? Or did he put his own needs—and Gracie's—on the back burner and let Em's desires take precedence?

He tapped the heel of his palm against the steering wheel. He'd never felt so torn before.

Maybe the better question was why did he feel this way about a woman he'd just met yesterday?

He knew why. And it was stupid. Stupid, ridiculous infatuation. Plain and simple. He was letting dumb emotions get the best of him. Because she was pretty and kind and funny.

The worst of it was, infatuation wore off. It always did. Love—which this wasn't even remotely—took a long time. Longer than two days, that was for sure.

"You're awfully quiet."

He looked up and realized she was staring at him.

She bent her head a little like she was trying to see him better. "Did I say something to upset you?"

He shook his head. "No. I just got lost in thought is all."

"I see. So is there more you want to show me?"

He rested both hands on the wheel. "I was supposed to show you Robin Gallow's house."

"Who's that?"

"Deposed goblin king. Now he's the mine foreman."

"Goblin king? Mines?" She raised her hands. "You want to back up a little?"

"To where?"

"There's a king living here?"

173

"Deposed king. His ex-wife, the queen, decided she wanted to be the sole ruler, so she poisoned him, dumped him at the Shadowvale gates, and said she'd only deliver the antidote if he agreed never to return or attempt to retake the throne. He did, so she did, and now he's stuck here."

Em's eyes went wide. "Holy crow. I bet he's still mad about that."

"Yeah, you could say that."

"And the mines? What kind of mines?"

"The gem mines. They're how Shadowvale sustains itself. Your aunt owns them, but she's never been shy about pouring the money they earn into the town."

"What kind of gems?"

He shrugged. "Rubies, sapphires, emeralds, moonstones, tourmalines, quartz, all kinds. Even diamonds. There are over twenty members of the Lapidary Guild. It's a full-time industry, although I think some of the gems are sent out uncut, too."

She blinked. "This town just gets more and more interesting. It's a weird mix of cool and creepy."

He snorted. "Which one am I?"

She smiled slyly. "I'm not answering that." Then her smile faded. "You really want me to leave, huh? Why? It can't be that you're worried about me. You've known me for two days."

He couldn't tell her. He wouldn't. Not after she'd just confessed to never having anyone watch out for her. Finding out that he basically had ulterior motives would just reinforce what she'd said about her life.

But he had to tell her something. "I think anyone who doesn't have to live here should feel lucky."

She snorted. "Lucky, huh? Well, that would be a first. And look, I appreciate your opinion. You obviously have more experience with this town than I do, but with a job on the horizon…I can't turn that down."

"You could get a job somewhere else."

"I'm sure I could. Eventually. But my aunt is about the last family I have left. Is it so wrong to want to be close to her? And to dig into the witchy side I apparently have? Wouldn't it be kind of cruel of her to drop that bombshell on me, then kick me out?"

"Yeah, that would be uncool." He couldn't argue with that.

Then she sighed. "Sad thing is, I think she's avoiding me. On purpose. She was pretty much unavailable all night last night."

"You were both at breakfast."

"She only came in a few minutes before you did. And I'm not sure how much personal stuff I want to discuss in front of her staff. I like Beckett, but I don't know Helen at all. It's just weird. Like Aunt Amelia is reluctant to get to know me. Which sucks, because I was really anticipating that she'd see what a decent person I am and want to give me a chance."

Deacon knew exactly what was going on. Amelia was hoping he'd scare Em off enough that she wouldn't have to get to know her niece and have her heart broken again.

Well, that was a crappy way to treat family. Even if Em was only going to be here a few days, why not at least spend time with her? Again, his protective instinct wound through him with fresh fire.

He reminded himself that it wasn't his place to get involved. "I'm sorry. Maybe you'll catch her tonight."

"Yeah, we're supposed to have dinner, but I'm not holding my breath." She looked out the window. "So you want to show me this goblin king's house?"

"Okay." He took the truck out of park and drove on, feeling more and more like he was becoming the bad guy. He hated that feeling. He was coming up against a hard decision, and he knew it.

He turned onto Candlewick Court.

Em gasped as they came through the first thicket of trees. "That's a house? That's not a house."

"No, it is. Really something, huh?"

"It's exactly how I described this town. Cool and creepy."

"You're right, it is." He'd never paid much attention to Gallow's home, having lived here for so long that such things got taken for granted, but now he tried to see it through Em's eyes.

With its deep-purple roof, curved gray stone walls, and imbedded gems, the house was a very unique dwelling. He had a feeling nothing like it existed beyond the gates of Shadowvale.

And he knew that Gallow lived there alone, except for some staff, but the man had been a king. Accustomed to a palace. Deacon supposed the size and grandeur of this place was Gallow's attempt to make up for the loss of his previous life.

Em leaned forward. "I see skulls. Do I really see skulls?"

"Yes. Goblins are fierce creatures."

She grimaced. "Are they, like, from people he's killed?"

"No. They might have been in his homeland, but here in Shadowvale those are just carved decorations like the gargoyles on the corners."

"Good to know." She kept staring at the house. "It's hard to look away from, isn't it?"

He studied it, too. "It is. Like a train wreck. Sort of."

His phone buzzed. He checked the screen and saw a message from Gracie.

On my way to the diner. See you in 15.

"We'd better get going. I promised Gracie we'd meet her for lunch at the diner."

"Oh, cool." She looked at her watch. "Hey, it's almost noon. Time flies, huh?"

"Yeah, it does."

She looked at the house again. "I'm not really sad to be leaving Dark Acres, though. This is my least favorite area of Shadowvale so far. There's something very curious about it, but there's a vibe here I don't love. Makes my skin itch. Like I'm on the verge of getting a rash."

"It's because you're a witch." He turned around in the cul-de-sac. He wasn't unhappy to leave Dark Acres either. "I'm sure you can feel the magic leaking through the meridian line, even if you don't really know what it is."

She tipped her head. "I thought it was just a bad vibe, but yeah, maybe it's more than that."

"Ask Amelia. She can probably explain it better than I can."

"Sure, if I ever see her."

"You will. You know, your aunt has been alone for years. Decades, really. She's probably forgotten how to be around people."

"Maybe. But she has Beckett. It's not like she's been completely alone."

"No, but from what I understand, the loss of Pasqual nearly destroyed her."

Em nodded, going silent.

The silence stretched out awhile longer, then she spoke again. "That had to be very hard."

"No doubt."

She was looking at him again. He could feel her eyes on him. Feel the questions just building up inside her.

"Have you ever had your heart broken like that?"

He gripped the steering wheel tighter. "That's kind of a personal question."

She ignored his comment. "I haven't. Not like that anyway. I just asked because I can't imagine what it feels like to put everything you have into someone only to be rejected by them. I've been through a lot in my life, but nothing like that. Nothing where I felt so torn down that I wasn't sure if I could get up again."

"I know his loss changed her. She was friends with my mother, and I remember my mother coming back from visiting with her on one of her bad days, and my mother would just hurt for her."

"That was kind of your mom. Do they still visit?"

"No." He swallowed. "My mother doesn't live here anymore." He wasn't sure she lived at all, but that was too hard a subject to dig into.

"Oh." She hesitated. "Is your father still around?"

He shook his head. "My father left us right before Gracie was born. Couldn't take life in Shadowvale anymore, I guess. Decided the world of men was a better option. My mother used to call the world beyond the gates that. He died a couple years after he left."

She looked horrified. "He left your mother with three kids and one on the way?"

"Two on the way, actually. Gracie's twin didn't survive."

Em inhaled, her soft gasp filling the cab. "That's awful."

Deacon frowned. "I shouldn't have said anything about that. Don't mention it to Gracie."

"I won't. I promise. It's forgotten." She stared out the windshield. "Sorry about your dad. That's pretty awful, too."

Deacon nodded. "Yep. All because this place was too much for him."

"Do you know where he went?"

"He sent a check at Christmas the first year. The address on it was Titusville, Florida. But nothing after that ever again."

Deacon planned to head there as soon as he was free of this town. Just to see if there was any trace of his father. Maybe find out what happened to him. How he'd died. Then maybe he'd hunt down their mother, even though Gracie had made him promise not to.

"Sorry," Em said. "I've upset you."

"I'm fine. It's history. We've moved on."

She smiled weakly. "Okay." A few minutes passed, then she straightened. "So where are we going for lunch?"

"The Sunshine Diner."

"Ironic. I like it."

"It's not entirely ironic. There are UV bulbs in the lighting over every booth. Pretty much means there are never any vampires there, but a lot of us go to get a little dose of vitamin D."

"Cool. Do the people that own it not like vampires?"

"I don't think they have anything against them. Just is what it is."

"Are they supernaturals?"

"No. They're humans with curses. Well, Mr. Applegate has a curse. His wife is fine, as far as I know."

"What's his curse?"

Deacon shot her a look.

"What? I'm asking you, not him."

He couldn't argue with that. "His moods tend to affect the weather. Fortunately, the diner makes him happy, so things haven't been too bad since he and his wife moved here. His son seems to have inherited the trait, however, and Carter isn't quite as even-keeled. Doesn't help that he's a teenager."

"I suppose it doesn't." She seemed to ponder that a moment. "Does that mean we could get rained on during lunch?"

Deacon shook his head. "In Shadowvale, you just never know."

CHAPTER NINETEEN

Amelia tossed Thoreau another steak. He caught it midair and gobbled it down in a few big bites. She folded the butcher paper to be put in recycling. "That's all for now, pet."

The beast stretched out his front legs, bending low as he arched his back, then plopped down in the grass, rolled over, and closed his eyes with a happy sigh.

She walked back to the patio, took a seat, and contented herself with watching him. She could do it for hours without growing bored. He was just so beautiful, and the amazement that this incredible creature shared space with her never grew old.

Footsteps scraped the stone patio behind her, coming to a stop within arm's length. "You're spoiling him."

She didn't turn to look at Beckett. "I should hope so."

"I can think of someone else who could use some spoiling."

She glanced over her shoulder with a slightly perturbed expression. "If you're angling for a raise—"

"I was talking about your niece. Emeranth. Or have you forgotten about her? Because you certainly seem to be trying."

"I haven't forgotten she's here." On the contrary, it was all Amelia could think about. She blew out a slow breath, shifting her gaze back to the garden. Guilt at the thought of how she was treating Emeranth already hung over her. She didn't need Beckett adding to it. Her mood turned defensive. "You don't know what's at stake."

"I think I do. And regardless, that's no reason to shut her out. She's family. Maybe the last you have left. And you took it upon yourself to tell her she's a witch, but since that life-changing pronouncement you've done nothing about it. The poor girl has to wonder what's going on."

Amelia frowned. She didn't require a lecture from the man whose job satisfaction would be found only when her soul was in his hands. "Leave me alone."

"Why? Because you know I'm right?"

"When did you stop being the collector of my soul and decide to become my conscience instead?"

"When you decided to ignore Emeranth without reason."

Stubborn, stubborn reaper. She whipped around to glare at him. "I have a reason. I am trying to protect her."

"From what? Your fate? What happened to you isn't going to happen to her. Listen to yourself. It doesn't make sense. You're scared of something." His eyes suddenly brightened with realization.

"You're afraid of getting your heart broken again, aren't you? That if you let her in, and she leaves you like Pasqual did…"

Amelia's throat squeezed with emotion. "That's not all." She slumped back in her chair. He wasn't wrong. "I won't survive it. But you should be happy about that. Then your job will be done."

"Amelia."

She knew that tone. What followed next was usually his explanation that he was not his job, that he took no pleasure in the inevitable, that he valued their friendship, such as it was, that his time here had given him a chance to experience life. She knew it all.

But that wasn't where he went. "She's a good girl. With a kind heart. She won't leave you."

"You don't know that."

"No, I can't say it for certain. No one really knows that kind of thing about someone else. But I like her, and she strikes me very much like a woman searching for a place to call home. Desperate for it, almost. And after talking to her, it seems to me that the last thing she wants to do is put down roots only to tear them up again." His voice softened. "If you talked to her, you'd see that for yourself."

She sighed. "Maybe." She stared at her hands. Despite the magic of this place, her knuckles were starting to gnarl. The hands and the neck were such traitors. They were always the first to betray a woman. "That's not all of it, though. The magic really will get its hooks in her. How can it not?

She's my descendant. It's inevitable. Especially if you complete your task. Someone has to take over."

"Maybe...maybe she'd be okay with that."

She squinted at him. "You know what it's done to me. What weight it's put on me. How great a burden I bear."

He nodded with great solemnity. "I do."

"And you think a young woman should have to handle that? She hasn't lived her life yet. She hasn't married and had children and found her place in this world."

"But I think she's trying to. At least that last part."

"And you think that place is here in Shadowvale? Because I don't."

He shrugged. "The gates let her in, didn't they?"

"That means nothing."

"It means something."

Amelia frowned and shifted her gaze back to the garden.

A soft noise left Beckett's throat. "You should at least initiate her. Make her a true witch. Give her a fighting chance before you toss her back out to the wolves."

Her frown deepened. "I'm not going to toss her out to the wolves. When I send her away, I'll make sure she's taken care of."

A new thought came to her, a gleaming, brassy idea. She sat up straighter. "That's it."

"What—oh no, you don't. I see it in your eyes. You're going to do something."

"Go away, Beckett. She's my niece, and I know what's best for her. And it's not life in this forsaken place, I know that much."

The Sunshine Diner was a sweet, cheery place that made Em happy the moment she walked in. The decor was sunflowers, which seemed appropriate, and the place was bustling, which she took as a good sign. Not surprisingly, the aromas out of the kitchen smelled divine. She watched a server go by with a tray laden with overflowing plates that included breakfast and lunch items.

Her stomach rumbled. "What's good here?"

"Everything," Deacon answered. "And you can get breakfast, lunch, or dinner twenty-four hours a day."

"This place never closes?"

"Nope."

Em thought that was promising.

He explained a little more. "Shadowvale's citizens don't all keep standard hours. There's a lot that goes on here when most towns would be shut down."

She thought about that. "The night I came in, things seemed pretty quiet."

A smirk bent his mouth. "It might have looked that way, but the town has a way of protecting its own. You only saw what it wanted you to see."

"Interesting." Which was a word she never seemed to run out of uses for in this place.

"Em, Deacon, over here." Gracie waved at them from a booth.

They walked over, and Em would have slid in next to Gracie, but she'd settled against the wall end of the bench seat with her purse and Tinkerbelle in her carrier on the other, taking up the remaining space.

Kind of like a blockade.

Which meant Em had no choice but to sit next to Deacon. Not a real hardship, but she could see Gracie's matchmaking at work.

Em slid in, then Deacon joined her. She put her small purse between them. Not much of a barrier, but it was something. Even so, as he settled in, his knee brushed hers.

She ignored it to nod at Tinkerbelle. "Hi there, pup. Are you having a nice day out?"

Gracie nodded nervously and gave her dog a scratch on the head. "Tink loves being out. Don't you, baby?"

Em looked around. There were at least two other small dogs in the restaurant. One in a carrier like Tinkerbelle and one in a large purse. And then there was a bigger brown dog, a Lab maybe, lying at his owner's feet. No meowls, though. "This is a pretty dog-friendly place, huh?"

Deacon unwrapped his silverware from his napkin roll. "We kind of make our own rules in Shadowvale. But yeah, no one really cares if you bring your dog as long as they're well behaved."

"So no hellhounds, then," Em said.

Gracie snorted. "No, no hellhounds."

A server came by with menus and glasses of water, then left again to give them time to decide.

Em liked the look of what was on the menu. Good, standard diner food. "What are you getting, Gracie?"

"Club sandwich and fries. It's my favorite. Deacon brings it home for me sometimes."

"Sounds good." Em glanced at that item on the menu. "What about you, Deacon?"

"Turkey potpie. And a slice of lemon meringue for dessert."

"Oooh, pie and pie," Em said. "That sounds good, too."

"What about you?" Gracie asked.

"Not sure. Maybe the soup and sandwich combo." All of the prices were reasonable, but the soup and half sandwich were a real deal.

Deacon closed his menu and folded his hands on top of it. "This is our treat, by the way."

Em looked at him. "That's not necessary."

"No, it's not, but this was Gracie's idea, so she's paying."

"Hey," Gracie said, her whole body moving toward the same side of the booth as Deacon.

"Ow." Deacon made a face at her. "Kicking me under the table is not a good way to get a birthday present out of me."

Gracie laughed and seemed to relax a little. "So you haven't bought my present yet, then? Good to know."

"I bought it," Deacon said. "Jury's still out on whether you're getting it."

Em smiled. The back-and-forth banter of the siblings was sweet and wonderful in a way that made her heart clench with longing. Funny how you could yearn for something you'd never experienced.

The server came back and took their order. Em stuck to the soup and sandwich. Even if they were paying, no point in spending more than was necessary.

As the server left, Em leaned forward. "So what do you do, Gracie?"

"I work from home doing accounting." She smiled. "I'm a bookkeeper for a couple of the businesses in town, including my brother Bishop's tree-trimming service."

Em nodded. "I bet he gets a lot of calls. There are trees everywhere here. I like it, though. All that green really helps take your mind off the overcast sky."

"It does, doesn't it?" Gracie peeled the paper off her straw and stuck it in her water. "How's your day been so far?"

"Good. I guess." Em laughed. "We went to the Dark Acres."

Gracie's eyes widened, and she looked at her brother. "Deacon, why on earth would you take her there?"

"Because it's a part of Shadowvale that she needs to see if she's going to live here."

Gracie frowned. "It's also dangerous. And scary."

Em laughed softly. "It wasn't so bad. I did enjoy seeing the goblin king's house."

Gracie nodded. "Really something, isn't it?"

Em leaned forward a bit. "Have you met him?"

"King Robin? Yes, I have actually."

"A real king. I can't imagine." Em was fascinated with the idea of royalty here in town, but then, who wouldn't be? "What's he like?"

"He's incredibly handsome and regal and—" Gracie stopped speaking to make a face at her brother. "Don't roll your eyes, Deacon. Lots of people find royalty interesting."

Em made a face at him, too. "I realize you're too cool to be impressed, but I haven't reached that stage of enlightenment yet, so humor me."

Gracie barked out a laugh and pointed at Deacon. "You've got your hands full with this one."

"I don't have my—" He shook his head. "You know what? I see someone I need to talk to. You two carry on."

He got up and left them, heading for someone seated at the counter.

Gracie snorted. "Wow. He's jealous."

"Of what?" Em looked around.

"Of you being interested in King Robin."

Now it was Em's turn to snort. "I don't think so."

"I do. And I know my brother better, so you're going to have to trust me on this one." Gracie narrowed her eyes, her gaze on Deacon. "He likes you. A lot more than he's willing to let on."

Something fluttered inside Em. Something that felt very much like butterflies in her stomach. But that couldn't be right. She wasn't falling for Deacon. Just like he wasn't falling for her.

Had to be more of this town's crazy magic.

Because that was the only explanation she was willing to accept.

CHAPTER TWENTY

Deacon didn't really need to talk to Oluf about Sunday afternoon's rugby match, but it was the only excuse he could come up with to leave the table.

And he needed to leave the table.

He had no desire to hear Emeranth ooh and aah over King Robin. He also didn't want to think about why that bothered him so much. Deep down, he knew why. But putting a name to that emotion wasn't going to happen.

Because it was nonsense. He wasn't feeling anything for her. Except that he wanted her to leave.

Which might have also been a lie.

He clapped Oluf on the back. "You good to go for Sunday's match? We play the wolves this week. Rico and his crew are a tough bunch." Rico Martinez was the alpha of the local wolf pack, and those boys could throw down.

The Viking warrior looked up from his pot roast and met Deacon with a toothy grin. "Very much so. I'm looking forward to breaking some bones."

Deacon grimaced. You couldn't take the berserker out of a man, no matter what century he'd accidentally time-traveled to. "So long as they're not mine."

Oluf laughed. "We're on the same team. Nothing to worry about."

"Right. Tell that to Zeke. You knocked one of his teeth out last week."

"An accident. It will grow back." Oluf shrugged and looked over Deacon's shoulder. "Who is that with Gracie?"

An odd prickle went up Deacon's spine. "Amelia's niece. Emeranth."

Oluf nodded appreciatively. "Emeranth. Very pretty. New in town, then?"

"Just visiting," Deacon answered with more edge than he'd meant to.

"Too bad. I wouldn't mind—" Oluf looked at Deacon and chuckled. "You like her."

Deacon frowned. "No. I mean, she's a nice enough person, but I don't, that is, I'm not..."

"You like her a lot." Oluf scooped up a forkful of pot roast. "About time you had a woman."

"I don't need a woman. I need to get out of—"

"Deacon."

Gracie's voice turned him around. Their food had arrived. He nodded at Oluf. "See you Sunday."

"I will see you Saturday. At the party," Oluf answered with a devilish twinkle in his eyes. "But bring your new woman Sunday. She will enjoy watching you play."

"She's not my—" Deacon sighed and went back to his table. There was no point in arguing with Oluf. The man was as stubborn as a stone.

He slid in next to Em, happy to focus on the food in front of him.

Em nudged him gently. "Who was that you were talking to?"

"Oluf Erikson."

Her brows lifted as if to say, *And?*

"He's a Viking berserker. A great warrior."

She seemed to take that in without question. Except for the one he should have known she'd ask. "What's his curse?"

"Em," Gracie hissed with a little grin. "You're not supposed to ask that."

Em shrugged as she picked up her sandwich. "I know, but I can't help myself. I'm a very curious person." She leaned in toward Deacon. "Just whisper it to me."

He took a breath to tell her no and inhaled the heady scent of her perfume, a mix of bright florals and fruit that smelled unmistakably like a sunny day.

Whatever he'd been about to say, the words stuck in his throat.

She nudged him with her elbow again. "Come on, just a hint."

Deacon had no clue what she was talking about. All he could think of was how close she was, how the slope of her neck was the sexiest thing he'd seen in a long time, and how easy it would be to press a kiss to the tender spot behind her ear.

"Cat got your tongue, Deac?" Gracie chewed a french fry with a very knowing look in her eyes.

He snapped out of it, surprised to find himself leaning toward Em. He straightened. "Oluf has time-traveling issues."

Em's eyes widened. "Wow. That's crazy."

"Yeah, well, if you're thinking about dating him, don't get any big ideas. He's not an easy guy to pin down."

She stared at him, then burst out laughing. Gracie joined her a split second later. Em shook her head. "Look at you, being punny."

He blinked, trying to understand what she meant. Then it registered. "I was being...never mind."

Gracie made a little noise, then ate another fry with a look on her face like she was already planning their wedding.

Little sisters. Gah.

He glanced at his watch, desperate for a reason to end this lunch. But the truth was, Em was his only job at the moment.

Why couldn't someone burst into flames, or cause it to hail, or have some kind of curse-related emergency when he needed them to?

He stabbed his potpie with his fork, letting out an eruption of steam.

"How do you know Oluf?" Em asked. "Is he one of the people you've helped?"

"We're on the same rugby team." He dug out a bite of flaky crust and turkey already knowing there would be more questions. "It's just for fun. Nothing serious."

"Really?" She blinked innocently at him. "I didn't think you went in for fun."

"Ha-ha." Was that really the impression he'd given her? That he was all work, no play? Apparently so. But doing anything else wasn't going to help him turn her off Shadowvale. "I can have fun. This just isn't the kind of town where that can always happen."

Gracie pointed a fry at him. "That's not true and you know it. What about movies in the park? And midnight sales? And Founding Day? And the arts and crafts festival? The fun runs? Bark in the Park? There are lots of cool things to do in this town, so stop making it all doom and gloom." Suddenly, she snickered. "Okay, it is always gloom, but you get used to it."

Em nodded. "I'm sure I will. And coming here certainly helps. Although the lack of sunshine isn't really bothering me so far."

Deacon sighed. He'd known this lunch was going to be a bad idea. And it was. Maybe time to just call it and tell Amelia that he'd done what he could. Em's desire to stay was stronger than the truth about Shadowvale. It was sometimes an okay place to live.

At least Gracie sure seemed to think so, and she was the one of them who had the most at stake in a place like this. Her curse made her so vulnerable here.

He had to get her out. But the chances of that were looking less likely by the minute.

Should he tell Amelia that he'd done all he could? That would be admitting defeat. Not something he liked to do.

He growled at the prospect. No. He was not ready to give up. Not when a better life for him and Gracie was a possibility. He would think of something.

He just didn't know what that something was.

After a great lunch and falling more in love with Shadowvale than she had the day before, Em walked back into her aunt's house, determined to find Amelia and have an honest talk with her. Em had come to a realization at lunch today. One she wasn't all that happy about.

Her aunt had set Deacon up to deliberately turn Em off of this town. She was sure about it. Especially after seeing how different Gracie's attitude about Shadowvale was. Gracie seemed to truly enjoy living here.

But really, Em had spent her life with a woman who went from one grift to another, and thanks to her mother's conniving ways, she had developed a gut feeling for when someone was trying to pull something over on her. She'd vowed never to let it happen again.

"Aunt Amelia?" She stuck her head in the library. "Are you around?"

No sign of her there. She wandered deeper into the house, down hallways she'd yet to explore. She found all kinds of spaces. A ballroom, more sitting rooms, a music room paneled in beautiful walnut, a game room complete with a pool table and darts, a theater room done in navy velvet with touches of gold, and closer to the kitchen some offices and a wine-tasting room.

But no sign of her aunt.

Em went out to look in the garden, but stayed on the patio in case Thoreau was out there again. Aunt Amelia might not be intimidated by that enormous cat, but Em was still on the fence. "Aunt Amelia?"

Nothing. Thankfully, that included no sign of a tiger either.

Finally, she went back outside and walked to the garage. She knew there had to be a way to get there from inside the house, but since she didn't know it, going outside was faster.

The wide doors were up, and Beckett was in the first bay talking to a man in a jumpsuit. A mechanic, from the looks of him.

Beckett smiled as she approached. "Hello, Miss Em."

"Hi. Do you have any idea where my aunt is?"

"In her quarters, I'd imagine."

"And those are?"

"Upstairs."

"That would explain why I couldn't find her." She sighed. "I guess I'll have to wait until she comes down."

"Why? You want to talk to her, go on up."

"I don't know if I should. Go up there, I mean."

"You should." The muscles in his jaw tightened. He looked at the mechanic. "Thanks, George. I'll talk to you later." He put a hand on Em's elbow. "Let's go back to the house."

"Okay." Something was afoot.

As they walked, he spoke. "Listen, your aunt, for all her power in this town, is sometimes too fearful for her own good. Sometimes she needs a push in the right direction. If you leave her alone, she may not ever come down."

Em nodded. "Except...she intimidates me."

"Part of her would be happy to hear that. And part of her would be heartbroken about it. Especially from you. No matter the front she puts on, she is desperate for company. And, I think, even more desperate for that family connection."

"But I don't want to be a bother. If she wants time alone—"

"She's had more alone time in her life than any one person could need if they lived to be a thousand. Go talk to her. She might seem bothered at first, but it's exactly what she needs."

Em didn't want to sound ungrateful, but disturbing Aunt Amelia could backfire on her. She needed her aunt to want her around, not think she was a nuisance. "You're sure?"

"I know her better than anyone else. Yes, I'm sure."

They stopped outside the front doors.

"Okay." She took a deep, cleansing breath. "Where's her room?"

Beckett pointed up. "Second floor, opposite end of the house from the guest rooms. Other side of the rotunda. Double doors."

"I've seen those doors. But I've never seen her use them. I guess we've just missed each other."

Beckett snorted. "Her quarters also have a second stairwell and private elevator. She rarely uses those doors, if at all."

"That would explain it."

He opened the front door for her. "You can do this."

She nodded, a little nervous. "I hope you're right."

Then she headed in and up the steps to the second floor. She walked around the rotunda, stopping at the double doors that led to her aunt's quarters. She stood there, rehearsing different opening lines and trying to find one that would set the right tone and mood.

None of them seemed quite right.

Then the door opened, and Aunt Amelia was in front of her. "Yes?"

Em went with the first thing that came to mind. "Can we talk?"

CHAPTER TWENTY-ONE

Amelia could sense the girl's hesitancy, just like she'd sensed her niece's presence at her door. Em was nervous, too, and Amelia felt for her. A little guilt came over her, knowing she'd caused that.

She nodded and smiled gently. "Of course. Come in."

"Thanks." Em looked around as she walked through the doors. "This is beautiful. Your whole house is, so it's no surprise your quarters are, too."

Amelia led her into the sitting room. "They say a man's home is his castle, but a woman's home is her sanctuary."

They took seats near the fireplace, which had a few glowing coals in it but was putting out very little heat.

Amelia adjusted the fabric of her caftan. "What would you like to talk about?"

Em smiled weakly, then clasped her hands so tightly that her knuckles paled. "I...I know you don't want me here. But I really, really need the chance to start over. I'm pouring my heart out to you, asking you to please allow me to stay. I promise not to be a bother. I'll stay out of your hair. You won't see me unless you want to. I just need a little time to get back on my feet. That's all. Please."

The heartfelt plea touched Amelia deeply. She knew the courage it had taken for Emeranth to speak her case. "Emeranth, if it weren't an issue of personal safety, I wouldn't give it a second thought. But there are forces at work here that you cannot possibly understand. Forces that would change the course of your life forever if—"

"Why couldn't I understand them?" The pleading tone of Emeranth's voice now carried an underlying edge of exasperation.

"Because they involve things beyond your experience."

It had all been beyond Amelia's experience, too, but she'd learned hard and fast what was going to be required of her. And she'd accepted it, without really understanding the scope of the cost. She would not allow that to happen to Emeranth.

"How do you know they're beyond my experience? With great respect, I have to say that you don't know what my life has been like. I've been through a lot. And survived. I've had far more experiences than most people my age."

Amelia wanted to hug the girl. "I know because I'm not talking about life experience. I'm talking about your experience as a witch. Your knowledge of all things great and magical. And in that regard, you aren't there yet."

Emeranth's mouth bent, and for a moment, Amelia thought she might cry, then realized it wasn't a sign of weakness but of determination. "And how am I supposed to get that experience when I haven't been initiated? You told me I'm a witch, and I believed you, but to leave me hanging..." She shook her head and looked away. "Maybe you're right. Maybe it was a mistake to come here. But I thought the fact that we're family would mean something."

The weight of Amelia's guilt increased. "It does mean something. It means that I want to protect you by keeping you free of this place."

Emeranth barked out a bitter laugh. "I've been free all my life. Free of a place to call home. Free of connections. Free of real friends. I don't want to be free. I want to belong. But I guess you can't imagine that. After all, you have a whole town to call your own."

Amelia had no idea what the girl's life had been like, but from Emeranth's words and knowing Manda as she did, Amelia was getting a picture. "I'm sorry your life hasn't been different. But it wouldn't be better here. This place would become your prison. Just as it has for me."

Emeranth looked at Amelia, narrowing her eyes. "Do you want to leave, then?"

"Yes. And no, I suppose. But it's a pointless question."

"Because if you leave, you die."

Amelia sat back a bit. "How do you know that?"

"I ask a lot of questions. Enough to wear Beckett down."

"Beckett." Amelia shook her head.

"I like him. Even if he is here to claim your soul."

Amelia's next inhale was sudden and sharp. "He really did talk to you."

"He did. And the truth didn't scare me any more than anything else that's happened in my life." She sighed. "Aunt Amelia, why won't you let me in? What are you afraid of? That I'll betray you in some way? That I'm here for your money? I'm not, I swear it on everything you hold holy. All I want from you is a place to stay until I can afford my own. Charge me rent if you want. I'll gladly repay you."

Amelia felt herself waver. She stared at her hands. Having Emeranth around would be glorious. But not for Emeranth. Not for what it would cost her. "I—"

"You know what?" Emeranth said. "I lied. That's not all I want from you. I forgot the most important thing I'm after."

Amelia's head came up, and she was instantly on alert. She braced herself for whatever truth Emeranth was about to give her. "What is that?"

"Family," Emeranth whispered in a voice husky with emotion. "My mother isn't…" She looked away, eyes shining with unshed tears.

Amelia put her hand to her throat as memories came swarming back. "To some extent, I know what your mother is and is not. I'm very sorry for that."

Emeranth's head whipped around. "You know my mother?"

"I do. She came here once. Looking for…help. Which I refused to give her because ultimately I thought it would do you both more harm than good. You, especially."

Emeranth cleared her throat. "That sounds like her."

They were both silent for a moment until Amelia couldn't bear it any longer. "I can give you all the money you need if you just promise me to leave this place."

Emeranth shook her head. "That's very kind of you. And it would solve a lot of my problems, but not the ones that need fixing the most, so thank you, but no. I don't want your money."

"What if I promise to initiate you? To finally put you in touch with your birthright powers?"

Emeranth's gaze narrowed. "I would have hoped you'd do that anyway, seeing as how you sprang the whole witch thing on me to begin with."

Amelia sighed. "Yes, you're right. I will do that much for you."

"But you won't let me stay here. Is that what I'm reading between the lines?"

Amelia wanted to give her a different answer, but a different answer would come at too high a price. "No, I cannot let you stay here."

Emeranth frowned and sat back, crossing her arms. "You can tell Deacon he can drop the act, then."

"What act?" Did Emeranth know?

"The one you hired him to put on. The one where he's supposed to make me think Shadowvale is the worst place in the world for anyone to live."

"It is. For you. I'm sorry."

Emeranth got to her feet, the defiant set of her jaw reminding Amelia very much of herself. "I hope someday you think differently. That you want to have a relationship with me, because I would very much like to have a relationship with you, but I can't let you decide my life for me. I'm staying in Shadowvale."

Amelia admired the girl's courage, but she refused to reward it. "I will not help you in that endeavor. Not financially or otherwise."

"I don't need your help. I've already found a job, and I'll sleep in my car if I—"

"You found a job?" Amelia grabbed the arms of her chair as a chill swept through her. She'd had no idea things had progressed so far.

"I did. And it might not land me a house like this, but it's a start."

Amelia dug her fingers into the upholstery. Her options were disappearing. "You are determined to stay here, then? Your mind is made up?"

"It is."

"Is there anything I can offer you that would change your mind?"

"Nothing. I need this fresh start. My mind won't change even if you withhold the initiation from me." Emeranth shrugged. "I've made it this far in life without being a real witch. I can survive the rest of it just the same."

"Then there is no point in my keeping the truth from you any longer."

Emeranth blinked a few times. "What does that mean?"

Amelia stood. "It means that you need to know the real cost of living here. At least the real cost for you, my descendant."

"Excellent, thank you. I'm sure it's all going to be fine."

The sparkle in Emeranth's eyes told Amelia that the woman had no idea what she was about to learn. "It won't be fine. By sharing all this with you, your fate will be sealed."

"That's kind of dramatic, don't you think?"

"Perhaps. But once all is revealed, you won't be allowed to leave."

The sparkle disappeared. "Do you mean the house? Or the town?"

"Shadowvale. You'll have to remain here for the rest of your life, which will be quite long, as mine has been."

Emeranth rubbed her brow. "This got really heavy really fast."

Amelia understood that. So much so, she offered her niece an option she herself hadn't been given. "You can think about it until the morning, if you'd like."

"No. More time isn't going to change the way I feel. I can live here for the rest of my life. I can do it."

"You'll never see your mother again, unless she comes here."

"That won't happen for another six to ten years anyway." Emeranth nodded. "My answer isn't going to change."

"Very few of your friends will be able to visit you here. The gates are notoriously particular about who they open for."

"I like that you assume I have friends." She smiled. "Still good on that decision."

Yes, Amelia thought. Emeranth was so very much like herself at an earlier age. So sure of what she wanted. So headstrong and independent and fierce.

If only she'd known then what she knew now. But then again, maybe it wouldn't have made any difference. Pasqual was all that had mattered to her.

Thankfully, Emeranth was going into this without the encumbrance of love.

"All right," Amelia said. "Come with me."

CHAPTER TWENTY-TWO

Emeranth recognized where they were headed a few minutes before they arrived. The enchanted forest. She couldn't imagine what this had to do with Aunt Amelia's big reveal, but she was too giddy with the news that she was being allowed to stay to care.

Her life was about to be so different. So much better. No one knew her past here. She could be herself, not Manda Greer's daughter, with all the sideways glances and disapproving stares that brought.

And she already had a job. Things were really falling into place.

Maybe she'd even give a relationship with Deacon a shot.

Joy overflowed in her, bubbling up like fizzy champagne. This, she thought, was what freedom felt like. True freedom.

She glanced at her aunt. The woman's solemn expression seemed more suitable for a funeral than anything else.

Why? What was she about to show Emeranth?

Even Beckett hadn't said a word since he'd gotten behind the wheel to drive them.

But Em still couldn't manage to feel worried. Whatever it was, she'd deal with it. And truth be told, she didn't fully believe Aunt Amelia's claim that she'd never be able to leave.

How could that be possible?

Beckett turned down a road that Em didn't remember seeing from her drive earlier with Deacon, but then, she'd been too busy looking for faces on trees and winged foxes to be sure she'd seen every road.

Another couple minutes and he slowed, then brought the car to a stop on a wide area of the shoulder. "Here?"

"This will do," Amelia answered.

Em didn't see a sign marking the spot as anything special. In fact, this section of the forest looked no different than any of the rest they'd passed.

He exited the car to open Aunt Amelia's door.

Em got out on her side, then waited for her aunt's next move. The air smelled deeply green and earthy, the way things did after a good rain.

Beckett shut the passenger door before speaking to Amelia. "You shouldn't go in alone."

"I'm not alone," she said. "I have Emeranth with me."

He frowned. "You know what I mean."

Amelia patted his arm in the most affectionate gesture Em had seen her make toward the reaper. "I do. And I appreciate it. But this is for Marchand eyes only."

"I understand." He looked at Em. "Be careful."

She nodded, not really understanding what she needed to be careful about, but wanting to assure him anyway. "Always."

Aunt Amelia started forward. Em spotted a break in the forest. A narrow, barely noticeable footpath. Amelia scooped her hand through the air. "Follow me."

Em gave Beckett a little wave and went after her aunt.

Who proved to be far more fit than Em would have imagined. Her pace required Em to walk briskly and didn't give her any time to dawdle for a better look at the interesting flora and fauna along the way.

Em imagined that was the point.

The path disappeared after a while. The forest, already dim, darkened further, but the light that filtered through stayed green and inviting. Plus, sprite moss dotted the trees at almost regular intervals, and green fireflies (no red lightning bugs, thankfully) danced in the air just out of reach.

At no time did she feel like they were in any danger, so Beckett's words of caution remained a mystery.

As they got deeper in, a new light source appeared. Slightly bigger than the fireflies and farther away, the spots of glowing blue intrigued Em. "What kind of fireflies are the blue ones?"

"They're not fireflies. They're fairies."

"Oh, that is cool." Em was glad Aunt Amelia couldn't see her mouth fall open. She tried to look closer at one, to see if she could make out the form of it, but they stayed too far away.

She would have loved to talk about them some more, but Amelia was still focused on the impending doom of it all.

"I'm bringing you here now, as an uninitiated witch, because I'm hoping that will give you some protection." Amelia spoke as she moved. "But your choice to stay in Shadowvale and your eventual initiation will change that. The magic will find you, and when it does, there won't be any going back. You must understand that."

"I do. I promise."

Suddenly, Amelia stopped, turned, and took Emeranth's hand. "It's not a bad life, but it can be a very lonely one."

Em smiled and squeezed her aunt's hand. "But we'll have each other, right?"

Amelia held her gaze for a moment, then dropped Em's hand to pat her cheek. "You're a good girl. You deserve a different life than this."

Em smiled back. "Maybe this is exactly the life I deserve." Impulsively, she hugged her aunt. "Thank you for trusting me with all this."

Amelia held on to her. "I hope you still think that when this is all said and done."

Em released her and leaned back. "I'm sure I will."

Amelia let out a breath, then turned and started walking again.

A mist rose up from the ground, making it harder to see more than a few feet in any direction, and yet Amelia kept going at the same pace.

Minutes passed, and the fog thickened. It stayed that way for what seemed like an eternity until suddenly it fell away.

Em's brows lifted, and she let out a small gasp.

They were in a grove of trees. Beneath their feet was a spongy carpet of blue-green moss. Around them stood a perfect circle of twelve thick trunks that stretched far above them. The branches made a dome, covering every bit of the sky except for another perfect circle that showed a disc of blue-black night sky sparkling with stars.

"It's night?" Em asked. "How long have we been walking?"

"A long time."

"I guess." But it wasn't the passing of time that Em was focused on.

It was what was in the center of the grove.

An open book about the size and thickness of a suitcase. It sat on an intricately carved pedestal and seemed to glow from an internal light.

Em pointed at it. "Is that *the* book?"

Amelia nodded. "I take it Deacon told you about it. That is the book."

"He mentioned it. I got the sense he doesn't really believe it exists. Obviously, it does. Amazing," Em breathed out. She took a step toward it, hand outstretched.

Twelve fierce warrior women stepped out of the trees, bows taut with arrows drawn and pointed at Em. They wore slim breeches of leather and tunics of pale silk that highlighted their bark-brown skin.

Too late, she realized the trees in the grove all wore faces. Or had. Those faces were surrounding her now. She put her hands in the air. "I mean no harm."

One of the women looked at Amelia. "All is well?"

Amelia nodded. "All is well. This is my niece, Emeranth."

The woman smiled, and all twelve dropped their bows to their sides. "Good. But it's also important to establish boundaries."

Em nodded vigorously. "Boundary established, for sure."

Amelia bowed. "Lylianna."

The nymph bowed as well. "Amelia." She looked at Emeranth. "A pleasure to meet you."

"You, too," Em said.

Lylianna returned to her spot in the formation, then all twelve turned and disappeared back into their trees.

Em looked at her aunt. "Nymphs, right?"

"Right."

"That was terrifying and cool."

Amelia smiled briefly. "There is much yet to come."

She walked toward the book, glancing over her shoulder when she realized Em wasn't following her. "Come. This is your legacy. You need to know this."

Em joined her aunt, checking quickly to see if the nymphs appeared again. They didn't.

Amelia put her hand on the book as she spoke to Em. "Beneath this book is the source of Shadowvale's magic, both dark and light. That source is protected by this place, the grove nymphs, and my magic. This town was created to provide a safe haven for the man I loved, but to do so required me to make a great sacrifice."

Em nodded, hanging on every word.

"That sacrifice was my agreement to protect a very dangerous object from mankind. To become its guardian. An object that was already failing and had been since ages past. And while Shadowvale was built to contain it as much as possible, the magic within it continues to seep out, drawing the most desperate to these gates."

"What is the object?" Em asked. Although she wasn't sure she'd get an answer, she was suddenly desperate to know. What could such a thing be?

Amelia hesitated as if she knew her next actions would be the point of no return. She gently closed the book and lifted it off its base with such ease that Em wondered how that was possible when it must weigh an enormous amount.

Amelia carefully set the book on the ground. The pedestal was hollow. Amelia reached inside and lifted out a lidded jar covered in designs that looked ancient and Greek to Em.

"This is the object," Amelia answered.

A hairline crack ran from where the lid met the mouth of the vessel. "What is it?" Em asked again.

Amelia took a breath, her grip firm on the jar. "The one and only Pandora's box."

♪

Deacon's head snapped up like he'd heard a shot, but there hadn't been a sound. Just a feeling that something, somewhere was being disturbed. A ripple in the magic pool that was Shadowvale.

"Something wrong?" Shepherd asked before taking a long pull of his beer.

Deacon shook his head. "No."

They were sitting at the bar of the Five Bells Pub, their favorite watering hole. The multiple televisions showed a wide variety of sports, the beers were cold, and the nachos were piled high with toppings.

It was the kind of night Deacon normally enjoyed. But not tonight. Tonight all he could think about was how he'd failed. Because there was no more pretending that Em was going to leave.

Not when she had a job and the kind of determination that overthrew governments.

The woman was as beautiful as she was stubborn. And she was really beautiful.

Shep nudged him. "What are you smiling about?"

Deacon frowned. "I'm not smiling."

"You were." Shep turned his gaze back to the television closest to them. "It's that woman, isn't it?"

"What woman?"

Shep snorted. "Nice try. Gracie already told me about her."

Deacon rolled his eyes. "Gracie needs to zip it. There's nothing to tell. Amelia gave me a job to do, and that was that."

Shep side-eyed him. "What job? And isn't she Amelia's niece?"

"The job of turning her off this place. Yes, she is Amelia's niece, but Amelia doesn't want her here."

"You would be the perfect person to do that."

Deacon held his tongue. Shep didn't know what Amelia had offered him in exchange, and telling him wouldn't help anything. Shep already thought leaving would be stupid.

Shep sipped his beer. "You're not going to find him, you know."

The muscles in Deacon's jaw tensed. He didn't like talking about their father, even though he spent an inordinate amount of time thinking about the man. "You don't know that."

"I do. With him, I know."

Maisie Sweeney, one of the pub's bartenders, came by to check on them. "You boys doing okay?"

Shep nodded. "Right as rain."

She gave him a big smile. "You holler if you need me."

She sashayed away, and Deacon snorted. "How come you haven't asked her out yet? You know she'd say yes."

"Don't try to change the subject." Shep planted his elbows on the bar. "What's Amelia's niece like?"

Pretty, smart, quick with a comeback, built like a—

Deacon's phone went off. He checked the screen. "Sorry, I'd love to stay and talk about what a fine couple you and Maisie would make, but Jerry Washington just had a flare-up. Gotta go."

"Oh, sure." Shep laughed. "Nice save."

"It's what I do." Deacon slapped a twenty on the bar. Sometimes, curses were great things to have.

CHAPTER TWENTY-THREE

Em stared at the jar. "*The* Pandora's box?"

Amelia tapped a finger on the lid even as she maintained her grip. "The very one."

"I hate to nitpick at a time like this, but shouldn't it actually be a box?"

"No. That name came about due to an error in translation. It's always been a jar."

Em nodded, unable to take her eyes off it. "And it really contains all the troubles of the world? Or was that an error in translation, too?"

"No, that part is absolutely spot-on. Except there aren't quite as many in there as there used to be. As you can see by the crack there, they've been leaking out for quite a while."

Em wanted to touch it, but was a little afraid to. "And you're its guardian. That's kind of awe-inspiring."

"I am. It's a big job, but I've been doing it so long it doesn't seem that way. After all, my magic built this place, and in return this place powers my magic. To a certain extent, we're symbiotic, Shadowvale and me."

"Is that why if you leave here, you'll…cease to exist?"

Amelia smiled. "Yes. If I leave Shadowvale, I'll die. This town keeps me alive. For its own purposes, but it is what it is."

"What would happen to the town? To Pandora's box?"

"It would be vulnerable. As for the town…I'm not really sure. But I don't think it would let me leave." She looked at Em. "At least not until my replacement has been found."

Em swallowed, understanding that her aunt fully believed Em was that replacement.

Aunt Amelia looked at the jar. "This has been out long enough." She slid it back into the pedestal and replaced the book on top.

"No one knows that's here?"

Amelia brushed off her hands. "No one. Not even Beckett. Not even the Evermores, who were the first residents to move to Shadowvale when the gates opened. And it has to stay that way, understand?"

"Yes." Em had more questions about that, but something her aunt had said stuck out. "When you said the Evermores, you meant Deacon's parents, right?"

"Deacon's grandparents, actually. Although I know his grandmother knew of this grove."

"What are they? He wouldn't tell me."

Amelia's eyes narrowed a bit. "Then I won't either. Some things are meant to be revealed at certain times. You'll find out soon enough, I'm sure."

Em wanted to sigh in frustration, but didn't. "Is it true what Deacon told me about the book? That if you write your name in it, your curse is removed?"

"Yes. The book and the jar are connected. Whatever's written in the book gets funneled back into the jar."

"Then why not just write your name in it? You could be free of whatever's holding you here."

"My magic created this place. Writing my name in the book would have no effect. I'm sure writing your name wouldn't either, although you have no curse to be rid of."

"We could write other people's names in it. You must know some people who'd like to be free. Or does the person with the curse have to be the one to write their name in the book?"

"I don't think that matters. But I know that each person gets one chance to add a name. And only one name at a time can be added. Absorbing the curses of too many at once would weaken the jar. The crack would worsen. It would become harder to contain the troubles already within it. That's part of why this grove is so hard to find."

"I understand. I think. Everything needs balance, right?"

"Yes. Very true." Aunt Amelia put her hand on the book again. "I hope you will truly be happy here. Because you understand that, with what I've revealed to you, there's not much chance the town will let you leave now."

Em laughed a little nervously. "You really believe that?"

"I don't just believe it, I've seen evidence to support it." Aunt Amelia's eyes narrowed. "If you've changed your mind, there might still be a chance for you to leave. It would take a lot of magic, but since you're not yet a full-fledged witch we could try it."

Em gave that a few seconds of thought. "But once I am a witch, then it's a done deal?"

"You'll be in possession of your magic. You'll be capable of taking my place."

Em bit her lip.

"We should go back. Beckett will be on edge until we return."

Em's feet didn't move.

Aunt Amelia pressed a hand to Em's arm and spoke softly. "We don't have to do the initiation right away. You take a few days and think about it."

"I want to do it..." Em hesitated.

"But it comes with strings attached now." Aunt Amelia guided them out of the grove. "I completely understand. More than anyone else could."

Em walked with her in silence, her head swirling with thoughts. She'd gotten what she wanted, the chance to start over fresh in a new town. With family. That was the best part.

Of course, she hadn't really anticipated that this new town would also be her last town. But she wanted the use of her powers. Even more so if she was going to be a permanent resident of this place.

There was no way she was going to walk away from all this now. If she was going to live here, and she was, then she had to be all in.

Taking on Jerry's curse meant Deacon couldn't use his truck to get home. Not with a halo of white-hot flame surrounding him. But Jerry had been very appreciative, and Deacon wasn't opposed to walking.

He thought briefly about shifting into his raven form and flying home, but curses didn't always mix well with his own personal magic, and the last thing he wanted was singed feathers. So he put one foot in front of the other and started moving.

The temperature had dropped, but he couldn't really feel it inside his personal furnace. He stuck his hands in his pockets and strolled toward home, mindful to keep a safe distance from anything that might catch fire from contact with him.

His mind wandered from subject to subject, but kept coming back to Emeranth. And what a terrible job he'd done of persuading her to leave.

Maybe it was for the best. Maybe she needed the new beginning more than he did. Although he was sad for Gracie. She might never have a real life outside of this place until her curse was lifted.

Who was he kidding? She'd never have much of a life *here* until her curse was lifted. No man had ever wanted to date her after finding out about her curse.

She might never marry because of it. Might never get the chance to be a mom.

He knew that weighed on her. No matter how much of a happy face she put on, she was a nurturer at heart. Having a family of her own was something she'd talked about since she was a little girl.

Except that talk had become a lot less frequent the older she'd gotten. Like she knew her chances of realizing that dream were so slim there was no point in putting it into words.

His heart ached for her. And his feelings of helplessness only compounded that.

He'd failed her so far. And he hated to fail.

Although, if he was completely honest, he wasn't that unhappy about failing where Em was concerned.

If he was going to be stuck in Shadowvale, it would be nice to have her around.

He realized he was smiling. Funny. He couldn't remember a woman who'd had that effect on him before. Em was something special, though. Something special indeed.

"Deacon."

For a second, he thought he'd heard her voice. That's how focused his mind had been on her.

"Deacon."

He turned to see he was passing Amelia's house, and Em was waving at him from the driveway. He stopped and waved back. "Hey."

She jogged toward him until only the wrought-iron fence separated them. "Why are you on fire? Someone's curse?"

"Yep." He looked past her to where Beckett was pulling a car into the garage. "You go out for a drive?"

She nodded. "Yep. Also had a long talk with my aunt." A grin spread across her face. "She's letting me stay."

"That's...great."

"Is it?" She gave him a funny look. "Because you certainly seem like you've been trying to get me to leave. And honestly, you don't look all that thrilled right now."

He glanced at the house again. He didn't want to throw Amelia under the bus, but he didn't want to lie to Em either. There was no point in it. And lies were a kind of curse all on their own. Nothing he wanted to dabble in. "I...uh...I was trying to help your aunt out, a little."

"By showing me the worst this town has to offer." She nodded. "I know."

"You do? Did she tell you?"

"Nope. Figured it out on my own. You're not exactly subtle."

He laughed, causing the flames to dance a little higher. "Yeah, I guess not."

She looped her hands around the bars and leaned in. "So are you just out for a walk, then?"

"Walking home, actually. Can't drive my truck like this unless I want to buy a new one."

"I suppose not." She dropped her head to look at him through her lashes. "You want some company?"

Her company? More than anything. But he wasn't the safest guy to be around at the moment. He spread his arms wide. "Walking next to me right now would probably be hazardous to your health."

"I'm a Marchand witch." She stuck her foot in one of the loops of wrought iron and climbed the fence, vaulting over the top and landing on her feet with catlike grace. "We're immune to fire."

"Yeah, I don't know about—"

She grabbed his hand. "See?"

Heat charged through his body that had nothing to do with the flames covering him. A second later, he snapped out of it and reflexively yanked his hand back. "You're going to get burned."

"But I can't be." She held her hand up, wiggling her fingers. "No burns, no blisters, nothing."

He peered closer. "How about that." He took a step closer. "Am I hot?"

She gave him a wry little smile. "Didn't we already have this conversation in your truck?"

He repeated his last sentence in his head, then snorted. "That's not what I meant. I meant can you feel my heat? Wait, that sounds like—these flames are putting out heat, they have to be." The woman muddled his thoughts to the point he worried he might be turning a little red. Hopefully, the flames covered that. "Are you affected by the temperature at all?"

She held her palms up to him the way someone might approach a campfire. "I can feel how hot you are, but it doesn't bother me."

He nodded, wondering what it would take to get her to hold his hand again. "Great."

"You want company, then?"

"I'd love some." To anyone else, he would have said no. He didn't really want *company*. He wanted Em.

CHAPTER TWENTY-FOUR

Em had a sudden light, fizzy feeling in her belly as she walked with Deacon. It had started the moment she'd spotted him from the driveway.

And had only increased once she'd joined him on the sidewalk, a move that had been completely impulsive. Driven, perhaps, by the weight of what had just been laid on her. She needed something to take her mind off all this new information, just for a little bit.

But that didn't explain why she caught herself flirting with him, too, tossing her hair back and giving him coy looks. What was going on with her?

Was it because she was feeling a little reckless, knowing that once she was initiated there was no going back? Or because she knew that she was staying? Had that flipped some internal switch that said it was okay to get involved?

Maybe. But then, why Deacon? Sure, he was hot. And not just because he was currently on fire. She let out a little laugh at the joke.

Deacon shot her a glance. "What's so funny?"

She shook it off. "Nothing, just thinking."

"About?"

Answering truthfully wasn't hard. "How my life has changed. I came here in desperate need of a new start, and now I'm getting it. And more. It's amazing."

He nodded. "I'm happy for you."

"But you're not happy about something else." She rolled that around in her head. What was it about her staying that could be upsetting him? Then it hit her. "You're not getting your reward."

He squinted through the flames. "What's that supposed to mean?"

"I'm just saying people usually do things in hopes of a payoff. Not saying there's anything wrong with that. It's how the world works. But I'm guessing you were hoping for something from my aunt in exchange for convincing me to leave."

His squint deepened. "It's nothing."

"Nothing you want to tell me, you mean."

He scowled a bit. "Why are you so perceptive?"

She shrugged. "I've had to be to survive. And I'm not always. But it's pretty hard to pull something over on me. Not saying that's what you were doing—"

"But I was. In a way." He stared straight ahead, like making eye contact was suddenly too much. "For my own ends. Nothing bad, I promise."

She nodded. "It's okay. You really do believe that Shadowvale isn't such a great place to live, don't you?"

He nodded, still frowning. "It has a lot of downsides. For me anyway. Doesn't mean it will for you."

He seemed so unhappy about what he'd done that words didn't feel like enough of a reassurance. She impulsively took his hand and gave it a squeeze. "Really, I'm not mad."

"Good. Thanks."

She went to let go of his hand, but he hung on.

She grinned, a half smile just to herself, and relaxed her hand in his. They walked that way for a few minutes, not saying anything. It was remarkably comfortable and, for Em, stupidly exciting.

So much so, she almost giggled. Wow, how sad was she that holding a man's hand got her this worked up? Sure, it had been ages since she'd been on a date, but this was *just* holding hands.

Granted, Deacon was crazy handsome and definitely had an untouchable vibe going on that made this sudden contact feel like a big thing, but it was still just holding hands.

She glanced at him. He was looking straight ahead, acting like Mr. Cool.

As much as someone who was on fire could anyway.

She couldn't stand it. "Gracie would lose it if she saw us."

He looked down at their hands and smirked. "She would. Best we don't tell her, hmm?"

"Right."

Another few moments passed before he spoke again. "I'm glad you're staying."

Happiness made her tongue loose and her mood buoyant. "Why? So you can take me out on a date?"

He stopped walking, which brought her to a stop as well. The look in his eyes was hard to decipher through the flames, but it seemed to Em that the fire would have been there either way.

He nodded. "You want to go out with me?"

She stared into his eyes. What would it hurt? She had a job and a place to stay. Why not go out with him? "Yes."

"You're coming to my sister's party, right? So come as my date."

"You think Gracie can handle that?"

He laughed. "If you say yes, I guess we'll find out."

That giddy, shuddery, lighter-than-air feeling came back. Like she was floating. Like she was outside herself looking in. "I'm saying yes."

"I'll pick you up at five, then. You can come get the cake with me."

"Deal." Impulsively, she leaned in to kiss him. A split second into the forward motion of it, she realized what she was doing. Realized that it was too soon, too much, that she'd only scare him off.

She tried to stop herself, but physics had taken over and there was no going back. Her mouth met his.

She put her hands to his chest to push back.

But he took hold of her shoulders and pulled her closer.

And then her world went up in flames.

Hot, delicious, Deacon-flavored flames.

Emeranth tasted like the best bad idea Deacon had ever had. He shouldn't be kissing her. She was Amelia's niece, and that could only lead to trouble. She was also the woman who had cost him his chance at freedom.

And yet he couldn't make himself care about anything but the feel of her mouth on his.

Then reality kicked in and reminded him that he was standing on the sidewalk in one of the nicest parts of town. While on fire.

Not exactly inconspicuous.

Reluctantly, he broke the kiss with a sigh. "We shouldn't have done that."

"That was exactly what I was hoping to hear." She crossed her arms and gave him a perturbed look. "So romantic. No wonder you're single."

"I just meant we shouldn't have done that here. On the sidewalk."

"Why? Is kissing illegal in Shadowvale? Because that might actually stop me from moving here."

Her teasing tone and glinting eyes told him she knew better, but this was no joking matter. "No. But your aunt might not like it."

"You know I'm a grown woman, right?"

He gave her a quick once-over. "I am aware." Very. Aware.

She gave him the same once-over, but there was nothing quick about the way her gaze raked him. "Good, because I know that you're a grown man. And that means we can do as we like."

His body temperature continued to rise and still had nothing to do with the flames bathing him. Where had this side of her come from? He didn't know. And wasn't sure he should question it. He nodded. "It does. But your aunt's probably already mad at me for failing to scare you off."

"I don't think so. Now that she knows I'm cool with everything living here means, I think she's happy to have the company."

"In that case, I'm glad for both of you. She's been alone a long time."

Em took a step toward him, close enough that the flames licked at her. "So have I."

Gracie's words, about having his hands full with Em, suddenly came back to him. And having his hands full of her was all he could think about. "Well," he breathed out, "I can fix that."

She smiled and bit her lip. "I should head back before my aunt thinks you kidnapped me."

"I'll walk you back."

"And risk setting her house on fire?" She shook her head. "That's not a good idea."

"I guess not."

A car drove past, slowing as it went by. Probably for a better look. Even in Shadowvale, a man on fire was worth a second glance. But that also meant they'd been seen together. What was done was done.

He closed the small gap between them with a single step, reached up, and cupped her jaw to pull her close for one more kiss. Hard and claiming, the kind of kiss he'd wanted to plant on her since the first time he'd laid eyes on her. "Have a good night. See you tomorrow at five."

She nodded, backing away with a sweetly stunned expression. "Five," she managed.

With a grin, he turned and headed for home again.

Tomorrow night might be Gracie's party, but he felt like he was the one getting the present.

Maybe staying in Shadowvale wasn't such a bad idea after all.

CHAPTER TWENTY-FIVE

Em ran into the house. "Aunt Amelia, where are you? I want to do the initiation now. Aunt Amelia?"

"What's all the yelling?" Amelia came out of the library.

Em nearly skidded into her. "Hi, sorry. I want to do the initiation. Now. Tonight. Can we?"

"Slow down." Amelia gave her a stern look. "What's all this about?"

"I'm just ready. I want to be here. There's no point in putting off the initiation. I want full access to my powers. I want to be the me I'm supposed to be."

Amelia's eyes narrowed. "Something's got you all wound up."

Deacon's kisses, but she wasn't about to tell her aunt that. "I'm just ready, that's all."

Amelia leaned in. "And you smell like smoke."

"Do I?" Em did her best innocent look. "Pretty sure the neighbors have a fire going. Lots of woodsmoke in the air."

Amelia didn't look quite convinced. "You know going through this initiation means your fate is sealed."

"I know." Em made herself stop smiling like an infatuated teenager, even though that's what she felt like. This was a serious matter they were discussing, and she wanted Aunt Amelia to know she understood that. "But how would you feel if you'd found out a part of yourself had been kept away from you all your life?"

"I suppose very much the same way you do." Amelia sighed. "All right. We'll do it."

"Thank you." Em hugged her. "Where? What do I need to do? Should I change?"

"What you have on is fine. We'll do it in my sanctum."

Em's brows went up. "And that is?"

"My personal space for practicing my craft. You'll have one. It might be an entire room, a dedicated closet, or just a space on a shelf. Whatever works for you. But having a space that you can dedicate is important to learning your art."

"Good to know." Em smiled. "See? I'm learning already."

Amelia nodded. "So you are. I just need to prepare a few things. Some of them I'll need help with. Beck—"

"Yes?"

The reaper spoke from over Em's right shoulder, causing her to jump. "Do you have to be so quiet?" She clapped her hand to her heart, laughing a little.

"I want to live long enough to get initiated, thank you very much."

He grinned. "My apologies. I'll endeavor to make more noise in the future."

"You'll do no such thing." Amelia pursed her lips. "I like quiet."

Beckett blinked innocently. "As you wish. What can I help you with?"

"I need four unbleached beeswax candles from Spellbound. The tall ones. Thoreau chewed up most of my supply, the naughty boy. And get a few large sage bundles. The organic kind, not that cheap stuff. I have a few, but since you're going anyway, might as well get some more."

"Got it," Beckett said. "Anything else?"

"I have everything else we'll need."

"Then I'll be back as quickly as I can. I'll bring them to you when I return."

"Thank you," Amelia said.

He left them with a quick nod.

Em rubbed her hands together. "This is very exciting. What's next?"

"Next we go to my sanctum and prepare by casting a circle."

Em didn't really know what that meant, but she was eager to find out. She followed her aunt through the house to a locked door near the kitchen. Odd, but Em didn't remember seeing the door before.

Amelia waved her hand over the lock, and it clicked open.

"Impressive," Em said.

"It's a simple spell, but a very useful one." Amelia opened the door, and they went down a flight of stone steps.

"This place has a basement?" The air was noticeably cooler, but Em wasn't uncomfortable.

"Most houses here do. Except those in the bayous."

"Right." Em glanced back toward the door. "Will that lock itself again? Because Beckett won't be able to get in if it does."

"Not until I wish it to lock." They hit flat ground, and Amelia whispered, "Luminos."

Lights blinked on.

"Hey, this is really nice."

The stone steps had given way to a tiled slate floor covered with a rich woven rug. Two walls were paneled with dark wood shelves, and a beautiful Edison bulb chandelier hung from the ceiling. Matching sconces illuminated the rest of the room.

A large fireplace took up another wall. Two leather chairs sat before it with a small table between them.

Another great reading spot, Em thought.

A long, gleaming, wood table was positioned closer to the walls of shelves. It sat at an angle so the ends pointed at the shelves. Behind it was a tall-backed stool of metal and wood with a padded leather seat. Apparently Aunt Amelia's desk, as it were.

The table held a few items. A well-used candle in a pretty brass holder. Notebooks, pens, a fancy box inlaid with enamel and stones. A short cranberry glass vase filled with feathers and quills.

But what really caught Em's eye were the shelves. Or rather, what was on them. Books of all descriptions. Magical books, Em guessed. Grimoires, Deacon had called them.

And then there were the containers. Glass and pottery jars, boxes of wood and metal. All labeled. Tiger Tears. Brimstone. Lightning Bug Wings. Dragon Scales. Hemlock Root. Ashes of Saints. Pixie Dust. Silver Filings. Misc Claws.

Herbs took up at least a shelf and a half. The other half of that shelf held small glass jars of precious stones, all faceted and sparkling in the light.

It was, like many things Em had already seen, hard to believe. She approached one of the shelves. "This almost seems like a movie set."

"I suppose it would, seeing as how you've never been in a sanctum before. But the movies never get it right. Too much eye of newt and wing of bat. Most spells rarely call for such outlandish ingredients."

"You know you have a box up there that's labeled Dried Newt Lungs, right?"

"I have a love-hate relationship with that box." Amelia stepped onto a footstool and retrieved the container. She took the lid off. "My weakness."

Em laughed. Hard. The box was filled with gold-wrapped chocolate hazelnut truffles. "Okay, that's a riot."

Aunt Amelia stared longingly into the box. "I love those things, but at my age they go straight to my hips. So I keep them down here on a high shelf in the hopes of avoiding temptation."

"But you want one right now, don't you?" The sweet, chocolaty smell rising off them was making her mouth water.

Her aunt frowned. "I do. But now is not the time." She put the lid back on and replaced the box in its spot. "Maybe after your initiation is done. Right now, we have work to do. A circle to cast, for one thing. Which means this rug has to come up."

Together, they rolled it up and carried it back to the base of the wall.

Amelia brushed off her hands, then got a large container off of another shelf. "Salt. It's the basis for a lot of work. I like Celtic sea salt, but you can use whatever you like."

"Table salt?"

"Salt is salt." Amelia took a handful. "Now I will cast the circle and name the elements. Even though fire is the one we're most concerned with, all four are important. The circle is almost always cast clockwise, and we tie the elements to the four points of the compass to ground them to our work."

Em nodded, fascinated. "Okay." All of this was so foreign, and yet something in her seemed to already understand what her aunt was telling her.

Amelia began drawing a large circle on the floor with the salt. At north, she made a small circle for earth; at east, one for air; at south, the circle for fire; and at west, a circle for water. Then she closed the larger circle at north, never once stepping inside it.

The whole process was slow and deliberate and done with a sense of respect that made Em feel very glad to be a part of something so ancient and solemn.

Soft footfalls reached them, and a second later, Beckett appeared at the bottom of the stairs, packages in hand. "Your candles and your sage."

Em took them from him. "Thank you."

"You're welcome. I hope it goes well."

"Me, too."

He gave her a quick smile and went back upstairs, shutting the door with a firm *thunk*.

Aunt Amelia waved her hand. Nothing happened that Em could see, so maybe she'd locked the door.

Aunt Amelia pointed to the bag Beckett had brought. "Place a candle at each small circle. Speak the name of the element as you place it and light it."

"What should I light them with?"

Amelia shook her head. "Ideally, your magic, but I realize that's not possible for you yet. There is a book of matches on my desk, in the enamel box. Use those. Leave the sage on my desk as well."

Em did as her aunt asked, taking the box of matches out, then placing the candles and lighting them as she spoke the element names. The candles were pale gold and smelled of honey from the beeswax.

When they had all been lighted, she stepped back to await her aunt's next instructions.

Aunt Amelia came around to stand in front of the south point. She looked at Em. "Step into the circle."

"Okay." Em did, careful not to displace any of the salt. She was nervous now, little tremors zinging through her, but they were mostly the excited kind.

Aunt Amelia stretched out her arms. "Emeranth Marchand Greer, do you enter this circle of your own free will?"

"I do."

"And do you promise to use your magic for good? To keep to the side of light? To put right first?"

"I do."

"This circle binds you even as it opens to you a new path. And while I guide the formation of that path, only you can walk it. The journey is yours alone to take. Are you ready to walk that path?"

"I am."

"Then with great love and honor in the trust you've placed in me, I hereby call fire to initiate you and bring your power fully upon you."

At that, the candle flames sprang up and spread, forming a dome of fire over Em. Her pulse kicked up, her heart racing, but she held on to the belief that the fire wouldn't hurt her. It hadn't when she'd kissed Deacon, so why should it now?

The memory of that kiss did nothing to slow her pulse, but she had this.

Until fire covered the ground beneath her and filled the rest of the space inside the dome. She held her breath for a moment, a panicked reaction, but a second later, she realized that the fire felt no different than air. A little warm, maybe, but there was no burning, no pain, no intense heat.

Just like that kiss.

She smiled and started breathing again.

As if sensing her acceptance, the fire disappeared.

She stared at her aunt. "Is that it? Is it over? Am I initiated?"

"You are. Welcome to your new life."

Em just stood there, a little breathless from it all. "What do I do now?"

"You study and learn and practice. But first, we're going to release this circle, then burn sage and clear the room so it's ready to use again."

"Okay," Em said. She thought about what her aunt had said. "Are you going to be my teacher?"

"I can be. If you wish."

"I do wish. That would be great."

Aunt Amelia smiled. "It's not going to be easy."

"That's okay. I'm not afraid of hard work."

"I sense that about you. It's a good quality." Aunt Amelia's gaze narrowed with sudden challenge. "You can start by extinguishing these candles."

Em took a step forward, fingers at the ready to pinch the flames out.

Aunt Amelia raised her hand. "No. From where you are. Use your magic."

Em nodded, a little unsure, but wanting very much to show her aunt that she could do this. She focused on the candle in front of her, the one at the south point representing fire. She calmed her mind and said, "Out."

The flame sputtered, but remained.

"Believe in yourself and in the power of the word," Aunt Amelia said.

Em repeated it with more feeling. "*Out.*"

The flame vanished in a wisp of smoke.

Em gasped. "I did it."

"You did," Amelia said. She smiled. "Now do it three more times."

CHAPTER TWENTY-SIX

Sleeping on the concrete garage floor was never Deacon's first choice, but when he was covered in flames, it was his only choice. A man on fire couldn't exactly climb into bed and hope to wake up with the house still standing. The downside to keeping the house from incinerating was how sleeping on the garage floor made him feel.

Stiff and achy. Like he was a hundred years older than he really was. Because of that, he lay there for a while, staring through the garage door windows.

It was still dark outside, but late enough that the moon had risen, releasing him from the curse he'd taken on.

He finally mustered the energy to push up to a seated position, thankful he was no longer covered in flames, but wishing every muscle in his body weren't rebelling. Slowly, he reached for his toes, rolling through his vertebrae as he moved forward.

Getting some flying time might help. He leaned back on his hands and sat for a minute longer, but that wasn't helping. Gradually, he got to his feet.

His joints cracked and snapped with the effort. Okay, a hot shower, then some flying time. Hopefully, Jerry wouldn't have another episode for a while.

Scorch marks blackened the floor where he'd been. Not much he could do about that. He toed his boots off, then picked them up and headed for the kitchen quietly so he wouldn't wake Gracie or Bishop. He had to eat something. He hadn't had a bite since taking on Jerry's curse.

Food didn't last long in hands that were eighteen hundred degrees. He knew the temperature, because the last time he'd absorbed Jerry's curse, Deacon had had Shep measure the flames with the infrared gun they had at the firehouse.

That level of heat pretty much made eating impossible. Besides, any food that would survive would be too burned to taste good.

His stomach grumbled in agreement as he opened the fridge. Lots of sandwich fixings, but he wasn't in the mood for that. He wanted a meal and was hoping for some of the roasted chicken from last night's dinner, but Bishop must have been here already, because the only thing left from last night's meal was the salad Gracie had made to go with it.

She always made salad. And she was the only one who ever ate it.

He shook his head as he closed the fridge. Old habits died hard.

Well, the diner was open. He could fly over there and get something. After he showered and put on clean clothes. He sniffed his shirt sleeve. It smelled like smoke. Not a bad price to pay, considering they hadn't burned off. That seemed to be the way of the curses, though. However they affected the original owner, they also affected him.

It could always be worse.

In general, taking on curses wasn't a fun experience for him, but this one had been different. This one had helped him discover that not only was Em not vulnerable to fire, she was also an exceptional kisser.

He smiled, thinking about that. He started up the stairs to his room, his steps light. There was no telling what the day would bring, but two things he knew for certain: He was going to see her again tonight for Gracie's party, and he was absolutely going to kiss her a second time.

After a long, hot shower that finally got the smoke smell off him and loosened up his stiff body, he changed into clean clothes, then walked out onto the back deck, shifted into his raven form, and took flight.

The air beneath his wings felt incredible, and when he landed in the park a few blocks from the diner, he felt like himself again. Still starving, too. He returned to his human form and headed for the diner, ready to chow down.

The overcast sky had started to lighten, signaling the sun was on its way up even if it wouldn't be visible.

Still early, though. Most of the houses he passed were dark. A couple lights here and there. One or two folks headed out to their jobs. An equal amount headed in from a night out. Weird hours weren't that weird in Shadowvale.

But the downtown wouldn't be waking up for a while, except for a few places like the diner. The rest of the shops had a few hours yet before their doors were unlocked, though some had special evening hours for citizens who really weren't daytime people.

Seemed to work out well with the after-hours crowd, who appreciated being able to shop like regular folks. As a result, those stores usually had a loyal clientele.

Wasn't all that surprising, really. Everything in Shadowvale worked out like that. After all, the entire place catered to those who lived here in a way that no town outside these gates ever could. There was no need to live your life any differently than anyone else, no matter if you were a cursed supernatural or a cursed human being.

Aside from the curses, the weird magical goings-on, and the lack of sunlight, this place was a freaking utopia.

He sighed as he walked.

If only he didn't feel so trapped here. If only he thought Gracie had a chance for a normal life here.

If only, if only, if only. Those words had become his life's mantra. And they were exactly what was keeping him from being happy. Always wondering what could be.

But now there was Em.

And he really wanted to know what could be with her. But that meant putting Gracie's best interests aside. At least temporarily.

Would he and Em get to the point someday where she might want to leave with him and Gracie? Because if that was the case, he could put his plans on the back burner for a little bit.

He went into the diner and grabbed a booth. It was worth finding out.

Em couldn't believe she was holding in her hand a key to the bakery. It felt like such an important thing. And it was, really. Not just because it was a sign of Nasha's trust in her, but because it represented the chance to earn a living. To finally take care of herself and make her own way.

That was a huge part of her new life.

Maybe not quite as big as the initiation she'd gone through last night, but still a major component.

She smiled at Nasha. "I won't let you down."

"I know." Nasha planted her flour-coated hands on her hips, smudging the sides of her full-body apron. "The fact that you were willing to come in so early on such short notice speaks volumes. It just never occurred to me that we ought to test that machine. I mean, what if it doesn't work? I've got a ton of beans on the way! I'm not sure I can come up with that many coffee-themed desserts if I have to use them up."

Em glanced back at the La Pavoni, gleaming like an enormous chrome jewel. "I'm sure it'll work. Those machines are built to a high standard, designed to work for years without issues."

"Good. Then make me a cup of coffee, and let's see what this thing can do. I hope those beans I brought from home will be all right. The order I placed is due in today, but probably not until noon or later."

"I'm on it, but it'll take about fifteen to twenty minutes for me to prep the machine before I can pull the espresso."

"No problem." Nasha grinned as she walked back to the prep table. "I'm here all day."

Em started for the machine, then paused, unable to stop thinking about something Nasha had said. "One question. How does stuff get delivered here without the town's secrets being revealed?"

Nasha looked up from the scone dough. "All part of the gate's magic."

"So...no one really knows how that works?"

Nasha laughed. "Nope. And none of us have tried to figure it out. At least not that we remember."

"Oh. *Oh.*" Em blinked at what that implied. "Got it."

Nasha returned to the scones she was making, and Em made a beeline straight for the espresso machine.

She went through the steps of prepping the machine. Adding filtered water, plugging it in, letting it warm up, then discharging the water. She was amazed at how it all came back to her even after not working as a barista for a while.

And what a joy it was to use a machine like this, even with the prep.

At last, she was ready. She ground the beans, filled the basket, tamped the grounds in, then pulled the espresso.

It smelled like heaven and looked like liquid silk. She grinned, unable to be anything but pleased with the first cup.

She walked it over to Nasha and presented it. "Here you are."

Nasha took a break from loading scones onto a baking tray. She lifted the cup off its tiny saucer and sipped the coffee. For a moment, she had no reaction.

Then her eyes lit up. "This is amazing. This came out of that machine?"

Em nodded. "It sure did."

"Oh, wow. I had no idea that machine could produce something so delicious." Nasha took another sip. "Deja Brew might be in trouble."

Em grimaced. "Is that going to be a problem?"

"Hah, no." Nasha wiggled her brows. "Nothing wrong with a little healthy competition. That's something we don't have much of in this town. So I'm all for it."

"I don't want to talk myself out of a job, but giving the coffee away like the baked goods could actually cause some bad feelings from the owners of Deja Brew."

Nasha pursed her lips. "Yeah, that's true. We'll sell the coffee. Can you work up some reasonable prices?"

"Sure, but do you have a register?"

"I do, believe it or not. I charge small amounts for special orders. It'll be easy to program in the drinks once you get them to me."

"Sounds good to me. I'll work them up right away. What else would you like me to do?"

"Nothing, really. Not until the shipment comes in. Which won't be for a while, so you might as well go home. Really, everything can wait until tomorrow. Besides, the machine won't be moved out to the coffee bar until then. I have a couple of guys coming in to do it."

"Okay, if you're sure."

"I'm sure. Gracie's party is this evening, and I know you're going to that, so don't worry about setting things up here. Tomorrow is fine for that. In fact, tomorrow can be your official first day if you like."

"Thank you. That sounds great. Are you going to the party?"

Nasha shook her head. "It would be a little awkward. I like Gracie, but since Shep and I didn't work out...you know. Could be weird. And not in a good way."

"Right." Em wasn't sure what *good weird* was, unless it was a Shadowvale thing. "I guess I'll see you tomorrow, then. Well, actually, I'll see you later today when I come back to pick up Gracie's cake with Deacon."

Nasha got a little twinkle in her eye. "So that's how it is now."

Em laughed. "Yeah, something like that."

"All right, see you then."

Before she left, Em turned the espresso machine off and wiped it down, even though it didn't need it. Once outside, she stood on the sidewalk for a moment, just enjoying the day. Since Aunt Amelia had done her initiation, it felt like she was seeing colors for the first time.

Everything was brighter and clearer and more...real. The thought sounded odd, but there was no other way to explain what she was feeling. Like she was just waking up from a long sleep. Or like her life had finally begun.

There was a new joy in her, and it gave her a lightness she'd never experienced before. Maybe it was the initiation. Maybe it was this place.

Maybe it was how, for once in her life, everything was coming together without the possibility of her mother uprooting her life, or doing something equally awful to ruin it all. Em's life was absolutely, positively hers now.

And that was amazing. So was this place.

She couldn't imagine being anywhere else. Her gratitude to her aunt was overflowing to the point that she wanted to do something nice for Amelia.

Em thought about flowers, but her aunt's garden was beyond anything a florist could top. Another loaf of pumpernickel raisin might be nice, but they weren't finished with the first one yet.

She glanced up and down the street, searching for ideas. Then it hit her. She'd hang out until Spellbound opened, then find the perfect witchy gift.

After that, she'd hit the thrift shop and see if she could come up with something fun to wear to Gracie's party. Oh! And she'd need to get a gift. Maybe a book? Gracie seemed like a reader.

Hmm. She should text Deacon.

Until the shops were open, however, she might as well have breakfast.

CHAPTER TWENTY-SEVEN

Deacon's phone buzzed just as he was about to sip his coffee. He braced himself, hoping that it wasn't another curse that needed taking care of. Not today of all days. Not on Gracie's birthday.

But when he looked at the screen, he saw a text from Em, a pleasant surprise that instantly put a smile on his face. He tapped the message to read it.

What does Gracie like? I need some ideas for a birthday present for her!!

His smile stayed put. He quickly texted back. *Your presence is all the present she'll want.*

Yeah, that's nice but for real. Women like gifts. ;)

He chuckled. *She'd be happy with anything.*

You're so helpful.

Fine, he responded. *How about a candle?*

"Yeah, that's not boring at all."

He looked up to see Em sliding into the booth across from him. Her phone was still in her hand. He shook his head. "Where did you come from?"

She grinned. "Magic?"

His brows lifted. "You're that good already, are you?"

"Nah." She tucked her phone away. "Nasha called me in to make sure the espresso machine works before we go live tomorrow. It does, and I finished up over there pretty quickly, so I figured I'd do some shopping. Of course, nothing's open yet, so breakfast seemed like the next logical step."

His day was getting better and better.

She caught her bottom lip between her teeth. "You don't mind me joining you, do you? I mean, if you're meeting someone—"

"Nope." He couldn't stop smiling. People were going to wonder what was wrong with him. Or maybe they'd assume it was someone's curse making him addlebrained. "I already ordered, but we can grab the server."

He stuck his hand up and waved at Lola, the woman who'd taken his order, to let her know they needed her.

She gave him a thumbs-up. "Be right over, Deacon."

Another server dropped off a menu on his way by.

"Great." Em slid it toward her and had a look. "What did you get?"

"Two eggs over easy with pancakes and bacon."

"Oooh, pancakes sound awesome. But if I eat that many carbs, I'm liable to go back to sleep." She perused the menu a little more. "Okay, that's me right there. Roast beef hash with a poached egg."

"I've had that. It's good."

She closed the menu and set it down. "Also, I need coffee. Lots of coffee."

"Didn't you make yourself a cup while you were at the bakery?"

Her mouth rounded into a little O. "Believe it or not, I didn't. It kind of slipped my mind." She laughed. "I was so focused on getting Nasha's right that I just forgot. I really should have made one for myself. Especially since I'll be selling it tomorrow. It's my first official day of work."

"I'll have to come by and try one, then. What did Nasha think of the one you made?"

"She loved it." Something dampened Em's happy expression. "You don't think she was just saying that, do you?"

"Nasha? Not a chance. She's not the type to hold anything like that back."

"Yeah, I guess you're right. Hey!" All of a sudden, she reached out and grabbed his hand. "How are you after being covered in flames? I meant to ask you that sooner, but I got distracted. Plus, you look okay, but were there any side effects?"

Her hand on his made it hard for him to concentrate, but he managed. Mostly. "No, I, uh, I'm good. The curses don't affect me."

"I know you said that, but it's so hard to believe. I'm glad, though." She let go of his hand. "Now back to our original topic."

He had no idea what that had been, but he'd talk to her all day if she wanted.

She laced her fingers together on top of the table. "You have to give me some ideas for Gracie. I want to get her something, even if it's just a little

257

thing. Which is all I can afford until my first paycheck."

"Okay." He thought some. Mostly about how he wanted to hold Em's hand again. "She loves dogs, obviously, so anything dog-related would probably be a hit."

"What else does she like? Does she have any hobbies?"

Mostly, she took care of him and his brothers. Not because she had to, but because she seemed to want to. That was the only reason he and Bishop hadn't moved out. And why Shepherd still came back most nights for dinner. "She likes to cook. She's really good at it. And she likes to read."

But what else did Gracie do? She worked. And took care of them. And other than the occasional lunch out, she stayed home and away from people. All because of her curse.

"Cooking, reading, and dogs? Okay, I can work with that." Em tipped her head. "You okay? You look...sad all of a sudden."

"It's nothing." He made himself smile again. "Just worried that everything goes okay for Gracie's party."

"I'm sure it will."

He nodded. Then Lola came over to bring Em coffee and take her order, leaving him to his thoughts for a moment.

This party was a bad idea. There would be people everywhere, inside and out. And a crowd meant a lot of opportunities for someone to accidentally touch Gracie. He and his brothers never should have given in to her.

But he knew how desperate she was for social interaction. And she'd known they'd be unable to refuse her on her birthday.

Now a sense of foreboding was starting to come over him. And in a place like Shadowvale, you didn't just brush off a feeling like that.

Maybe they could talk her into wearing gloves.

Lola put her hand on the table in front of him. "You need anything else, Deacon? Refill on your coffee? Your food should be right up."

He blinked at Lola's question, trying to think about what she'd said. "A refill would be great. Can you hold my food until Em's is ready?"

Lola smiled knowingly. "I can do that, and I'll be right back with your coffee." Then she was off to the kitchen.

Deacon rubbed his forehead. "What did you order? The hash? I was a little lost in thought there."

"Yes." She nodded. "Are you sure there isn't anything I can do to help you get ready for tonight?"

"No, not really. Around two, Shepherd's going to make up an excuse that he needs Gracie's help with the firehouse books, or something like that. Then once she's out of the house, Bishop and I are going to decorate."

Em gave him a stern look. "Um, I can help decorate, you know. Many hands make light work."

The corner of his mouth hitched up. "Yeah, I guess you could. But won't you want to go home to get ready?"

"I can bring everything with me. No big deal. Then we can still go get the cake together."

"Okay, that would be great."

"What about food? Besides cake, I mean."

He scratched at the stubble on his chin. "We were just going to put out some chips. Pretzels. That kind of thing. You know, plus the cake."

"Are you kidding me?" Em rolled her eyes. "You guys need more help than you realize."

"All right, then, help us. What else do we need?"

"More than chips. How about Bishop decorates while we go to the store? You do have a grocery store here, don't you?"

"Yes. The Green Grocer. It's also open twenty-four hours."

"Perfect. Do they have a deli?"

"Yes."

"Even better. Call them and order some platters. Sandwiches, deviled eggs, veggies and dip, stuff like that. You have to feed people."

"Hmm. I suppose you're right."

Lola came back with a carafe to top off both their coffees, and behind her was another server with their food.

Plates in front of them, they dug in, pausing occasionally to finish sorting out the party menu.

He was infinitely happy that Em had saved them from starving everyone, so when she gave him a coy look, he stopped a forkful of pancakes halfway to his mouth. "What's up?"

"I have some news to share."

"Do tell." He ate the pancakes, just catching a drip of syrup before it left the fork.

"I'm a real witch now. I went through the initiation last night."

"Oh?" For some reason, he found that very appealing. But then, he liked women who were ambitious. "That's really cool. Congratulations."

She looked very pleased. "Thanks. I don't really know much more about being a witch than I did yesterday, but I'm on my way to learning."

"What's your first big spell going to be?"

She blinked a few times. "I have no idea. I guess I should think about that."

He laughed. "I'm not sure you have to have a first big spell, but then, I'm not a witch, so what do I know?"

"Speaking of…" Her eyes narrowed. "What are you? The not-knowing is killing me."

There was no point in not telling her. She was staying. And she'd find out sooner or later. Everyone in town knew. He was kind of surprised no one had told her. "I'm a raven shifter. My whole family is. Except…Gracie. I mean, she is one, but she's never been able to shift."

"Oh. I'm so sorry to hear that. Does it bother her?"

"It does, although she'd never let on that it does, but I know it's something she thinks about."

"I'm sure."

The look in Em's eyes was the same curious one he was getting used to. The one that said she had more questions. And since she was staying, he was happy to answer them. Some of them. "What else do you want to know?"

She pushed the hash around on her plate. "Your family has been here a long time, huh?"

"We have. Your aunt knew my grandmother and invited her to Shadowvale as soon as the town was established. My grandfather was one of the first to arrive at the gates. One of the called, as we say."

"The called?"

"Those who feel summoned here. Or those who somehow find their way here."

"Am I one of those?"

He thought about that. "Not really. You were trying to find this place. That doesn't happen as often."

"But the gates let me in."

He nodded. "True."

"So where do I fit?"

"I'm not sure." He stabbed another bite of pancake.

Lola came by and warmed up their coffees again. Neither spoke until she left, then Em had another question.

"Why tell me now about what you really are when you wouldn't tell me before?"

"Because before now I was convinced you'd be leaving. But since you're staying, not telling you makes no sense. It's not a secret. You could have asked just about anyone, and they could have told you."

She snorted. "I never thought about doing that. Except I did ask Beckett and my aunt, and both said it was up to you to tell me, which made me think it was a secret."

He smiled. "Beckett's good people."

"He is." She stirred sugar into her cup. "So what else didn't you tell me because you thought I was leaving?"

He picked up a strip of bacon, bit off the end of it, and gave her question some thought. He gestured with the remaining piece of bacon. "I might not have mentioned some of the more famous people that live here."

She leaned in. "You showed me Dr. Jekyll. He seems pretty famous. Who else is here?"

He paused a second. "You'll find out eventually, so I guess there's no point in holding back."

"Nope. None. Spill."

"Well, for one...Bianca Wynters."

Em made a face. "I have no idea who that is."

"She used to go by another name." He paused for dramatic effect. "Snow White."

Em's jaw dropped open. "Shut up. She's not real."

"Pretty sure she'd argue that with you." He grinned. "She runs the Red Apple Bed and Breakfast. Although it's really more of a boarding house."

"No way." Em was almost vibrating with interest. "How many rooms?"

He took another dramatic pause. "Seven."

"For real?"

He nodded, then leaned in for more impact. "And she only rents them to the miners. Who also happen to be—"

"If you say dwarfs, I'm going to lose it."

He shrugged. "I won't say it, then."

Her voice came out in a hushed tone, like she was trying to hold herself back from yelling. "Are you telling me the Seven Dwarfs work in the gem mines?"

"Yes. Of course, there are others. But this particular group is quite loyal to Bianca."

Em shook her head, eyes wide. "This place."

"She almost didn't move here, what with the Brothers Grimm living in the Dark Acres and them having history, but there's really no better place for a vampire, so she relented."

Em's mouth opened again. "Snow White is a *vampire*?"

Deacon chuckled. "Why else do you think an evil queen wanted her heart? Or how she gained such beauty? Or inspired such devotion from a troop of dwarfs, who could have been plying their trade as mercenaries anywhere else? Oh, she's something, all right."

Em went quiet for a moment. "Will she be at Gracie's party?"

Deacon almost choked on his food. "Uh, no. She rarely leaves the Red Apple. Trust me, it's for the best. The dwarfs would come with her, and they party like frat boys with nothing to lose."

Em blinked a few times. "What have I gotten myself into?"

CHAPTER TWENTY-EIGHT

Em's breakfast with Deacon had done nothing to dampen her enthusiasm for her new hometown. If anything, she'd decided that living in Shadowvale was never going to be dull. She'd kind of thought she wanted dull, but to her that meant a life without drama.

The kind her mother constantly produced. The kind that wore a person down and had them constantly looking over their shoulder, constantly waiting for the other shoe to drop.

Shadowvale drama was altogether different. For one thing, it didn't involve her. For another, it was all pretty interesting. And while some of the residents and their curses could be dangerous, she never felt like she was in danger.

Except maybe when facing down Thoreau in her aunt's garden, a situation she didn't intend to repeat.

No, breakfast with Deacon had only increased her sense of joy. Partly because getting to see him was an unexpected surprise. He'd been so open, too. Telling her about being a raven shifter.

How cool was that? He could fly.

Fly!

At that very moment, she was passing Bewitched Broomsticks, which halted her forward movement. She stared at the model in the window. The handle was a sleek metallic blue with scrolling silver pinstriping, and at the end, its silver-white bristles were bound with silver thread.

As brooms went, it was gorgeous. And clearly not made for sweeping.

But she was far too new a witch to invest in such a thing. At a minimum, she'd have to talk to her aunt about the subject. Em didn't even know if all witches could ride broomsticks. She'd certainly never seen her aunt on one. Maybe it was a skill only a few could master.

Although if that was the case, why would there be a shop selling them?

She wanted to go in and look around, but there'd be time for that later.

Right now, she had a present to buy for Gracie, a thank-you gift for Aunt Amelia, and a trip to the thrift store for a possible party outfit.

And all before she had to be at Deacon's.

First stop was the thrift store, Stella's Bargain Bin. From the outside, it looked more like a boutique than a secondhand shop.

A little bell jangled when she went in. The older woman behind the counter, with blazing-red hair and black cat-eye glasses, waved at her over the game of solitaire she had spread out before her. "Hi there, honey. Welcome to the Bin. I'm Stella Kittridge. You need help finding something?"

"Just looking around at the moment, thank you."

Stella nodded and went back to her game. "Just holler if you do."

"Okay."

A few racks in and Em realized that most of what was in the shop was designer goods. It was like poking around in a rich woman's closet.

Naturally, Em very quickly found a little black dress that called to her. It draped off one shoulder and had a spray of jet crystals across the front, making it sparkle with every movement. It seemed to be in pristine condition. She couldn't find a price tag on it, but she figured there was no point in asking if it didn't fit. She took it to the dressing room, fingers crossed that it worked.

It did. She slipped out to look at herself in the big full-length mirror.

"Oh, you look marvelous in that, darling." Stella came over. Her leopard-print pants and fuzzy pink sweater made for quite a combination, but Em couldn't help but like the woman.

Hard not to like someone who clearly didn't care what anyone else thought.

Em turned to see herself from another angle. She'd never had something this nice in her life. "It is really pretty."

"It was made for you."

"Thanks." As Em turned, she saw a little white tag dangling from a string near the side seam.

Funny, she could have sworn that wasn't there before. She crossed her fingers again that the price was made for her budget. She checked the tag. And swallowed. Fifty dollars. So much for bargains.

Stella waved a hand, her pink rhinestone nails throwing rainbow sparks in the light. "I forgot to tell you when you came in. All black clothes are seventy-five percent off today."

Em looked at the tag again and did the calculation. "So this dress would be twelve fifty?"

"I'd have to check my calculator." She laughed. "Math was my late husband's job. Say, I don't think I've seen you before. Are you new around here? We don't get a lot of new people."

"Yes, I'm Amelia's niece. I've just moved here."

"Oh, honey, then today is your lucky day. First-time customers get a twenty-dollar gift card. You'd better do some more shopping, or I'm going to owe you money."

Em wasn't sure what to say. "Really?"

"You betcha."

"Thank you. I'm definitely getting this dress."

"You'd better. No one's ever looked that good in it, I assure you." Stella went back to her cards.

Em changed out of the dress, then took it up to the counter. The glass display case held a variety of items, including an antique-looking tiger brooch.

She pointed at it. "Could I look at that pin?"

"Sure thing." Stella got it out and put it on a little black velvet pad. "You know, your aunt would love this. I keep meaning to call her and tell her about it."

Em checked the price. Ten dollars. "I'll take it. I've been looking for a gift for her, and this would be perfect."

"I'll put it in a little velvet pouch for you. Would that be good?"

"That would be great." Em glanced around. There was so much she hadn't looked at yet, but she lived here now, so she could come back anytime she liked. "I love your shop. It's really something. I have a feeling I'm going to become a regular."

Stella grinned, crinkling her gold-dusted eyelids. "Always love to hear that."

"I'm Emeranth, by the way. But I go by Em most of the time."

"Nice to meet you, Em. And nice to have you in the shop." Stella wrote up a quick receipt. "Here you go."

Em paid, amazed to be getting away so cheaply.

Stella handed her a pink shopping bag with the store name on the side in black. "You come back anytime you like."

"I will, thanks." Still smiling, she walked on a little farther and came to a home goods store. She went in and, after a little digging, found a cute apron with dogs on it that seemed like something Gracie might like.

Em bought that, then on her way back to her car, stopped into another shop and bought a birthday card. Hopefully, her aunt would have some wrapping paper.

Feeling very pleased with her purchases, she drove back to Indigo House. Today was a good day. A really good day.

She found Beckett in the kitchen settling down at the counter for lunch. "Hey."

"Hey to you, Miss Em." He glanced at her bags. "Doing some shopping?"

"Yes, and I need some wrapping paper for Gracie's gift. Please tell me there's some in the house?"

"You'll find everything you need in the wrapping room."

"There's a wrapping room?" Of course there was.

He nodded as he picked up his sandwich. "It's part of the craft room, really."

"Oh, I think I know where that is. Great, thank you."

Chef came in with a tray of ingredients. "Would you like some lunch?"

"No, thank you. I had a big breakfast. But I'll probably grab something later. No need to make me anything."

"As you wish." Chef set about organizing the things she'd brought in.

Em looked at Beckett again. "Is Aunt Amelia going to Gracie's party?"

"That's the plan so far. Although I think she'll probably only stay long enough to drop off her gift and wish Gracie a happy birthday. Gatherings like that are not her thing."

"Understood. Okay, I'm off to wrap and get ready. I'm helping Deacon and Bishop decorate and get the food set up."

"That's very kind of you." Beckett laughed. "Those boys could use the help, I have no doubt."

"Yeah, they were just going to serve chips." Em rolled her eyes before heading off to the craft room with a laugh.

In the next hour, she got Gracie's present wrapped, then packed a small bag for herself with her new black dress and all the accessories she'd need to get ready for the party. With that done, she went to find her aunt to give her the tiger brooch.

Aunt Amelia was on the back patio, reading.

Em approached with the little velvet bag held behind her back. "Hi."

Aunt Amelia looked up from her book. "Hello there. How has your day been?"

"Really good. I like it here very much."

"I'm glad to hear that. I hope that never changes." She tipped her book toward the chair next to her. "Sit."

Em took the seat. "I want to thank you again for everything you've done for me." She held out the little black pouch. "This isn't much, but I wanted to get you something."

"You didn't need to do that." But Aunt Amelia's smile told Em that it had still been a good idea.

"Like I said, it's nothing big."

Amelia took the bag and opened it. "How perfect. I love it." She opened the catch, reached up, and pinned it to her turban. "How does it look?"

"Very sparkly. And like something a woman with a pet tiger would definitely wear."

Amelia laughed. "Thank you. That was a thoughtful gift."

Her smile faded suddenly. Em frowned. "What's wrong?"

Amelia sighed and looked out at the garden. "I just worry that eventually you may not be as thankful for what I've done by allowing you to stay."

Em put her hand over her aunt's. "I promise, whatever happens, I will never blame you for anything that goes wrong. I'm an adult. It was my decision to stay here."

Amelia nodded, but looked unconvinced. "I hope you always think that."

CHAPTER TWENTY-NINE

Having breakfast with Em had put Deacon in such a good mood that he knew Gracie would pick up on it if she saw him. That meant she'd probably give him some grief about it, too.

Just like she'd really let him have it if she saw him polishing his good shoes. Fortunately, he was tucked away in his bedroom.

The thing was, his mood was so good he didn't care if she teased him about anything. In fact, he'd probably tell her all about his breakfast with Em, especially because it would be a great diversion if it seemed like Gracie suspected something was up concerning her birthday party.

After all, at the moment she thought her party was just her brothers making dinner for her, followed by cake from Black Horse.

She had no idea the house would be filled with people. The RSVPs were at close to seventy-five, and he had no doubt there would be plenty who would show up without having responded to the invite.

He couldn't wait to see her face. He wasn't sure what would surprise her more—the crowd they'd invited, or the sight of her brothers in suits. They'd all agreed to dress up, because one of the things Gracie always harped on was how they didn't have any nice family pictures. She'd get one tonight. They also had a photographer coming.

He sighed. The things he did for his sister. The last time he'd been in a suit had been for a funeral. At least this was a much better reason.

So far, though, he hadn't seen Gracie since getting back from breakfast. She was in her office working. Easy to tell, because the door was shut and he could hear the keyboard clicking away.

He checked the time. Shep would be calling very soon.

That meant Em would be arriving.

He smiled. He did a lot of that lately. Because of her.

He finished with his shoes, put the kit away, and heard Bishop's truck pull up outside.

Deacon washed his hands, then jogged downstairs to fill his brother in, meeting him in the foyer. "Hey, Em's coming over to help. And she says we need more than chips and dip."

Bishop made a face. "We have cake."

"We have almost eighty people coming over. We need food. Don't sweat it. Em's going to help me. I ordered a bunch of platters from the Green Grocer. Cold shrimp, little sandwiches, fruit and cheese, veggies with hummus, deviled eggs, some fancy olive-and-pickle tray, all kinds of stuff."

Bishop's brows went up. "That was probably a good idea."

"I know it was. Em's going with me to get the cake, too, then we'll be back to finish the decorating with you."

"Where's Gracie?"

Deacon jerked his thumb over his shoulder. "In her office working."

"Shep should be calling any—"

The phone rang.

The brothers went still, listening. The ringing stopped after the third. They looked at each other, but still said nothing. Shepherd would have to play his part convincingly to get Gracie out of the house, but once she got to the firehouse, he'd also have to work hard to keep her there.

She knew her stuff when it came to numbers and computers, but word had it one of the firemen was especially gifted at screwing up computers, and Shep had put him on it. Not before making a complete backup of everything, however. Shepherd hadn't become fire chief by being foolhardy.

A few more seconds and the sound of a door opening and closing could be heard from the other side of the house. Where Gracie's office was.

"The kitchen," Bishop said.

Deacon nodded, and both men took off for that room.

They were lounging against the counter, chatting with great nonchalance when she came in.

"There's our birthday girl," Bishop said. He went to hug her.

She put her hands up, cringing. "Don't hug me when you're all sweaty and covered in sawdust."

He laughed. "Hey, I was working."

She shot him a judgy look. "Shouldn't you still be working?"

"I'm not allowed to come home for a break?"

She eyed him suspiciously. "I guess." Then she looked at Deacon. "You're awfully smiley."

Deacon leaned back a little more. "Why shouldn't I be? It's a very special day."

Gracie grinned. "True."

He held on to his smile. "It's not every day I have breakfast with Em."

She swatted his arm. "For one thing, you've had breakfast with her three days in a row. For another, I want to be mad at you, but I'm very glad to hear you two are getting on so well. For a third, that wasn't the special day I was referring to."

"I know." He winked at her. "Happy birthday."

"Thanks, but don't change the subject. How was breakfast? And how did you end up eating with her? I thought the tour was over."

"It is, but we ran into each other at the diner. She's staying, you know. She got a job at Black Horse."

"She is? She did? That's great. I really like her." Gracie bit her lip. "How do you feel about her? I mean, you're spending a lot of time with her, so…"

Bishop snorted and tipped his head back. "Here we go."

She sighed. "Both of you settle down. I wish we could talk about this some more, Deacon, and we will later, but Shep says he's having major computer issues over at the station. For the record, though, I totally approve of Em. She's awesome. So try not to screw it up."

Deacon straightened. "Hey."

Bishop grinned. "What's going on at the firehouse?"

Gracie frowned. "I don't know. Shep said he can't find any of the payroll records, and his expense reports all look like they're in Chinese."

Deacon played dumb. "You're going over there?"

"I have to." She shook her head as she took her purse off a hook by the door and slung it over her shoulder. "If he plays with it anymore, he'll probably delete everything. I'll be lucky if he hasn't done that already."

Bishop nodded. "Sounds like a big job."

"I have no doubt it will be."

Deacon tried to look sympathetic. "Well, don't worry, we'll have dinner waiting for you when you're done."

She glanced at him. "Are you really not going to tell me what you're making?"

"Hey," Bishop said. "You already know you're getting a cake from Black Horse. Let's not ruin the surprise any further."

She frowned at both of them. "The surprise will be surviving my brothers' cooking." With a long-suffering sigh, she headed for the door. "Don't destroy my kitchen."

They looked at each other, trying not to laugh. "We won't."

As soon as she left, he and Bishop went upstairs to get out the decorations they'd hidden away.

A few minutes later, another car pulled into the driveway. Deacon turned toward the front of the house. That had to be Em.

He went back downstairs to get the door. It was her. She got out of her car and walked up the front steps. She'd changed into jeans and a T-shirt with a little cardigan over it, but had a small bag with her. Her clothes for the party, he assumed.

Really, he didn't care what she wore. She always looked great. "Hi."

She stopped at the door. A loose strand of hair dangled in her face. She blew it out of her eyes, pursing her lips in the most enticing way. "Hi."

He really needed to kiss her again. Instead, he pointed at the bag. "Is that your change of clothes?"

She lifted it a little. "Yep. And my present for Gracie."

"Good."

With a look of utter amusement on her face, she tipped her head at the house. "Are you going to let me in?"

He sighed. She made him so dumb. He was going to have to work on that. "Yes, sorry." He moved out of the way. "Gracie just left."

"I know." She walked into the foyer. "I got here too early, so I waited down on the next block until I saw her car go by."

"Good thinking. I'll show you the guest room. You can put your bag in there, then you can have that space to get ready in. There's a bathroom and everything." He sounded like a rambling idiot. A bathroom and everything. What was that supposed to mean?

No wonder Gracie had told him not to screw it up.

"That would be great, thanks."

He led her down the hall and past the kitchen. Well, almost past the kitchen.

Bishop popped out, all smiles and personality. "Hi there."

"Hi," Em said. "You must be Bishop."

His brows lifted a little. "Good guess. Or did one of my siblings make it easy and tell you I'm the handsome one?"

"No one mentioned that, no." She snorted. "And actually, it was pretty easy to figure out who you are. See, I'm *very* acquainted with Deacon, and I know Gracie is on her way to help Shepherd at the firehouse, so you have to be Bishop. Process of elimination, really."

A little of the sparkle left his eyes, but Deacon refrained from laughing. Bishop did so enjoy being admired. A weakness of his youthful ego.

Then Em laughed softly and tipped her head at Bishop. "Also, you have a leaf in your hair."

Bishop put his hand to his head and found the offending greenery. He muttered something about needing to shower and went off to his room.

A new fondness for Em sprang up in Deacon.

She leaned in closer, speaking softly. "Did I upset him? I didn't mean to."

Deacon laughed. "He probably expected you to be overwhelmed by his boyish charm and rakish good looks. Most women are. According to my sister, he's the one brother who doesn't need help with the fairer sex."

Em's mouth bent in a wry little smile, and she took a step toward him. There was something almost…wicked in her eyes. "Does that mean you do?"

His tongue stuck to the roof of his mouth as his core temperature shot up a few hundred degrees. Her perfume danced under his nose, enticing him to move closer. "I…probably."

She lightly placed a fingertip on his chest, a touch so soft it should have been barely noticeable.

It almost knocked him down.

Her smile turned coy. "What kind of help do you need, Deacon? What kind of help could I provide? Because I am *willing* to help."

He wanted to kiss her again, more than anything else in the world. Until they were both senseless. Until time disappeared. The urge was so great, he decided to go for broke and found his voice again. "All kinds."

"Like?"

He put his hands on her hips. "Kissing."

Her brows shot up in obvious amusement. "You need to practice that, do you?"

He nodded. And backed her against the wall.

She let out a soft little, "Oh."

He didn't need further encouragement. He leaned in, pressing against her as he captured her mouth.

Another sound escaped her, a mewl of pleasure. It fueled him. Made his grip more possessive.

Her hands cupped the back of his head, pulling him closer. Her teeth grazed his bottom lip, igniting every nerve in his body.

He couldn't breathe, couldn't think, couldn't do anything but kiss her. She had a power over him like no curse he'd ever felt before, but this woman was no curse. She was a gift.

But now was not the time or place to unwrap that gift.

Reluctantly, he ended the kiss. They had a lot of work to do, and kissing her wasn't going to accomplish any of it, unfortunately.

She gazed at him, dreamy-eyed and openmouthed. "You lied to me."

"I did?"

"You don't need to practice your kissing." She laughed suddenly, like something funny had just occurred to her. "Unless you want to practice it with me."

He laughed a little, too, then shook his head and pressed his lips to her temple, breaking the contact to whisper, "You do something to me, Em. Is it your magic? Are you putting a spell on me?"

She looked up at him, her gaze so bright it seemed filled with stars. "I wouldn't even know how."

He was in deep trouble. He liked her way too much. He took her hand. "I'm not sure I'd care if you were bewitching me at this point. I like you. A lot."

She grinned, glancing down at the floor for a moment. "I like you, too."

"Good. There's only one thing I ask if we're going to do this. Because it seems like we are, right? Doing this? Us?"

"Yes. It seems like we are." Earnestness shone in her eyes. "What's the one thing?"

"That we be honest with each other. No game playing. If things change, we talk about it."

She nodded. "Yes. One hundred percent. I want that, too."

"Okay, then we understand each other."

"We do."

He smiled. "Let's drop your bag in the guest room and go pick up some food. We have a party to get ready for."

Chapter Thirty

Cloud nine was for ordinary happiness, Em thought. She was on cloud ten. That's where the deliriously blissful, possibly-falling-in-love people hung out.

And she was right there with them.

Even though she was actually in Deacon's truck. She smiled over at him. "You ordered a bunch of platters?"

"I did. Probably a few more than we'll really need. You'll see."

"Did you already get ice cream?"

"Ice cream?"

"For the cake?" She snorted. "You boys don't throw a lot of birthday parties, do you?"

"No, we don't. None of us really celebrate ours. But you know, for Gracie we'd do anything."

Em nodded. "That's nice. It's very sweet how much you guys look after her."

"We have to."

He didn't say more on the subject, but it seemed like he'd been about to. Like he had been on the verge of telling her why Gracie needed so much care from her brothers. Maybe it was nothing. Maybe it was just how a family acted. Em wouldn't know, really.

It had to have something to do with Gracie's curse. Deacon hadn't come close to sharing that with Em, and she hadn't asked him. She wasn't going to ask Gracie either.

Em had already had it drilled into her that asking was rude. If people wanted you to know, they told you.

If she was going to fit in here, she had to abide by that.

And besides, Gracie would share when she was ready. Em felt certain of that. They were destined to become good friends. It was inevitable, really. Especially if she and Deacon kept going in the direction they were headed.

Which wasn't something she was going to spend hours thinking about. Whatever was going to happen...she was just going to let it. Easy was good. And that's what she wanted out of her new life. Easy. Low stress. No drama.

Even if Shadowvale was sort of all about drama, it was also the kind of place where being yourself was okay. No explanations, no excuses, just abide.

That part appealed to her immensely. Still wasn't going to make her suddenly start sharing her unfortunate past with everyone, though.

As far as Em was concerned, her history was just that—history. As gone as her mother was locked up.

Putting all that behind her was the only way she could move forward.

"You're awfully quiet," Deacon said.

She smiled. "Sorry. Just thinking about how much I like it here."

He nodded. "I'm glad you feel that way, but it's okay if you change your mind about this place, too, you know. Someday, I mean. Not now." He shrugged. "I just mean…"

"That if I ever want to leave, you won't fault me for it."

"Right. That." His mouth thinned for a moment, then he took a breath. "And when or if that day comes that you want to leave, I'm open to discussing it. Just so you know."

She studied him for a few seconds. "You really don't like it here, do you?"

"I like it more lately." He glanced at her, smiling. "But for the most part, I'd like to get free of here. Like to get Gracie out, too, but that's a tougher job to accomplish."

"Because of her curse?" Em held her hands up. "I'm not asking what it is, just assuming that's what makes it hard for her to leave."

He nodded. "At least here, people know to give her space. In the outside world, that won't be the case. We'd both need to be cured before we can go, but her especially. Hers is worse than mine, for sure. Your aunt said…"

"Said what?"

He shook his head, smiling again. This time, it looked a little forced. "Never mind. Let's not focus on all that today. We have a party to throw. And a ton of work to do."

As much as Em wanted to know what Amelia had said, she let it go and changed the subject. "You think Bishop will actually get anything done while we're gone?"

Deacon pulled into the Green Grocer's parking lot and found a spot. "I have my doubts." He put the truck in park and looked at her. "Which is why we need to get back as soon as we can. I love my brother, but when it comes to anything outside his own business or women, he sometimes lacks motivation."

"Even where Gracie is concerned?"

"No, not so much with her, but the thing is, he knows we're coming back to help. So why put in too much effort until we're there to pitch in?" Deacon raked a hand through his hair. "I don't mean to make it sound like he's lazy, but Bishop has definitely had an easier path in life than the rest of us. Things just seem to fall into his lap sometimes."

"Some people are like that."

They got out and went into the store. Deacon grabbed a shopping cart.

"Deli?" Em asked.

He nodded. "Yep. Then frozen foods for ice cream."

Em looked around. It was one of the nicest grocery stores she'd been in, but then, she was learning fast that Shadowvale didn't skimp on providing its citizens with the best of things. "You already have paper goods, then?"

Deacon slowed a little. "Paper goods?"

"Plates, cups, napkins, utensils. You have how many people coming?"

"At least eighty. And I see where you're going. We don't have enough for that many."

"Then we need a trip down whatever aisle stocks party supplies, too."

He rubbed his forehead. "I am so glad you showed up."

She grinned. "And I'm so glad you think that. Also happy to help."

Forty-five minutes later, they had everything they needed, and possibly more, which seemed to be what Deacon was aiming for. He'd said twice that he'd rather be oversupplied than run out of something.

Next stop was Black Horse for the cake.

As they were walking toward the bakery, Em turned to Deacon. "How big of a cake is this if it's going to feed eighty people?"

"It's just a standard cake, but then I ordered a sheet cake in the same flavors. That way, Gracie has a pretty cake and a practical cake."

"You thought of that, and yet you were just going to serve chips?"

He held the door for her. "Yeah, no. Nasha suggested that."

She paused, putting a hand on his chest and pretending like getting to touch him had anything to do with the conversation they were having. "I like how you listen to women. That's a very attractive quality in a man."

He smiled, looking very pleased with her compliment. "I do what I can."

Em went up to the counter. "We're here to pick up the cake for Gracie Evermore. Cakes, I guess I should say."

"Hey, Em." Brighton, one of the other employees, nodded. "They're on the racks ready to go. I'll go get them."

"Why don't you let me help?" Deacon said. "I know there's two."

"Sure," Brighton said. "Come on back."

Em hooked her thumb toward the street. "I'll get the door for you guys."

A couple minutes later, everything was loaded up. That put the cab of the truck almost at capacity. Several bags were already in the bed.

Deacon got them headed for home. "Bishop better have done something."

"Don't worry," Em said. "We'll get it all taken care of. I'll put all the food away if you like."

"That would be great."

She looked into the back seat. "There's no way all of this is going to fit in your fridge, is there?"

"No, but we have a second one in the garage, and it's mostly empty. That should take care of it."

"Okay, good."

By the time they pulled into the driveway, they had a game plan. Deacon would light a fire under

Bishop, as needed, and then the two of them would get to work decorating the deck and backyard. Em would take care of the food and setting up the dining room table for the buffet area, then she'd join them to finish decorating the inside of the house.

If all went well, Gracie would be totally surprised.

They got everything into the house and got to work. The next few hours passed in a whirlwind. Shep texted every so often to let them know Gracie was still stuck on his computer problems and showed no signs of giving up.

At last, there wasn't much left to be done except get themselves ready and greet the guests who would be arriving shortly.

The three of them went to change.

Deacon and Bishop made it back downstairs and into the kitchen, but Em wasn't out yet, so Deacon guessed she was still in the guest room getting ready.

Bishop adjusted his tie. "Is it supposed to be this tight? It feels like it's choking me."

"That's what ties do."

"Let's ditch them." Bishop nodded like he was trying to persuade Deacon what a good idea that was.

Deacon didn't need persuading. "I guess. But if Gracie wants them on for the picture—"

"We'll put them back on." Bishop already had his undone.

Deacon started loosening his, too.

The soft *click-clack* of heels came down the hall.

While Deacon was still working on his tie, Bishop let out a low whistle that was half human, half raven, a sure sign he'd spotted something noteworthy.

"Don't you both look nice?"

Deacon turned at the sound of Em's voice. His fingers fell away from the knot of silk at his throat as his jaw went south.

She'd piled her hair up on top of her head, exposing the slim column of her neck and, thanks to her body-hugging dress, the strong lines of one shoulder as well. A few tendrils of hair had escaped—on purpose or not, he had no idea—but they added a casualness to her look that made her seem very approachable. Very girl-next-door-who-just-happens-to-be-stunning.

And heart-stoppingly sexy.

Until now, he'd never realized how tantalizing a glimpse of a woman's collarbone could be. He swallowed, finding his voice. "Bishop, go check the front door for guests."

"There's no one at—"

"Go. Now." Deacon couldn't take his eyes off Em. He needed a moment alone with her.

"Fine." With a sigh, Bishop trudged off.

Deacon held his hands out to Em. "You look amazing. You're the most beautiful woman, witch or otherwise, I've ever seen."

She smiled and took his hands. "Thank you very much. I feel pretty. And by the way, you look pretty hot yourself."

He pulled her closer. "I know this is Gracie's night, but I'm going to have a hard time paying attention to anyone but you."

She slipped one hand free to rest it on his chest. "You're making me blush."

He softly kissed the tip of her nose. "Thank you for helping with all this, but more than that, thanks for not being put off by me. I know when we first met, I was…"

"Grumpy?" She laughed. "It's okay. I don't mind that side of you. You haven't seen me at my worst yet either, so don't fall in love just yet."

"Might be too late." The words were out before he could stop them, but he didn't care. They'd agreed to be honest with each other. That was about as honest as he could get.

Her eyes widened, and she let out a soft gasp. "Deacon."

He shook his head. "You don't have to say anything. In fact, I don't expect you to. But you deserve to know that I haven't been this happy, or this content, in a long time."

She smiled. "Me either."

Then she leaned in and kissed him on the mouth.

The doorbell chimed, breaking them apart.

They both laughed. She brushed her thumb across his bottom lip. "Lipstick," she said.

"That's okay. I don't mind being a marked man." He tipped his head toward the front of the house and the sound of Bishop greeting people. "Come on, let's get this party started."

She gave him an appraising look. "As far as I'm concerned, it already has."

CHAPTER THIRTY-ONE

Em stood by the gift table she'd decorated with pink crepe paper ribbon and silver paper stars, just taking a quick breather and admiring the festivities. The party had been in full swing for about two hours now.

Gracie had been well and truly surprised. She'd quickly run upstairs and changed into more celebratory attire, then had joined the mob and hadn't stopped smiling since.

Neither had Em, really.

She'd never been to a party like this. Between relocating constantly and her mother's con games, the only parties Em had gone to were typically orchestrated by Manda to set up a mark.

But this? This was a real party. With real people. And the only goal was to have a good time.

Which was happening in abundance. The big deck off the back of the house had become an impromptu dance floor, and all over the house people were clustered in groups having lively conversations. And Gracie, the party princess in her tiara (supplied by her brothers, along with a matching one for Tinkerbelle), held court in the main living room, with Tinkerbelle on her lap and surrounded by friends.

Em's cheeks hurt from laughing and smiling and talking to so many people. She'd never remember all their names, but she was working on it. Some she already knew, which was really cool.

Not just a real party, but a party where she knew people. Sure, one of them was her aunt, who'd shown up briefly in a gorgeous ivory caftan and matching turban with Em's tiger brooch proudly displayed on the knot.

Thankfully, she'd left the actual tiger at home.

And Stella, who'd worn a strapless leopard-print jumpsuit and gold heels, revealing a figure that seemed to defy her years.

But then, this was Shadowvale. And nothing was really that odd anymore.

Really, though, the best part of the party was how Deacon kept finding her to check in and see how she was doing. And sneak a kiss.

She smiled even as she noted the ice bucket needed refilling.

How quickly things had fallen into place here. How easily she'd begun this new life. It was, hands down, the best thing that had ever happened to her.

She closed her eyes for a second and took a breath, letting the upswell of gratitude wash over her.

When she opened her eyes, the ice bucket really needed refilling. She scooped it up and headed for the garage fridge where Shep had stored the extra bags of ice.

She filled the bucket, then headed back in.

As she turned down the hall from the garage, she ran smack into Gracie, knocking her down and sending a spray of ice cubes into the air. "Oh my gosh, I'm so sorry. I didn't see you. Are you all right?"

Gracie was on her butt and elbows, her tiara now sideways. "It-it's okay. I'm…fine. I was just going to see if there was another bottle of champagne in the garage fridge."

"There is, but I'll get it. And I'll clean this ice up. You go enjoy yourself. You're not supposed to be working. You're the guest of honor." But something was wrong. Gracie looked like she'd been punched in the gut. "Are you sure you're okay?"

She nodded unconvincingly. "Just, uh, had the breath knocked out of me." Then her mouth bent in a weak smile. "I'm good."

She started to get to her feet. Em shifted the ice bucket to the other side and offered Gracie a hand up.

Gracie didn't take it, just got up on her own. "I'm good," she repeated. Then she cleared her throat. "Thanks for all the help you gave the boys. I know you did a lot of this. That was very kind of you."

"I was happy to do it."

Gracie held on to her odd smile and backed away. "Well, thanks again. See you, uh, in there."

"Right. Gotta grab that champagne." Em stood there as Gracie disappeared, not entirely sure what had happened. Maybe she'd hit Gracie harder than she'd realized, but Gracie didn't want to let on. Em felt awful. She hadn't meant to run into her. Gracie had to know that.

She'd have to check with Deacon and make sure Gracie was all right.

She replaced the ice bucket, then got a towel from the kitchen and gathered up the loose ice, making sure there were no wet spots on the floor. Couldn't have anyone else falling because of a puddle.

She tossed the ice in the laundry room sink, left the wet towel on the washer, and went back to the garage for the champagne. She put the bottle into the cooler at the drink station and realized she hadn't seen Deacon in a little bit. He must be outside.

She did a quick spin through the house and the backyard and found no sign of him.

Oddly, no sign of Gracie either.

A small knot formed in Em's stomach, a feeling that something bad was happening, but she didn't know what it could be. Just that when she felt like this, there was always a reason to listen.

Always. The last time she'd felt like this, the police had shown up that evening to take her mother away.

*

Deacon couldn't imagine what was going on. "You're having a good time?"

Gracie nodded as she shut her office door. "Great time. Or at least I was until…"

Her hands twisted together.

"Until what?" Deacon asked. "What's wrong?"

Gracie sighed, her gaze dropping. "Someone touched me."

He sucked in a breath. "Long enough to—"

"Yes."

She still hadn't made eye contact again. That worried him. "Was it bad?"

She nodded.

He cursed, but in his head only. No need to upset Gracie further. "You going to be okay? I can send everyone home if you want."

"No." But the word was an unpersuasive whisper.

"How about I get Tink and you just hang out here for a while? I'll bring you some cake and ice cream."

She shook her head, finally lifting it to look at him. Her gaze seemed haunted, but then, it usually did when her curse had kicked in. "Don't go."

"Okay, I'll stay here with you." Whatever Gracie needed, he'd provide. Her curse might not be physically debilitating like some others, but it could be worse in some ways.

That was why he had to find a way to cure her and free her from this burden. No one should have to know another person's deepest, darkest secrets. Especially not his tender-hearted little sister.

A tear slipped down Gracie's cheek. "I think…I should tell you—"

"I thought you decided that was a bad idea. That it was an invasion of privacy for you to share what you found out. I mean, is it really bad? Like, do I need to detain someone?"

"Not bad like that, but..." She wiped at the tear, looking away again. "Deac, it was Emeranth. She didn't mean to touch me. In fact, I'm not sure she even realized she did. We just ran into each other in the garage hall."

She let out a deep, shuddering sigh. "I've been pushing you toward her, and I know you've gotten friendly with her so...I feel like I should tell you what I found out. Do you want to know?"

He couldn't answer immediately. Couldn't find the words. If Gracie thought he should know, he probably should. But was that betraying Em? It wasn't her fault that Gracie's curse meant that with a single touch, she could tell what darkness hid in a person's heart.

But he had feelings for Em already. Feelings that could very well translate into a future. How could he move forward knowing that whatever Gracie had found out had upset her this much?

He put his hand over his mouth for a second, weighing his options. "I want to know. But I don't want to know."

Gracie nodded. "I understand. I wish I didn't know."

Telling him would lighten her burden, he understood that. He was stronger than Gracie. He could bear it. "Okay," he said quietly. "Tell me what you found out."

She nodded, then hugged her arms around her torso. "Listen, I've had a couple of glasses of champagne. More than a couple. And some of that punch that Bishop made, and I know there's alcohol in that. All I'm saying is, don't take what I'm about to tell you as gospel. Research it first. I know you can do background checks on people."

"I can." As Shadowvale's peacekeeper, he had access to every criminal database known to mankind, including the big one, the National Crime Information Center. He used them only when he had a very compelling reason. Or sometimes when a new person appeared in town.

He hadn't even thought about doing it with Em. She was Amelia's niece, after all. That seemed to be background check enough. Maybe he'd been wrong.

"Say you'll do it on Em. Promise me. I don't want what I saw to be true. I want it to be some silly misinterpretation due to all the birthday fun I've had."

"I promise. I'll check it all out." He rolled his shoulders, which had gone very tense. "Tell me what you saw."

Gracie took a breath, then blew it out slowly. "Emeranth might not be her real name. She's gone by others. She's been involved in some shady things. She's conned a lot of people out of a lot of money. In fact, her mother is in prison right now."

The words rolled over him, making him numb. "I can't believe that." Em was a good, decent person.

Another tear slipped down Gracie's cheek. "I don't want to either. That's why you have to check it out."

He nodded. "I will."

Gracie wiped her face. "We have to pretend like nothing happened. We have to finish this party with smiles on our faces."

"Right," he said. "There's no reason to do otherwise, until I can run a background check on her."

"Could you do that now?"

"I can start it, but those things take time."

"How long?"

"At least overnight. Maybe longer." He was fortunate to have the kind of access few others had. He understood in the outside world, the kind of info he was after might take days to populate.

"Start it now. I want to know I was wrong. I need to be wrong."

"I want that, too. I'll get it underway."

"Good." She chewed on her bottom lip. "Should I tell Bishop and Shepherd?"

"No, let's keep this between us until we know for sure." He tried to keep his tone light. "Besides, Bishop sucks at hiding his feelings."

"He does, I agree." She let out a breath that she'd seemed to be holding. "In the meantime, until we do know for sure, you have to keep being sweet to her. No different than you've been."

"I will. But that's a hard thing to ask." Especially if she was hiding something like this from him.

Maybe even using him for her own means. And all at the cost of his and Gracie's freedom. What if she wasn't even really Amelia's niece? It would be pretty tough to fool Amelia. And he didn't want to go down that path.

Not yet.

"I know it's going to be hard. But what if I am wrong? I don't want to be the reason things fall apart between you two. I couldn't live with that, Deacon."

"You won't have to. We're going to figure this out." He hesitated.

Gracie's face fell again. "What is it?"

"Nothing." He didn't want to tell her what it would mean if Em was lying to Amelia, too. The chaos that would rain down on this town. He made himself smile. "You're probably right, it was just a false reading brought on by too many bubbly drinks."

A faint, hopeful smile finally curved her mouth. "That's right. That's all it was."

He kept up the optimistic expression. But it was hard to hold on to. Especially when they both knew that whatever Gracie learned from her curse had never been wrong yet.

CHAPTER THIRTY-TWO

Em finally found Gracie out on the deck with Bishop. Deacon was still nowhere to be found, but he'd probably been cornered by someone and was trying to escape the small talk. She smiled at the pair. "Hey there. Gracie, have you given any thought to when you want to open presents?"

Gracie turned stiffly. "I don't know. I guess I could do that now." She looked up at Bishop. "What do you think?"

"Sure." He shrugged. "Have at it."

"Okay." She looked at Em again, but there was something strained about her expression that Em couldn't quite figure out. "You want to gather everyone in the living room, then? We'll just be another minute."

Em nodded. "I'm on it. I haven't seen Deacon in a bit, though. I'm sure he's around. I'll just have to look harder."

"Oh," Gracie said. "He, uh, had to run upstairs to take a phone call. He'll be down as soon as he's done."

"Okay, great." But Em's internal crap detector was going off. What the heck was going on? Was Gracie mad that Em had accidentally knocked her down in the hall? That couldn't be it, could it? It seemed so petty. And so unlike Gracie.

Then it occurred to her what this was.

Gracie's curse. It must have something to do with social interactions, must make it hard for her in some way. That had to be why Deacon had been hesitant about the party.

And why Gracie didn't go out much. It all made sense now.

Poor kid. Em felt for her. If Gracie's curse was social anxiety, it was something a lot of people suffered from, but at least Gracie had the safety of Shadowvale to protect her. Here, people seemed to understand that being different was okay.

Everyone in Shadowvale was weird. Which meant no one was.

She smiled. Heaven help her, but she loved this place. Hard. "See you inside in a bit."

She found Deacon in the kitchen on her last sweep through to gather people for present opening. "Hey."

"Hey." He was cleaning up. Wiping down counters. Busy work that could wait until later.

"Everything okay?"

He nodded. "Yep." Then he smiled. Like he'd suddenly realized he hadn't been. "How's it going out there?"

"Good. Gracie's going to open presents, so we should get everyone into the living room."

"Sounds good. I'll gather whoever's outside."

"Everyone's pretty much gathered. We just need you. We're going to do the cake right after. Then I suspect people may start heading out." She glanced at her watch. "It's getting late. My aunt already left."

"She was here longer than I thought she'd be. She's not one for socializing much."

The socializing comment made Em want to ask about Gracie's curse, but she just smiled instead and kept the conversation on her aunt. "Maybe I can help change that. After all, she did show up tonight."

"True."

She leaned against the fridge. "Although I really don't know if that had anything to do with me or not."

"You must have had something to do with it. When I say she doesn't go out much, I mean I really can't remember the last time I saw her outside her home. I think she goes to council meetings, and that's about it."

Em shrugged. "I guess I'm a more powerful influence than I realized."

He gave her a long, odd look. "I suppose you are." He draped the dishrag over the arch of the faucet neck. "All right, let's get those presents open. Then we can cut into that cake."

And send everyone home was the next thing she expected him to say, but he didn't. Instead, he just gave her a terse smile as he went out to the back deck.

No kiss on the cheek. No wink. No sweet expression that was meant only for her. Something had changed in him, just like it had in Gracie.

Em was clueless as to what had happened. Unless Gracie had told Deacon about Em knocking her down. But again, that was an accident. He wouldn't hold that against her, would he?

She wished she knew. The not-knowing was causing a pit to grow in her stomach. She did her best to ignore it the rest of the evening. Fortunately, that wasn't for much longer. But as the night was drawing to a close, she didn't know anything more than she had earlier.

Gracie and Deacon still seemed slightly chilly toward her. Well, Deacon did. Gracie's attitude toward Em seemed to be more about pitying her for a reason she couldn't fathom.

Em did her best to pretend nothing had changed. She started to help clean up, gathering cups and plates from all over the house, but Deacon stopped her.

The smile she loved was there, but it didn't quite make it up to his eyes. "You don't have to do that."

She straightened. "I don't mind."

"That's kind of you, but you have to be exhausted. You worked all day helping us. We're tired, too. In fact, we're not even going to worry about this mess tonight. We'll tackle it in the morning. After coffee."

She straightened, her hands full. "You're sure?"

"Absolutely. Besides, don't you have your first day of work at Black Horse in the morning?"

She nodded. "I do."

"I don't want this mess to be the reason you're late. Go home and get a good night's sleep. You want to make a good impression with Nasha on your first day."

"For sure." She smiled. He was right. But she still felt like she was being sent home. "I'll just go grab my bag and head out. I should say good night to Gracie and your brothers, too."

"Gracie went up to bed already, and Bishop and Shep are in some deep conversation in the den. I'll tell them you said good night."

"Okay." Weird. But maybe they *really* were all just tired. She went back to the guest room, grabbed her bag, then walked to the front door.

Deacon was waiting there, door open. She went through, and he walked out onto the porch behind her.

He just stood there. She glanced at him. "Night."

"Night."

Impulsively, she leaned in to kiss him.

He turned at the same time so that she caught his cheek and not his mouth.

Her gut told her it wasn't by accident, but she wasn't in the mood to discuss it. Even though she wanted to.

She put it—and him—behind her and went down the steps to her car. She'd call Gracie tomorrow and flat out ask her what had happened. And maybe apologize again.

But right now, she needed to get home. Deacon was right. Tomorrow was important. Having a job was key to her survival.

Having a boyfriend wasn't.

Deacon was a wreck inside. The kind of chaotic mess he hadn't felt since his father had passed. And his mother had left.

That was crazy, though. Why should he have such strong emotions about a woman he just met?

He knew why.

And he refused to put it into words. Not until he had some truth about Em. Who she really was. What she really was.

Right now, he was in self-preservation mode. Walls up. Feelings off.

Except that wasn't totally possible with Em, and that was killing him. If she really was conning them, he was going to be crushed.

As much as it had hurt when their father had died, and then their mother had left, having to cut Em out of his life would be just as bad.

It would dump fuel on his desire to get out of this place, too. Gracie would probably feel the same way. Maybe in some small way, Em's betrayal could be good for them.

Devastating, but there was always a silver lining, right? He shook his head. Nothing felt very shiny at the moment.

As her car pulled out of the driveway, he turned and went back inside, closing and locking the door behind him.

The party had been great, much in part to Em's help. She'd been everywhere. Talking to people, making sure drinks were filled, food was replenished, and everyone was happy.

She'd been perfect. Too perfect? Was that even possible?

Had she been trying to ingratiate herself to them? But for what end goal? She'd already been given the green light from Amelia to stay.

He couldn't figure it out.

He jogged upstairs to check on Gracie. He knocked softly on her door. "You still up?"

"Yes. Come in."

He opened the door and leaned in. She was in bed, a book on her lap, Tinkerbelle at her side. "Did you have a fun night?"

"I did." Her smile only lasted a second. "Until…"

"I know."

Her face was scrubbed clean, making her look younger than her years. Reminding him that she was indeed his baby sister. "Anything come back on the computer yet?"

"I haven't checked since I came upstairs."

"Well, let me know."

He nodded. "I will. Love you. Night."

"Love you, too. Night."

He started to shut the door.

"Deacon?"

He looked back at her. "Yeah?"

"What are you going to do if…it's all true?"

He took a breath. "I don't know. Talk to her, I guess. There are two sides to everything. But those databases don't lie."

Neither did Gracie's curse. They both knew that.

She looked down at her book. "I don't want them to be true. I really, really don't. I like Em. She's one of the nicest people I've ever met."

"I know. I feel the same way."

"You like her, don't you?"

"I do. I did." He sighed. "I do. But I'm the law here. I can't be involved with someone with a criminal past. How would that look?"

"But if it's in her past, you could just let it be."

"I don't know, Gracie. I can't decide that yet."

She scratched Tinkerbelle's head. "You let me know."

"I will. Get some sleep."

She smiled weakly again.

He shut the door and went to his office. He stood at the door, hand on the knob, but couldn't bring himself to turn it. He didn't want confirmation of what Gracie had found out. Not tonight.

What would it matter if it waited until morning?

He took his hand off the knob and walked away.

CHAPTER THIRTY-THREE

But Deacon couldn't sleep. His thoughts wouldn't let him, and so, at five thirteen in the morning, after much tossing and turning, he got up, went to his office, and switched on his computer.

He logged into his National Crime Information Center database account. The reports he'd requested were waiting there.

He stared at them a long time before clicking on the first one to open it.

Immediately, he wished he hadn't.

A long, painful sigh slipped out of him, and he scrubbed a hand over his face. Then he cursed softly as the happiness of the last few days evaporated, only to be replaced by anger and the feeling of betrayal.

Gracie's curse had been right. Again. Just like it always was. Except in this case, it hadn't captured the whole story.

Emeranth Greer, aka Elizabeth Green, aka Emma Greyson, aka Ellen Garwood, had quite a past. Two arrests, both with her mother, Manda Greer, who had her own string of aliases and was indeed serving time at the moment. Both of Em's arrests had occurred when Em was a juvenile.

That was something to cling to.

But what stopped him cold was that Emeranth had an outstanding warrant. One that was extraditable. And now that he knew about it, he couldn't just do nothing.

He cursed again.

Then he dug into the report a little more, reading to find out what exactly had happened.

Her mother had been arrested a week prior, but it wasn't until a few days ago, maybe even the day that Em had arrived in Shadowvale, that the money her mother had been accused of stealing had been found.

Over five hundred thousand dollars. In three different accounts. All in Em's name. Which was what had caused the warrant to be issued.

He shook his head.

No wonder she'd wanted to stay in Shadowvale. She was untouchable here. Protected because this town basically didn't exist. What better place to hide from the law?

He squinted at the screen. Made sense why she was so desperate for a job, though. Those accounts would have been frozen instantly. The money unusable.

What a mess. He leaned back. A quick glance at the time told him he'd been at this nearly half an hour. Still too early to wake Gracie up and fill her in.

He didn't really want to tell her about all this. She liked Em so much, and he wanted Gracie to have a friend. But not a friend who was a liar and a thief and out to con her way through life.

He scowled at the screen.

Emeranth might be able to explain some of this, but five hundred thousand dollars? There wasn't an explanation that was going to make that right. Except for a confession.

He stood, stretched, then went back to his room. Motivation sped him up, because he would have rather lingered under the hot shower. Instead, he got dressed, then quietly left the house.

The air was cool and still. His truck would make a lot of noise when he started it up, so flying was his best option if he didn't want to wake Gracie and Bishop.

With a few quick steps, he shifted and took to the air.

He landed minutes later on Amelia's driveway and returned to his human form. He went straight to the door and knocked, then rang the bell, thinking that might be a better way to roust someone at this hour.

Beckett was that someone. He came to the door, somehow impeccably dressed even though it was early. He greeted Deacon with an odd look. "Were we expecting you this morning?"

"No, but I need to talk to Emeranth immediately."

"Then you'll have to head downtown. She left for the bakery five minutes ago."

Deacon hesitated. "They don't open this early."

"Apparently, they do now that they serve coffee." Beckett stepped back. "You'd better come in."

Deacon hooked a thumb over his shoulder. "I'll just go. There's no need for me to—"

Amelia's voice rang out. "Who's at the door?"

Beckett sighed. "I told you." Then he turned and nearly shouted, "Mr. Evermore is here."

Amelia walked into the foyer, dressed in a satin robe, her hair around her shoulders. "What's going on? What's happened? Is Emeranth all right?"

Deacon frowned. "I should go."

Amelia pinned him with a hard stare. "Not until you explain what's brought you here at such an hour."

There was no point in saying nothing. She'd know he was lying. "It's about Emeranth."

Amelia's hard stare softened, replaced by one of concern. "What happened?"

"She accidentally touched Gracie last night."

Amelia's brows lifted slightly. She understood what that meant. "I see. And now you want to talk to her. So what did Gracie find out that brought you here? Because it must be important for you to be on my doorstep this early."

"It is important. And because of what happened, I ran a background check on Emeranth. The reports came in this morning." He raked a hand through his hair. "They're...not good."

Amelia lifted her chin and sighed. "Beckett, coffee in the sitting room, please. Deacon, follow me."

He did, and Beckett left them to get the coffee, presumably.

As they entered the room, Amelia brought the lights and the fireplace to life with a wave of a hand. She took the seat nearest the flames, positioning herself to see him. "Out with it."

"Her mother—"

"Manda Greer."

"Yes."

"I thought this was about Emeranth."

"It is, but her mother's involved. She's in jail, by the way."

Amelia didn't seem surprised by that. "Again? No wonder Emeranth didn't want to talk about her. That woman has been a constant disappointment as a mother."

That made Deacon pause. He knew what it was like to have a disappointing parent.

Amelia gestured toward him. "Go on. What else has Manda done?"

"First-degree felony, for one thing. Scheming to defraud, for another. She's a grifter. A con artist. And apparently, she took someone for half a million dollars."

Amelia leaned back. "Are you sure? I know what she is, but that's quite a sum. She's never been that successful in anything she's done."

He wasn't that surprised at Amelia's cool reaction. "She had help. From Emeranth. In fact, the money is in accounts that are in Emeranth's name, which is why there's a warrant for her arrest and extradition back to Oklahoma."

Amelia's eyes narrowed. "Emeranth wasn't involved in this."

Deacon tried to be patient. "I know you want to protect your niece, but those accounts say otherwise."

"You don't know Manda. She's the worst kind of person. Beyond just being a con artist. She's willing to use her own child for whatever means necessary. Always has been. I don't know why things would have changed now. And I have no doubt she's behind those accounts, not Emeranth. Dig deeper. I want to see evidence."

"Amelia, I have dug deeper. I've read the reports, the case files. Everything points to them being in on this together. If you want to see evidence, I'll have to get Gracie to hack into the police department's files in Oklahoma."

"Then do it. Find out what they have exactly."

"But it's clear, isn't it?" He spread his hands. "Why else would Em come here? She knew the hammer was about to fall, and she needed a safe place to hide out. What better place than the invisible town of Shadowvale?"

"Except she knew nothing about this place until she got here. And if she and her mother made off with that much money, why wouldn't Emeranth have used those funds to disappear? At the very least, she would have come here with money. But she came here destitute. Nearly penniless."

"Maybe she was too afraid to touch it. Too worried the paper trail would lead the feds to her."

Amelia shook her head. "This was all Manda. I promise you." She exhaled a frustrated breath and glanced at the fire for a moment. "Manda came here once, years ago. Emeranth couldn't have been more than five or six then, although Manda left the child home."

Deacon sat back, listening.

"Manda was never one of the more gifted Marchand witches. The greatest bestowment of power tends to skip a generation. But she understood that. Understood that her daughter was the one who'd have the kind of magic that would be life-changing. If only Manda could get her hands on it."

Deacon got a sense where this was going.

Amelia twisted the large ruby ring on her finger. "She wanted me to transfer Emeranth's power into her. She said it was the only way she could give her daughter the kind of life she really deserved."

Amelia snorted. "What she meant was it would be the only way she could ever effectively run her scams. She didn't have the magic to do it. Couldn't muster up the kind of real power needed to pull off those long cons. But Emeranth could."

Amelia leaned forward, eyes dark with memory. "Emeranth has the kind of power in her that, if wielded without conscience, could do great damage."

He strummed his fingers on the arm of the couch. "You realize you're not making a great case for her innocence."

She frowned at him. "But you have to know by now that Emeranth isn't that kind of person. She's not her mother's child. Not at all. She has a good heart. A giving spirit. And a deep desire to leave that life behind her. That's why she came here. It wasn't to hide. It was to escape. And I don't mean from the law. From the life her mother saddled her with."

Deacon dropped his gaze to the table between them. He had seen firsthand what kind of person Em was, but if she really was a con artist like her mother, she could make him believe anything. He wasn't convinced he knew the real Emeranth. Not now that he'd seen the reports. Those facts in black and white made it hard to think otherwise. But if Amelia needed to see the police evidence, he'd get that, too.

"You don't believe me."

He made eye contact with Amelia. "I believe that you believe the story she's fed you."

Anger sparked in her eyes, and the flames in the fireplace jumped, snapping at the logs with new energy. "You're wrong."

"I hope I am. But Gracie's curse never is."

"Emeranth is not her mother. Just because Manda has done wrong, doesn't mean Emeranth should be punished, too."

"Pretty sure the police are after her for her part in this, not her mother's." He shook his head. "I'm sorry, Amelia. I don't want any of this to be true. I like Em. Or at least the Em I thought I knew. But we cannot knowingly harbor a fugitive."

Amelia practically vibrated with anger now. "The gates let her in. Would they let a criminal into this place? Would they give safe harbor to someone who could bring the law down on us? Think, Deacon. Who knows better? The outside world? Or the magic that protects us here?"

He didn't want to argue with her anymore. He understood why she was so upset. She'd been alone for so long that to suddenly have family at her side again must be such a gift, but he also knew she was blinded by that love.

He stood. "I don't disagree with you. But the magic that protects us is *your* magic. That makes it biased. And I'm the law in Shadowvale, which means I have to do what is right."

Her bottom lip trembled. She didn't look at him as she spoke. "What are you going to do?"

"To start with, I'm going to talk to her."

"Just talk?"

He couldn't promise that. "For now."

She got to her feet. "You're heading down a path you may not come back from."

He let that roll over him. He knew she was upset. "You put me in this job. Asked me to be the one to persuade Em not to stay here. Why me?"

She sighed. "Because I know how much you hate it here. How much you want a different life for you and your sister."

"And I tried, didn't I?"

She nodded.

"And now it looks like I'm going to get her out of here after all. So the job will be done. Just not in the manner you wanted."

"At least let her finish out the day at the bakery. Is that so much to ask?"

He hesitated. "I can do that. But if you use that time to hide her away or—"

"I won't. I swear on Thoreau's life."

"All right. End of shift. I'll give you that."

CHAPTER THIRTY-FOUR

The strong scent of coffee—and the lighter scent of baked goods—lingered in Em's hair and clothes, but she walked out of Black Horse a happy woman. Tired, but happy. There were worse things to smell like, that was for sure. And there wasn't much better than an honest day's work completed.

Now she just had to sort out what had actually happened at Gracie's party. She hadn't heard from her or Deacon today, but then, they'd known this was her first day on the job. So had they not reached out because of that? Or was everything okay? Or was it still a big mess?

Em was done not knowing. She wanted less drama, not more. Actually, she wanted no drama, but life probably wasn't going to let that happen.

As she headed for her car, she pulled out her phone and dialed Deacon. She figured she'd start with him and see what he would tell her.

The sound of ringing brought her head up.

Deacon was leaning against her car.

She smiled and hung up, then tucked her phone back in her purse. "Hey."

He didn't smile back. "Hey."

Was that all he had to say? "Is that it?"

He frowned. "We need to talk."

"Yeah, I'd say so." She stopped a few feet away. "Also, my first day was great, Deacon, thanks for asking."

His frown deepened, and he looked away.

She put her hands on her hips, a little peeved by his cool reception. "What on earth happened last night? I've spent every spare moment trying to figure it out, and I can't. All I can come up with is something to do with Gracie's curse. But you know, since it's not polite to ask and no one volunteered that information, I have no idea what that something might be."

He glanced down the street. "Yes, it has something to do with her curse. We should go somewhere more private—"

"Really? Is it that big of a secret?"

He looked at her again. "I'm not talking about Gracie's curse, I'm—can we just go somewhere?"

"Like?" She shrugged. "I don't know that many places."

"How about the park down the street?"

She crossed her arms. There weren't that many people walking around, and they were partially blocked by one of the big trees that lined the streets. It was private enough to her. "How about right here?"

He didn't seem happy with that, but he straightened and pointed to a bench one parking spot away. "Let's sit."

"Okay."

Once they were settled, she didn't say a word. Just waited for him.

He didn't disappoint. "Tell me about your mother."

That made her inhale a little sharper than normal. "She's, uh...not a very good person, to be honest. What does this have to do with last night?"

He sat with his elbows on his knees, but he turned his head to look at her. "You and Gracie collided in the hall last night."

She nodded. "I know. I apologized. It was an accident."

"I understand. And so does she. It's not about the collision, it's about the contact that happened because of it."

"Contact?"

"You touched Gracie. Long enough to activate her curse."

Em just stared at him. "Which is?"

He let out a breath. "With contact, she sees a person's deepest, darkest secret."

"That has to suck. No wonder she—what did she get from me? This is why you're asking about my mother? So you know, then, don't you?" She swallowed hard. Everything she'd fought to put behind her was staring her in the face once again.

"She saw your mother and she saw you. In trouble. Arrested. Saw the other names you've used. Knows you've conned people out of a lot of money."

Every word was a dagger in her heart, but she couldn't let the last statement lie. "Wait a second, I have never knowingly conned anyone out of anything. And those other names of mine? All my mother's doing. Just like the arrests."

She blinked back angry tears. Some because her mother's awful influence still persisted, some because her fresh start had gone stale so soon. "She's a con artist. A decent one. Good enough that I didn't realize how elaborate a story she'd woven to get me to go along with her games."

"Like what? How do you explain all those names?"

"For years, she led me to believe that my father was an angry, abusive, manipulative man hunting for us. That he wanted to take me away from her. That he would punish her because she'd gotten me away from him. She told me those names were to protect me. Used the same story for why we had to move so often."

He didn't say anything at first. Then he nodded. "Pretty good story."

"It was. She even came home once with bruises. Said he'd found her at her job and almost killed her. Told me to pack whatever I could. We left almost immediately with only the things we could fit in the car."

One of many memories that haunted her. "I know now that she'd probably been made by the mark she was conning. And either got those bruises from him or gave them to herself to sell her story to me." Em shrugged and looked away. "Whichever. It worked."

"Okay, I'll accept that. The names weren't your doing. What about the two arrests?"

Boy, he'd really done his homework. "Wrong place at the wrong time. And I did something she asked me to, only to find out after the fact it wasn't kosher. She conned me into a lot of stuff when I was younger. I'm not proud of that. Makes me look like a fool." She grimaced. "So much for a sealed juvi record."

He looked away then. "Nothing stays secret for long."

"Apparently not. Is that enough to convince you that I'm not a criminal? Or do you need more proof? My mother's in jail, you know."

"I know."

"Well, there's a reason for that. She's the one who's made a career out of bilking people. All I wanted to do was get away from her and her lies. Her getting arrested finally made that possible. Sad when that's the best shot you've had for an independent life in a long time."

"Just one more question." He sat up, staring straight at her. "How do you explain the half million dollars? The security cam footage of you walking into the bank?"

She stared right back. "What half million dollars? What bank? What footage?"

He shook his head. "Don't start with the games now."

"This isn't a game. I have no idea what you're talking about, and trust me, that's not a sum of money I'd soon forget."

His mouth bent like he was disgusted. "Stop lying, Em. It's over. I ran reports on you. I know about your warrant. I know you came here to save your skin. And today Gracie hacked into the Bethany, Oklahoma, police department's files on you. We saw the footage of you walking into the bank where you set up the accounts for the money."

She gaped at him. "I'm not lying. I don't know anything about any of this. And who gave you the right to go digging into my past? Or to hack into the police department?"

"Your aunt did when she made me peacekeeper of Shadowvale."

Em jumped up, beyond angry and not sure what else to do but get away from him. Her aunt couldn't have possibly been behind this, could she?

He stood and went after her, grabbing her arm. "Hey, wait a sec—"

She turned, flinging her hands up. And with the movement, she sent out a burst of magic that surprised both of them.

It knocked Deacon off his feet and onto his back a couple yards away.

She gasped. "I'm so sorry. I didn't mean to do that."

325

Slowly, he pushed up to a sitting position, his expression a little dazed. The few people who were out had started to gather. Apparently, there were a few things in Shadowvale that could still draw a crowd.

She inched toward him. "Are you okay?"

He nodded. "I'm okay."

But he didn't get up either. Like he was waiting to see if she was going to strike again.

"Crap. I really am sorry. I don't know how I did that. I'm sure I couldn't do it again if I tried."

"Well, don't." He finally stood up and brushed himself off. "That's quite a punch you're packing." He glanced toward the people who were watching, giving them a nod and a wave. "All good here, carry on. Just practicing a little magic."

As they dispersed, she moved closer.

"Listen, I don't know what your reports told you, and I don't care what footage you saw, but I am *not* lying. I don't know anything about a warrant, or this money you're talking about, or setting up accounts in some bank. Nothing. If I did, I would say so. Remember?" She pointed back and forth between them. "Honesty?"

"I'll show you the reports. And the footage."

She thought about that. "Okay. Then I'll show you I have no money."

Asking Em to drive was an uncomfortable request, but since Deacon had flown here, he didn't have much choice. He also didn't want to let her out of his sight. Not until this was all sorted.

Or he'd taken her into custody.

Something he had no desire to do. It weighed heavy on him. On his heart. He couldn't imagine doing that to her. And yet, if she really was guilty of these things…he'd have no choice.

He'd taken an oath when he'd become peacekeeper. If he broke it for her, what would that say about his integrity? About his own moral compass?

"You're awfully quiet for someone who had so much to say a few minutes ago."

He glanced at her. "I don't want you to be guilty."

"Then you should be happy, since I'm not."

"The evidence says otherwise."

"I understand that, but my mother is a very manipulative woman. I'm sure she told the police whatever she thought would result in the best possible outcome for her."

"Maybe. But that still doesn't explain the three accounts in your name with the five hundred thousand dollars in them. And your face on the bank's cameras."

She adjusted her grip on the steering wheel. "No, but that doesn't mean there isn't an explanation. My mother does come from a long line of witches, after all. Couldn't she have some magical abilities?"

"I suppose."

From the lines bracketing her mouth to the furrows above her brows, she looked miserable.

He wanted to comfort her. But how could he? He was the peacekeeper. He was the law in Shadowvale. And he was supposed to remain impartial.

But his heart was aching for the woman next to him, and there was nothing impartial about that. "I'm sorry."

She frowned at him. "Yeah, you seem really torn up."

"I am." He didn't blame her for the attitude. "But I'm also supposed to protect this town from people like…"

Her brows shot up. "Me?" She snorted with derision. "Yeah, I'm clearly a threat."

"Em. I am doing my job."

Her bitter expression lasted another three seconds. Then she sighed. "I know."

They both went silent for a few moments, then she spoke again. "My mother has been a weight around my neck my entire life. I didn't find out her story about my father was a lie until I was eighteen and able to do some digging, including getting a copy of my birth certificate. You know what it says on the line for father? Nothing. It says nothing."

She shook her head. "My mother genuinely doesn't know who my father is."

"Maybe she just didn't want to say."

Again, Em snorted. "No, I promise you if she knew, she'd be draining that man for support."

"You're what, twenty-seven?"

"Twenty-eight. Why?"

"You could have left before now."

"I tried. Twice. Once, I managed to save up enough money for first and last month's rent for a tiny little shoebox of an apartment. She called the management company and told them I was running drugs out of the place. I came home and found the locks changed and all my stuff on the sidewalk. I had to beg her to let me come back home with the promise never to leave again."

He grimaced. "And the second time?"

"The second time, I just packed a bag and bought a bus ticket to the West Coast. I was literally ready to be homeless as opposed to being pulled into another one of her schemes."

He waited.

Em sighed like the world was upon her shoulders. "She called the bus company, told them I was off my meds and mentally unable to make decisions for myself, threatening to sue them if they didn't tell her where I'd gone."

She shook her head. "She was waiting for me at the station when my bus arrived."

"So you gave up."

"I didn't give up so much as I decided to bide my time. Wait for another opportunity. So when she got arrested, it was like a bright shining light telling me this was my chance. Maybe the best one I'd ever get."

"How did you end up in Shadowvale?"

"I was going through my mother's things—she was big on hiding money. Rainy day fund, she called it. Anyway, I found my mother's address book and started paging through it. I knew I had an aunt Amelia, but also that my mother didn't like her and didn't like talking about her. Which made it seem odd to me that her name and address were still in my mother's book."

She shrugged. "I figured if my mother didn't like her, there had to be a good reason. Like maybe she was wise to my mother's ways. I thought that meant she might take pity on me."

"Good call."

She gave him a long, hard side-eye. "Until recently, yes."

CHAPTER THIRTY-FIVE

Em sat at Deacon's desk and stared at his computer with him looking over her shoulder. The charges were there on the screen in black and white, along with the report on her supposed windfall and the details of her warrant.

And then there was the bank footage in evidence.

After watching it for a third time, she put her hand over her mouth and shook her head. "That looks just like me. But it can't be. I'm done for. I don't know how she did it, but I'm done for."

Deacon put his hand on her shoulder. "Maybe we can figure this out."

She looked up at him. "You sure you want to help me?"

"I am. And I want to know the truth. Figuring this out will do that." Then his gaze softened. "I want you to be innocent. More than anything."

That was reassuring. "Me, too. And I'm thinking I really need to talk to my aunt. Tell her about this. There might be something she can do. Something she can suggest. She's lived a lot longer than me, she ought to have some idea I haven't thought of."

"She already knows about this."

Em stood to face him, perplexed. "She does? How? You told her before you came to see me?"

"I went to Indigo House first, after the reports came in. I was hoping to talk to you there, but you were already gone. Your aunt saw me and made me come in and explain why I'd shown up. She's not happy with me. She thinks I should just let this go."

Em stared at him. The man she'd started to have future thoughts about. "I'm not thrilled with you either." She put her hands up. "But I understand you're doing your job."

"Thank you for that." He studied her for a moment, looking very much like a man who wanted to kiss her.

"Don't," she said.

"Don't what?"

"Don't look at me like you wish things were different. I wish they were, too, but you started this."

"Actually, you started it when you bumped into Gracie."

"It was an accident. And you should have told me not to touch her."

"I told you not to touch *anyone*."

"Not the same thing. Not exactly." She glanced back at the computer while she put one hand on the back of her neck and rubbed at the tense muscles. "There has to be a way to fix this. Some way to prove I didn't open those accounts. I've never even been in that bank."

"Accounts have to be opened in person. That footage proves you were there. I'm sorry, but that's pretty clear evidence that you have been at that bank."

Em snarled out a word she almost never used.

Deacon's brows lifted.

"Oh, don't look so surprised. You already think I'm a criminal. What's a little swearing?"

He nodded, trying to look serious and failing. "If it helps, I'm starting to believe less and less that you're a criminal."

"A resounding endorsement if I ever heard one."

"That didn't come out the way I meant it. Listen, would you be willing to do something for me?"

She crossed her arms. "I have no idea until I know what that something is."

His hesitation told her it wasn't something she was going to like. He grimaced, then said, "Take a lie detector."

"For real?"

He nodded. "It would help us both."

"I already know I'm innocent."

"I meant me and Gracie."

"Oh." She gave it a second of thought. She really wanted them both to have confidence in her innocence. So why not? "Sure. Fine. What do I have to lose?" She looked around. "Where is this machine?"

"It's not a machine. It's a person."

"Someone's curse?"

"Yes."

"Do you want to take Gracie along?"

"No, she's in her office working. It's a good distraction, and she needs that right now."

"Is that why you didn't tell her I was here?"

"Something like that."

She sighed. Sounded like Gracie didn't want to see her. That would change if Em could prove she was innocent. "Lead the way to the lie detector."

This time, he drove. And curiously, the way happened to lead to Stella's Bargain Bin.

She peered out of the truck window. "Are we shopping?"

"Stella's curse is the ability to always know when someone's lying."

The things you learned about a person. "Interesting. I bet no one ever tries to return something and claim they never wore it."

"Probably not. On the flip side, she keeps a secret like no one's business."

"Also good to know." She glanced at him. "This is where I got my party dress."

A glint shone in his eyes. "That little black dress?"

She nodded.

He took a deep breath. "That was a good dress."

She kept her smile to herself as they got out of the truck and made their way inside.

Stella was behind the counter, perched on a stool. Her billowy zebra-print top was balanced with black skinny jeans and red cowboy boots that matched the color of her hair. Black tassel earrings swung as she turned. "Howdy, kids."

"Hi." Em gave a little wave. "My aunt loved the tiger pin."

Stella's smile expanded. "I saw she had it on at Gracie's party. Always nice to know a gift has hit the spot."

She gathered up the game of solitaire in front of her. "But you're not here to shop, are you?"

Deacon grunted something Em couldn't make out. "We need your gift."

Stella snorted. "When it's useful, it's a gift. When it's not, it's a curse." She tapped the playing cards on the counter to even them out, then slid them back into their box. "Which one of you?"

Em raised her hand. "Me. And thank you."

"Don't thank me yet." Stella laid her hand on the counter, palm up. "Put your hand in mine."

Em did as asked. Stella's palm was warm and soft. Comforting, actually.

Stella folded her fingers around Em's hand. "Go ahead, ask your questions."

Deacon nodded. "Did you steal the five hundred thousand?"

"No. And I didn't know anything about it until you told me."

Deacon looked at Stella.

She nodded. "Truth."

He asked a second question. "Have you ever knowingly been involved in your mother's schemes?"

Em lifted her chin. "Once. I thought if I went along, she'd leave me alone. She told me she would." She shook her head. "Another lie."

335

Stella glanced at Deacon. "Truth."

He asked another one. "Have you ever been in Oklahoma First Federal."

"Never."

"Also the truth," Stella said.

He seemed to relax. "Did you come here to hide from the law?"

"No. I came here in hopes my aunt would have pity on me and give me a place to stay so that I could get my life back on track. So that I could have a fresh start. A life without my mother and all the baggage that comes with being her daughter."

Stella looked at Em this time. "You poor kid." She sighed and shifted her gaze to Deacon. "All true."

"Good." He smiled. "Very good."

"Good?" Em slipped her hand out of Stella's. "I'd say it's great."

"It would be great if we could prove it to the police." Deacon put his hands in his pockets. "But we'll find a way to get you out of this. Innocent is innocent."

Em narrowed her eyes. "And fair is fair. Put your hand on Stella's."

Stella laughed. "She's a clever one."

Deacon squinted. "Why?"

"So I can ask you some questions."

He didn't budge. "One question."

She cocked her head. "I didn't limit you. Two questions."

He sighed and put his hand on Stella's.

Who immediately got a brand-new grin on her face. "Long time since I held hands with such a handsome fella."

He smiled. But only a little.

For the first time since Em had met Deacon, he seemed nervous. She liked that. She leaned one elbow on the counter as casually as she could and asked her first question.

"How do you really feel about me?"

He didn't answer right away. Instead, he looked at Stella.

She nodded. "Go on, tell her."

"I like you. A lot."

Stella nodded vigorously. "He does."

Em gave careful thought to her next question. There were a thousand things she could have asked, making it almost impossible to pick the right one. "What do you want more than anything else in the world?"

A muscle in his jaw twitched, and his mouth firmed up. "For Gracie to be free of her curse."

Stella gave Em a thumbs-up, then cupped her hand around the side of her mouth and whispered, "But that's not all of it."

Deacon frowned. "That's all I'm telling you."

Em could understand that, but there was so much more she still wanted to know. "Why is that so important to you? Shadowvale is full of cursed people. She seems to be happy living here."

Frustration darkened his eyes. "Happy is relative. I know what she really wants, and that's to be a wife and mother. But she refuses to get involved with anyone anymore because of her curse."

Em nodded. "I can understand that. It would be like living on the brink of a chasm. Always waiting to find out the thing that would push you in."

Deacon took his hand off Stella's. "Gracie has enough burdens to bear in this life. She deserves to have her heart's desires. But won't. Not as long as she lives here. Not as long as she's chained to her curse."

A light came on in Em's head. "Which is why you tried so hard to get me to leave. My aunt was going to help you with Gracie's curse."

He didn't give a response, but the answer was on his face. When Em had decided to stay, Deacon had lost the chance to help his sister.

No wonder he'd tried so hard to turn Em against this town.

"Thanks, Stella," Em said softly.

"You're welcome." Stella patted the side of her hair, even though it hadn't moved since they'd arrived. "You have a good day, now."

"You, too."

Deacon grunted and headed for the door. He held it open for Em, but didn't say another word, even after they'd gotten into the car.

Em looked at him. "You don't seem happy. And I thought you would be now that you know I'm innocent."

He blinked. "I am happy. Just thinking about how to get you out of the mess you're still in."

"That's what you do, isn't it? Fix things. Keep peace. No wonder you got the job. You're very good at it."

He sighed. "Not always."

"You're just saying that because nothing went the way you thought it would."

He turned the engine on. "What do you mean?"

"You didn't get rid of me, you didn't get help for your sister, and then you fell for the woman who ruined that for you."

He rested his arm on the steering wheel, his other hand braced on the seat between them. "I don't regret falling for you."

"Even with my terrible past?"

"Your mother's mistakes aren't yours, and you shouldn't be judged for them." He tapped a finger on the wheel. "I didn't react well when I first heard what Gracie had found out. I'm sorry."

"Thank you. I appreciate that. And you're forgiven." She reached out and touched his hand. "Do you have any ideas on how to prove my innocence?"

"Not yet. That security cam footage is a killer." He tried to smile. "Sorry."

"It's okay." She gave his hand a squeeze. "In the meantime, I have an idea on how to solve something else."

CHAPTER THIRTY-SIX

Deacon parked the truck where Em asked, then got out and met her on the side of the road. "This is impossible, you know. It's really just a myth. One of the great urban legends of Shadowvale."

"No," she said. "It's not. Now follow me."

"Em, you can't just traipse into the woods and—"

She was already traipsing into the woods.

With a sigh, he went after her. "This is the enchanted forest, woman. People get lost in here. Like, really lost. Search-party lost. Never-to-be-found-again lost."

She turned abruptly. "Just trust me, okay? You know I was telling you the truth before, right? So trust that I'm telling you the truth again. After all, why would this time be any different?"

She had him there. "Lead on."

And lead she did. With a confidence that surprised him. They went deep into the enchanted forest, following a lightly worn footpath.

They walked through drifts of fog, causing little eddies of vapor to spin up in their wake. As they came through it, Deacon realized the footpath they'd been following was gone.

Still, Em kept going. She took his hand, glancing at him as if to ask if that was okay. He squeezed her hand in response and chastised himself for ever doubting her.

Fireflies danced past, and sprite moss lit their way.

Then they went deeper still. What little light had been filtering down dimmed further. Sprite moss and fireflies were all they had to go by.

Until the glowing blue orbs appeared.

Deacon stopped, tugging on Em's hand. "Fairies," he whispered.

"I know," she said, smiling. "Aren't they beautiful?"

He nodded, unable to say more. In all the years he'd lived here, he'd never been this deep in the enchanted forest. Not for lack of trying.

Every attempt he'd made had ended up in him going in circles. Once, he'd gotten into a thick patch of mist that had rendered sight beyond a few feet impossible.

He'd been lucky to get home that time.

But he'd never found his way to the fairy realm.

"C'mon." Em pulled him along.

She resumed her pace.

It was hard not to stare at the interesting plants and insects in this part of the woods. He even thought he caught a glimpse of a drox, too. At least the end of its bushy green-blue tail.

But a few feet more and a mist rose up around them, eliminating visibility in all directions.

"Em, this isn't good. We should go back. While we can still figure out which way back is."

"It's fine, I promise." She tugged at him to move again.

He stayed where he was. "It's not fine. I've been in this forest before. A long time ago, but not so long that I don't remember how I almost didn't make it out of here. I know what you're trying to do, and I appreciate it, I really do. But we can't risk our lives—"

"Deacon. Trust me."

Her eyes held the kind of earnest promise that made her impossible to deny. "I guess if I'm going to get lost in here, you're the person I'd most like to get lost with."

She laughed. "That's very sweet. But we're not going to get lost. You'll see."

They started moving again. He held tight to her hand, afraid if she let go, he'd lose her. But she moved with such sure steps that he felt at peace, no matter what happened.

The mist cleared, revealing something he'd only ever heard about in his grandmother's whispered stories.

He stared up at the circle of trees. "The grove."

She stood at his side, nodding. "Isn't it beautiful?"

"More than I could have imagined. How did you know how to find it?"

"I can't tell you that." She smiled at him. "Come on, there's more."

They slipped between two of the thick trunks to stand in the perfect ring of trees. Overhead, the branches covered the circle except for a small opening at the center.

Beneath which sat the thing Deacon had long ago stopped believing in.

"The book." The carved pedestal it sat on was beautiful. He put his hand on his head. "Is that really it?"

"It is." She grinned. "Pretty cool, huh?"

"Cool? It's—"

Twelve warrior maidens emerged from the trees, bows drawn, arrows pointed at Deacon's heart.

He'd been a fool not to notice sooner that the twelve trees had faces. He raised his hands. "I mean no harm."

Em stepped in front of him. "Lylianna, this is my friend Deacon. I vouch for him."

The nymph in front of them lowered her bow a few inches. "He hasn't forced you to bring him here?"

Em shook her head, smiling. "No. He didn't even know where I was taking him. He's a good man. I promise. He's an Evermore."

Lylianna dropped her bow to her side, then nodded to the others, who did the same. Deacon let out a relieved breath.

Em gave him a quick smile over her shoulder, then moved to his side, allowing him to see the nymph leader better.

The fact that Em had stepped in front of him, to protect him, wasn't lost on him. No one had done anything like that on his behalf since his mother had left. From that day on, he'd always been the protector, not the protected. Em's gesture wasn't something he'd soon forget.

Lylianna nodded at him. "My apologies, Evermore. We knew your grandmother. She was a good woman. A friend. Be at peace, both of you."

He nodded back. "Thank you."

Lylianna turned to Em. "Be well, Emeranth."

"You, too, Lylianna."

The nymphs disappeared back into their trees.

Deacon shook his head, amazed by what he'd just seen. "That was crazy. And that's not something I say lightly in this town."

Em smiled. "Let's go see the book."

"Definitely." He followed her to it. The book was already open. And there were lines where names had been added, but when he tried to read them, the letters scrambled and turned into little meaningless symbols. "Interesting."

"What is?" Em asked.

"I can't read any of the names already written here."

"I can't either. It's a protection spell, to safeguard those who've already shed their curses."

"I like that. A lot." He glanced around. "This whole grove is amazing."

"Isn't it?" She picked up the feather pen resting in the middle of the book, put one hand on the edge of the pedestal, then leaned in and started to write.

He straightened. "What are you doing?"

She ended with a flourish, then put the pen back where she'd found it. "I put Gracie's name in the book."

"Are you—did you really?" He tried to read what she'd written, but the line was as blurred and undecipherable as the rest of them. "You only get one shot. One person, one name. That's the legend anyway. Why wouldn't you put your own name in? I thought that's what we came here for."

She made a face. "Why would I put my own name in the book? I'm not cursed. Wait, do you want to put your name in?"

He didn't even need to think about that. "No. Not if I'm staying in this town. I wouldn't be able to help the citizens then."

She smiled. "Good."

"But you really should have put your name in."

She shook her head. "Again, I'm not cursed."

He stared at her. "Are you serious? There's a major warrant out for your arrest, and your mother is—"

"Okay, right, there's all that. But that's not a curse. Not like Gracie's thing." Her lower lip trembled just a tiny bit. "And saving myself was never my goal. I wanted to prove to you that I am not who that warrant says I am. That I'm not the kind of person that would take advantage of someone. Or only look out for myself. That I really do care for you and Gracie."

He couldn't believe what she'd done. "I already knew that."

"But you had doubts. I could see it in your eyes. And who could blame you? The evidence against me is pretty convincing." She sniffed, shaking her hair back at the same time. "I wanted to take away all those doubts."

"You've done that. You've done something I've been trying to do for years, actually. I don't know how to repay you for this."

"I don't want you to repay me. I didn't do this to get something in return. I did this to mend the trust that was broken between us."

He shook his head. "I'm sorry. I shouldn't have doubted you. And I am going to repay you. I'm going to find a way to prove your innocence. I'm the peacekeeper. It's my job to protect the citizens of Shadowvale. Especially the pretty, witchy ones."

She smiled a little. "How are you going to do that?"

He paused to think. Amelia had said Em's mother was a witch, too. Although not a very good one. "What's your mother's magical situation? How adept is she?"

Em shrugged. "I don't think very. I never saw her use magic in my life, but then, she purposely suppressed my gifts. Maybe because she couldn't find a way to use them for herself."

He did a little more thinking. "Do you think that could have been a con, too?"

Em squinted. "Meaning?"

"Meaning maybe like you said in the car, she has some magical abilities. But maybe she's more powerful than either you or Amelia could even guess. Maybe she didn't want either of you aware of what her skill level is."

"Anything is possible when it comes to my mother. Why? What are you thinking?"

"I'm thinking I have a valid reason to get out of Shadowvale."

CHAPTER THIRTY-SEVEN

Em crossed her arms and gave Deacon a hard stare from her spot on Aunt Amelia's sitting room couch. "I'm going, too."

Deacon frowned and leaned against the fireplace. "That would not be a wise decision."

In her usual chair, Aunt Amelia smoothed the extra fabric of her peacock-colored caftan. "You cannot leave Shadowvale, Emeranth. I made that clear to you. And even if you could, Deacon is right that it would be unwise. You are a wanted woman. I won't have you taken away from us."

Em couldn't argue with that, so she took a different tact. "But he doesn't know what he's looking for."

Amelia's right brow lifted in clear amusement. "Neither do you. Your powers are far too young to be of any help. And he'll have the help he needs in the spell I'm giving him."

Em sighed louder than necessary.

Deacon was trying not to look happy and failing. She knew he didn't want her to go for the same reasons her aunt had stated. Mainly, the chance that she'd be arrested.

He gave her a consolatory look. "I'll miss you. But I won't be gone long."

Amelia pointed at him. "Remember that. Because if you don't come back, this place will suffer."

He kept his eyes on Em. "I'm coming back. Don't worry about that." Then he glanced at Amelia. "When will the spell be ready?"

She got to her feet. "Soon. Em and I are going to work on it the moment you leave, which you should do shortly, because you need to pack."

He stopped leaning. "Right. I guess I'll go and let you get to it."

Em stood. She wanted to hug him and kiss him and say goodbye, but he'd be back before he headed to Oklahoma. And also, her aunt was watching them. Which made Em feel a little like she was sixteen.

Amelia laughed softly. "Just kiss him already."

Em shot her aunt a look. "Can you read minds?"

"No, but it's not hard to tell what you're thinking with the way you're looking at him."

Deacon was trying not to smile again.

Amelia walked toward the door. "I'll be in my sanctum. Come down after you say goodbye."

She left, giving Em a moment alone with Deacon. "I'll say goodbye to you when you get back."

He walked to her, putting himself in her personal space. "Does that mean I'm not getting kissed?"

She grinned. "I'll still kiss you now. If you want."

"I want."

She put her hands on his chest and smiled up at him. "Are you going to tell Gracie about her curse being lifted?"

He shook his head. "I'd love to, but I think you should do it. You're the reason it happened, after all."

"You can tell her. In fact, I think you should. Then if she wants to talk to me again…"

"If she wants to talk to you again? You may never be rid of her after what you did."

She stared at one of the buttons on his flannel shirt. "I don't want to be rid of her. I want to be friends again."

He cupped her face in his hands. "You will be." Then he leaned in and kissed her gently. "You're not going to be rid of me either."

She leaned into him, her temple against his cheek. "I don't want to be."

He wrapped his arms around her. "Good."

"You think going to the apartment I shared with my mother is really going to solve anything?"

"If your mother has any kind of power at all, then she used it to open those accounts in your name with your image. And if I can find evidence of that, we can clear your name."

"But it's magic. And the outside world doesn't accept magic as real. Look at me. I was a witch and didn't even know it. Wouldn't have believed it if Aunt Amelia hadn't shown me the truth by using her abilities in front of me."

He pulled back to look her in the eyes. "We'll figure it out."

"I hope so."

"We will." He kissed her forehead. "Now I have to go pack, and you have to help your aunt with whatever spell she's sending off with me."

Em nodded. "See you in a bit, then."

"In a bit."

He left, and she went to join her aunt in her sanctum.

A variety of items were laid out across the worktable, but at the center was a bright copper bowl.

Aunt Amelia looked up from a spell book as Em came down the stairs. "There you are. Let's get to work."

"What are we doing exactly?"

"Building two spells for Deacon to take with him. Well, one spell and one potion."

"To get through the gates?"

Amelia shook her head. "No. I'll take care of that. The potion will allow him to temporarily see magic."

"You can see magic?"

"In general, it can't be seen. There have been cases of witches born with the ability to see it, but they claim it's very distracting. In Deacon's case, the potion will show him any magic in your house. Magic your mother would have created." She paused. "Actually, it'll show him whether or not anything has been magically tampered with as well."

"And the spell?"

"It's a removal spell. Not something ever cast by someone who isn't a witch, to my knowledge, so it needs to be perfect."

Em came to stand by the table. "Removal?"

Amelia took a glass vial off of a shelf. "Yes. It will allow him to strip the magic from anything he finds."

Em pondered that for a moment. "So if my mother has hidden something, or disguised it, he'll be able to…unhide it."

"Essentially, yes." Amelia scanned the table, then, seemingly pleased, looked at Em. "Are you ready to begin?"

"Absolutely. Just tell me what you want me to do."

Amelia produced a long silver needle. "Prick your finger. I need three drops of a young witch's blood. Into the copper bowl, please."

Em grimaced, but did as she was told. For Deacon, and to prove her innocence, she'd do whatever was necessary.

They spent the next forty-five minutes on the potion and the spell. When they were done, Em felt like she'd just been through a master class in magic. Also a little exhausted. Mentally and physically.

"Magic is tiring," she said to Amelia.

Her aunt nodded. "It can be. Especially when it's done right. But it should be. The use of magic isn't something to take lightly. It's work. Worth the effort, but not without some cost. Anything good is the same way."

Em nodded. "I agree."

Together, they went upstairs. Em carried the small bottle that held the potion, and Aunt Amelia carried the slip of paper that had the removal spell written on it. She'd also imbued the paper with additional magic that would cause it to incinerate itself once the spell had been spoken. It was all very *Mission: Impossible*, and Em was secretly thrilled that this was part of her new life.

But that didn't stop her from being worried about Deacon.

Beckett met them in the library with a manila folder. "Mr. Evermore has just arrived."

"Thank you," Amelia said.

He handed her the folder, then went to stand by the door.

Amelia went to her favorite chair near the fireplace, waving her hand at the logs within as she sat. A cheery blaze shot up.

"Are you cold?" Em asked.

Amelia nodded. "It's the spell work. And my age, I'm sure."

"It does get cool here at night this time of year, doesn't it?"

"It does. Thoreau likes it, though."

Deacon walked in. "I'm packed and ready."

Amelia held out the manila folder to him. "Your ticket and rental car are all arranged."

He took the folder. "Thank you."

"Thank Beckett. He took care of it."

"But you paid for it."

She shrugged. "That's the easy part."

He glanced back at Beckett. "Thank you."

Beckett smiled and whispered, "First class."

Deacon nodded. "Nice."

Amelia held out the paper with the spell on it next. "This will remove any magic you find. Read it aloud, then drop the paper. It'll combust instantly and leave no trace."

His brows shot up. "Very *Mission: Impossible*."

Em snorted. "I had the same thought."

Amelia frowned. "This isn't Hollywood fakery. This is real magic."

Deacon went serious again. "Understood."

She pointed to her niece. "Emeranth has the potion that will allow you to see any magic in use. Don't drink it until you get there. It won't last more than an hour or so."

Em offered him the small vial.

He took it and held it up to the light. "Less than three ounces? I have to get it through airport security."

"It'll pass," Amelia said. "Once you've taken it, anything that's been touched by magic will have a green light around it. The brighter the light, the stronger the magic that's been applied."

"Got it." He smiled at Em. "Guess I should get going."

Amelia checked the time on the mantel clock. "Yes, you should. The airport is an hour away, and your flight leaves in less than three." She got to her feet. "Thank you for doing this. Be safe."

"I will." He looked at Em. "Happy to do it."

Amelia stood. "I'll leave you to say goodbye. Again."

She left, but Deacon didn't wait for her to be completely out of the room before he pulled Em into his arms. "I'll be back as soon as I can."

She nodded. "I know. But please, like Aunt Amelia said, be safe. I know you're doing this for me, but—"

"For us."

"What?"

"I'm doing this for us. So you don't have to live the rest of your life looking over your shoulder. So you can have peace." He tucked a loose strand of hair behind one of her ears. "I'm the peacekeeper. It's what I do. And I want the woman I love to have peace."

She stared at him. She knew what he'd just said. She just couldn't quite process it. "You just said…"

"I know. And I do." He kissed her on the mouth. Hard. Then he let her go. "Don't get into any more trouble while I'm gone, okay?"

"I won't."

Then he was gone, and she was left to stare after him and replay his words in her head. *He* loved her. He *loved* her. He loved *her*.

She smiled. She loved him, too.

CHAPTER THIRTY-EIGHT

Finding Manda and Em's apartment wasn't hard. He had the address from Em, and the car Amelia had rented for him had GPS. So did his phone.

Getting into the apartment was a different story.

He'd arrived just as the sun was setting. He'd taken a few moments to watch the sunset. He probably shouldn't have, but it wasn't something he'd seen in a very long while, and he indulged the urge.

But then he was all business again. Once it was properly dark, he found a secluded part of the stairwell and shifted into raven form, then he flew onto the balcony of the apartment and returned to his human form.

The sliding door was locked, but the small window that looked into the kitchen wasn't. That saved him from breaking the glass. After making sure no one was watching, he pushed it up, shifted again, and flew inside.

Once back to his human self, he glanced around as he walked from the kitchen to the living room.

The police had been here. That much was obvious from the disheveled state of things from their search.

What was left for him to find, he wasn't sure. But hopefully, the potion would help. He pulled the small vial from the pocket of his jeans, unscrewed the top, and drank it down.

It tasted of herbs, bitter and sharp and earthy.

His head went light for a moment, then his chest felt like it was on fire. The sensation passed quickly.

And all around him, things gave off a soft green glow.

Manda Greer had indeed lied about her abilities. Magic was evident everywhere.

He pulled on a pair of latex gloves and started his investigation.

He found a high concentration of magic in the first bedroom. Had to be Manda's room. The clothes in the closet weren't Em's size or style, and the scent wasn't hers either. He rummaged through the space, but everything in here had already been touched by the cops. And nothing gave off more than a faint green glow, even though there was a lot of it.

He wasn't an expert on spells or witches, but it seemed to him that the magic she'd used had been focused on enhancing herself. The glow lingered on her clothes, the makeup bag on her vanity, her perfume bottles. Maybe she'd used the magic to make herself look younger? More beautiful? Or maybe she'd used magic to make herself more believable to the marks she was trying to scam?

Both made sense for a con artist. Being more attractive and coming off as genuine could only help her.

But the discovery wasn't something that would prove Em's innocence, so he moved on.

The hall bath had nothing to offer, so he went to the next door. He put his hand on the knob, then hesitated. This would be Em's room. Her personal space. No longer, he realized, but it had been.

He opened the door and went in. The room had been rummaged through, just like the rest of the house, but it was easy to see that it had started out much neater. It was sparse compared to Manda's room, which had a loud, boisterous feel to it with scarves and jewelry draped on everything.

Maybe it was because Em had packed up her things and left. But as he looked around, he didn't think that was why. More likely, it was because Em had wanted to separate herself from her mother.

He wondered if he should bring any of her things back. She couldn't have possibly taken it all with her to Shadowvale. But if something turned up missing, the police could get suspicious. Even so, he opened the closet to see if anything she'd left looked important.

The only thing that caught his eye was the insistent green light coming from the back wall. He pushed the remaining clothes out of the way to reveal an access panel. It probably went to the plumbing on the other side where the bathroom was.

The light leaked out from the panel with a brightness that had to mean strong magic.

He didn't have time to search for a screwdriver, so he went back to the kitchen and got a butter knife. That popped the panel off just as easily.

The glow lit up the closet.

Nothing was immediately visible inside the opening. He reached in, felt around, and found a small fabric-wrapped bundle attached to the wall's interior above the panel. No wonder the police hadn't found it. He pulled the bundle out.

The deep-blue fabric felt like silk through his gloves. It was a little pouch, secured with red cord. He untied the cord and dumped the contents onto the bed.

A few things fell out. One was a lock of hair, tied with red thread. There was a sprig of something green and woody. And a small polished rock that was sort of a milky pink.

All of it was glowing like crazy.

He picked up the hair. Looked like Em's. He wasn't sure what the significance was, but Amelia would know. He took out his cell phone and called her.

She answered immediately. "Have you found something?"

"I have, but I have no idea what it is. It's a lock of hair. I found it hidden in a little fabric bag."

She inhaled softly. "Tied with red silk thread?"

"I don't know if it's silk, but it's red thread, all right."

"Just a moment."

He heard her shift the phone, maybe to her shoulder or just away from her mouth. Either way, he could still hear her.

"Emeranth, come here."

Em's voice came through a little more muffled, but still understandable. "I'm here. What's going on? Is that Deacon?"

"Yes. Do you know if your mother might have a lock of your hair? Is that possible?"

"Sure, it's possible. She had one in my baby book. She always made sure that went with us whenever we moved."

"Thank you." Amelia's voice came in loud and clear again. "Deacon, could that be Emeranth's hair?"

"It was my first thought, actually. And it's the right color."

Amelia sighed. "Was there anything else in the pouch?"

"Yes. A stem of a plant. Looks like pine."

"Smell it. Could it be rosemary?"

He did. "Yep, that's what it is."

"Anything else?"

"A small polished rock. It's light pink, kind of milky, but also clear in places. It's not a solid pink."

"Rose quartz." Amelia let out a frustrated noise. "Manda has cast a glamour. And she's using Emeranth as her focus."

"In nonwitch terms, what does that mean?"

"Manda used a magic spell to make herself look like Emeranth. That's why there's security camera footage of Emeranth going into the bank. It was Manda, glamoured to look like Emeranth."

"In Manda's bedroom, her clothes, her makeup, and her perfume all have a green glow, too."

"No doubt all imbued with the same spell. All part of her ruse to look like Emeranth."

Deacon's gut went cold. "She framed her own daughter."

"Essentially, yes."

He felt sick that he'd ever doubted Em's innocence. "Will the spell you gave me undo all this?"

"It should, yes. But then the police will have to be alerted somehow. They'll have to be prodded to view the evidence again so they can see it's really Manda in that video and not Em."

"Don't worry about that. I'll take care of it. Tell Em this is all going to be over very soon."

"I will. Get those spell components out of the apartment. Throw them away somewhere else."

"At the airport?"

"That's fine. Safe travels, Deacon. And thank you."

"Happy to help." He hung up and pulled out the scrap of paper with the spell on it. He read it once silently to be sure he wouldn't make a mistake, then read it out loud.

The instant he finished speaking, the edge of the paper ignited. He dropped it just as it went up in a flash of smoke and flame. Nothing remained. Not even a hint of ash.

And on the bed, the lock of hair had lost its green glow.

Everything had.

He gathered up the contents of the pouch, tucked them into his pocket, then went back to Manda's room to double-check. No green glow anywhere.

He had one more thing to do before he could go home. One more thing to clear Em's name. Then she'd be free.

He took his cell phone out, found the number for the Bethany Police Department, and dialed.

In less than two hours, he was back on a plane and headed to the one place he'd never thought he'd be happy to return to. Shadowvale.

He stared out the window, but there was nothing to see in the blackness of the night sky. At least in Shadowvale there were stars.

And Em.

He smiled. He was going home. To a woman he was crazy about. And to a sister who was no longer cursed to bear the heavy burdens of others.

Amazing how his life had changed in a matter of days.

It almost seemed like magic.

CHAPTER THIRTY-NINE

Em stood frozen as she watched over Gracie's shoulder.

Gracie typed away, expertly finding her way into the Bethany Police Department's case files. She emphatically hit the enter key. "There."

"Bring up the footage," Deacon said.

She tapped a few more things, and a video screen popped up. The security footage from the bank started to play.

Em held her breath, waiting for the damning moment.

And then her mother came into view as she walked into the bank.

Em exhaled. "You did it. She doesn't look like me anymore."

Deacon shook his head, smiling. "Your aunt's spell did the trick."

Em looked at him. "But you made it possible."

Gracie twisted back to see them. "Pretty cool, huh?"

"Very," Deacon said. "Here, let me check the warrant."

Gracie got up and let him have the seat. She grinned at Em. "I want to hug you."

Em opened her arms. "Go for it."

With a little squee, Gracie wrapped her arms around Em. "Thank you for writing my name in the book. And thank you for making this hug possible. And thank you for making my brother so happy."

Deacon snorted. "Oh boy, here we go. Gracie's never been so touchy-feely in her life."

She gave his shoulder a playful push. "Because I couldn't be. And now I can. So I'm going to hug people all the time now." She winked at Em. "And find a man to hold hands with. That's next."

"Slow your roll, G." He tapped a few more keys. "You can hold hands with me if that's what you want."

Gracie rolled her eyes. "Yeah, no."

Em laughed. "Well, you're welcome. I was happy to do it."

Gracie looked like she was about to tear up. "You changed my life, you know. Our lives, really."

Deacon leaned back. "You know what else is life-changing? Not having a warrant out for your arrest." He smiled at Em. "It's gone. And new charges have been filed against your mother. It's all over. Nothing more for you to worry about."

Em put her hand over her mouth, trying to take it all in. "That's amazing. Thank you."

He got up and faced her. "Thank your aunt. It was her magic."

"But you went there. You took the risk." She wanted to hold on to him and never let him go.

"And you made Gracie whole. I'd say we're even."

Gracie snorted. "I'd say you still owe her. Fixing my curse was a much bigger deal."

Deacon looked at his little sister. "Oh? So how do you propose I repay her?"

Gracie's eyes sparkled with the most mischievous gleam. "Proposing is a great idea."

A flush of heat washed up through Em's body with such intensity that there was no way she hadn't turned bright red. "I...uh..."

Deacon narrowed his eyes at Gracie. "Tinkerbelle needs to go out."

She pursed her lips, still amused. "Sure. Okay. You kids have fun." She left them alone, but not without one final, knowing glance over her shoulder.

When she'd shut the door, Deacon took Em into his arms. "It's not a bad idea."

Em just stared at him, unable to make words come out of her mouth.

He smiled. "Do you think it's a bad idea?"

She shook her head.

"Good." He kissed her, short and sweet, then went back to holding her against him. "We could have a long engagement. Or a short one. I'm easy."

She laughed. "You're the exact opposite of easy." He opened his mouth to respond, but she pressed her finger to his lips. "Fortunately for you, I enjoy a challenge."

"Is that a yes, then?"

"No." She grinned. "You have to actually ask first."

He let out a little chuckle. "Okay, got it."

"You should probably clear things with my aunt, too."

"Good thinking. Maybe Thoreau can be the ring bearer."

Em gave him a strained look. "I'd prefer Tinkerbelle."

"We can work out the details." He went quiet for a moment. "I love you, Emeranth Greer."

"I love you, too, Deacon Evermore." She leaned in a little closer. "But you know I can't leave Shadowvale. And I know you want to. So how do we work that out?"

He pressed his forehead to hers. "I don't want to leave anymore. I just want to be with you."

"You're sure?"

"Never more sure about anything in my life."

"Good." She reached up and took his jaw in her hands, then kissed him soundly. "In that case, my answer's yes."

Want to be up to date on all books and release dates by Kristen Painter? Sign-up for my newsletter on my website, www.kristenpainter.com. No spam, just news (sales, freebies, releases, you know, all that jazz.)

If you loved the book and want to help the series grow, tell a friend about the book and take time to leave a review!

OTHER BOOKS BY KRISTEN PAINTER

PARANORMAL ROMANCE
Shadowvale series
The Trouble with Witches
The Vampire's Cursed Kiss
The Forgettable Miss French

Nocturne Falls series
The Vampire's Mail Order Bride
The Werewolf Meets His Match
The Gargoyle Gets His Girl
The Professor Woos the Witch
The Witch's Halloween Hero – short story
The Werewolf's Christmas Wish – short story
The Vampire's Fake Fiancée
The Vampire's Valentine Surprise – short story
The Shifter Romances the Writer
The Vampire's True Love Trials – short story
The Dragon Finds Forever
The Vampire's Accidental Wife
The Reaper Rescues the Genie

For more Nocturne Falls
Try the Nocturne Falls Universe Books
New stories, new authors, same Nocturne Falls world!
kristenpainter.com/nocturne-falls-universe/

Sin City Collectors series
Queen of Hearts
Dead Man's Hand
Double or Nothing

STAND-ALONE PARANORMAL ROMANCE
Dark Kiss of the Reaper
Heart of Fire
Recipe for Magic
Miss Bramble and the Leviathan

COZY PARANORMAL MYSTERY
Jayne Frost series
Miss Frost Solves a Cold Case: A Nocturne Falls Mystery
Miss Frost Ices the Imp: A Nocturne Falls Mystery
Miss Frost Saves the Sandman: A Nocturne Falls Mystery
Miss Frost Cracks a Caper: A Nocturne Falls Mystery
When Birdie Babysat Spider: A Jayne Frost Short
Miss Frost Braves the Blizzard – A Nocturne Falls Mystery
Miss Frost Chills the Cheater – A Nocturne Falls Mystery

Happily Everlasting series
Witchful Thinking

URBAN FANTASY
The House of Comarré series:
Forbidden Blood
Blood Rights
Flesh and Blood
Bad Blood
Out For Blood
Last Blood

Crescent City series:
House of the Rising Sun
City of Eternal Night
Garden of Dreams and Desires

Nothing is completed without an amazing team.

Many thanks to:

Cover design: Design & derivative cover art by Janet
Holmes using images under license from
Shutterstock.com
Interior formatting: Author E.M.S
Editor: Joyce Lamb
Copyedits/proofs: Marlene Engel/Lisa Bateman

ABOUT THE AUTHOR

USA Today Best Selling Author Kristen Painter is a little obsessed with cats, books, chocolate, and shoes. It's a healthy mix. She loves to entertain her readers with interesting twists and unforgettable characters. In addition to Shadowvale, she currently writes the best-selling paranormal romance series, Nocturne Falls, and the cozy mystery spin off series, Jayne Frost. The former college English teacher can often be found all over social media where she loves to interact with readers.

www.kristenpainter.com

26787332R00215

Printed in Great Britain
by Amazon